Debits and Credits
A Grace Edna Edge Mystery

by

Lyn Fraser

Lyn Fraser

Mainly Murder Press, LLC
PO Box 290586
Wethersfield, CT 06129-0586
www.mainlymurderpress.com

Mainly Murder Press

Copy Editor: Jennafer Sprankle
Executive Editor: Judith K. Ivie
Cover Designer: Karen A. Phillips

Copyright © 2014 by Lyn Fraser
Paperback ISBN 978-0-9895804-7-2
Ebook ISBN 978-0-9895804-8-9

Published in the United States of America

Mainly Murder Press
PO Box 290586
Wethersfield, CT 06129-0586
www.MainlyMurderPress.com

Dedication and Acknowledgments

For Reenie, Eleanor and Andrew

~

My thanks go out to the many people who have contributed to the publication of this book. I would like to start with my delightfully creative colleague and longtime friend from the Bennington Writing Seminars, Sharon Love Cook, who, along with mystery writer Suzanne Young, introduced me and my work to Mainly Murder Press. I am grateful to my fiction writing group, Waiting for a Swell, for their support, encouragement and general irreverence: Sandra Dorr, Michele Hanson, Di Herald, Carrie Kellerby, Melinda Rice and Linda Skinner. So what if they call me The Little Red Hen?

Spiritual connection is important to this story on many levels, and I would like to express grateful appreciation to the communities of Nativity and St. Matthew's in Grand Junction, St. Hildegard's and St. James in Austin. Several people have provided encouragement at critical times through this process, including Karen Gilleland, Mary Green, Lois Jarre, Jacqueline Hansen, Judith Liro, Julia Dorsey Loomis, Aileen Ormiston and Emily Parker. There's no way I could have written this book without my golfing friends, and I would like particularly to thank the women in the golfing leagues of Lincoln Park and Tiara Rado in Grand Junction, Lions Muny and the "lovely ladies" of Morris Williams in Austin. My thanks to Nancy Patay and Lori Prader for introducing me to needed help on the pharmaceutical issues in the novel and to Adele Cummings for her expertise on cement mixers, but I am solely responsible for any errors related to these topics.

I am appreciative beyond measure for my family: Eleanor, Andrew, Quin, Marti, Kackie, JuJu, Jason, Web, Tina, David, Fitz, Laurel, and most especially for Reenie, who has read and encouraged this manuscript in so many versions she can speak in the voices of the characters. Many thanks also to Toot, Addie Mae and the intrepid explorer-cat Escalante.

~ One ~
Death in the Dewey Decimals

My eyes glaze over as C. Granger Dockery cracks yet another egg. With one hand raised to shoulder level, he streams the white into a copper bowl, dropping the yolk into a smaller bowl. Now twenty minutes into funneling and speaking, he tips the containers forward to show the audience, audibly ooh-ing over his collection of golden dollops and slithery whites.

Scanning for admirers, he can see me but not Aunt Arrow, because her seat remains vacant. That's cost me quite a few glares, holding a place for her in the second row. With C. Granger's presentation at the top of her do-not-miss list, Aunt Arrow intended to be up front and insisted we meet at ten before two to get a prime seat. She considers C. Granger the *crème de la crème* of thriller writers, which, translated, means that the two of them likely found the same watering hole after they appeared together on a "Celebration of Ink" panel several years ago.

Today C. Granger's promoting *The Soufflé Conspiracy*, and I'm astonished Aunt Arrow's late. She and I go our separate ways on quite a few issues, but punctuality isn't one of them.

I check my watch again. It's a new one with flower petals in different colors and sizes instead of numbers. The big hand now sits on the medium-sized yellow daisy, which means Aunt Arrow's thirty minutes late. The book signing, pastries and wine spritzers follow C. Granger's talk, scheduled for the big hand's arrival at the purple pansies. Which isn't yet, so she still has some time to make it back for the soufflé puffing and assorted post-speech activities.

Aunt Arrow persuaded me to attend this all-day writers' conference because I'm an aspirant. Along with several hundred others, we're spread around a University of Texas ballroom, better known as the Brazos Belle, gem of Texas dance palaces. Authors have a special appreciation for names like that. Mine, by the way, is Jasmine McPherson—my pen name, that is. My real name is Grace Edna Edge, but that makes me sound more like a mystery writer, which wouldn't work at all for promoting my romance fiction. I think marketing is one of the keys to success in this business, finding that promotional specialty, something I've managed to do quite cleverly in my paying work.

Professionally, I'm a forensic accountant, which involves helping individuals, nonprofits, educational institutions and companies detect fraud, check forging, embezzlement, disappearing endowments, hyped financial performance, hidden assets, that kind of thing. Unfortunately, I thrive, because fraud is a growth industry.

The subject of my most recent case was a woman who took thousands of dollars from the Parent Teachers Organization at her son's middle school and then went on to teach there. No longer. I solved the case, as I often do, by tracing transactions—this one beginning small by siphoning funds intended to buy punch for the parent-teachers conference night, then moving on to renovation of the science lab and book donations for the school's library. Next week I testify on behalf of a woman divorcing a well-known area businessman who's managed to conceal almost four million dollars in property holdings abroad. And just this morning during a break, I tentatively accepted the case of a university professor who's lost a bundle in a suspected hedge fund fraud perpetuated by a member of his church.

Surfaces can mislead. If I hadn't read the conference program, I would have thought from this bizarre presentation that C. Granger writes cookbooks; but the program notes reveal that his newest tome "offers a Cordon Bleu chef whose personal relationships run amok in tandem with those of a sinister international cartel attempting to infiltrate Indian casinos in the southwestern United States." I might have preferred the cookbook. Perhaps there'll still be something useful for me after all, as he's begun talking about his writing process, the alleged topic.

C. Granger tells us the idea for his current project began when he searched Native American lore for a puberty ceremony to help his own pubescent son deal with fallout from the second divorce. Enthralled, he then wanted to use the ceremony in a book, "but I had to make up a story where it would fit, where it would be essential to the plot."

I'm on the edge of my padded folding chair, because that's one of the areas I want to improve, my plotting. But instead of going ahead with the story he's made up that requires the ceremonial, he tells us how he's trying to stop smoking. Hypnosis. The patch. Nicotine gum. E-cigarettes. And taking up gourmet cookery. That's where the eggs come in. He warns us that the soufflé will be ruined from the outset without proper utensils. "Use only a large whisk with thin steel wires," he demonstrates on the unadulterated whites.

I look around, hoping Aunt Arrow might have slipped into a seat behind me, not wanting to squeeze by disgruntled participants eyeing her empty chair. She's easy to spot today, wearing the violet and tangerine headscarf that she's arrayed as a turban for her public appearance. But she's not among the sitters, and all I see moving in the background are a couple of waiters carrying large trays of wine glasses.

The other reason I've come with Aunt Arrow today is that she's part of the conference program. She led a breakout session this morning on "The Colon: Where Journalism and Literature Meet." Aunt Arrow's recently retired as an op-ed columnist for the *Austin Times*. There were five breakout sessions, and we could only choose one, so I didn't go to Aunt Arrow's. Since that may have may have peeved her, I was glad to hear women in the restroom between sessions rate it highly for self-deprecating humor and practicality of content.

I attended the nuts and bolts panel on the effective use of detail in fiction, which turned out to be extraneous because I'm already quite accomplished in detail integration, something that's essential to my writing. It's not just getting the detail right, like whether my Scottish warrior is eating kippers on shortbread or bangers and mash, but making sure each detail is there for a reason, like considering whether he really needs to be eating at all if he's going to die in the next battle scene.

I set all my stories in Scotland because I like to write about rising mist and men going forth to battle in kilts, through fields of heather and rising mist. Then, when they return to the maidens, there are some built-in efficiencies to the love scenes because I can get them right into the physical stuff without a lot of undressing of the men. So my unique offering as a writer combines undergarment efficiency and epaulets. I am the only romance writer I know of who has her male soldiers wearing both kilts and epaulets.

Although my avocation brought me to this book event, it parallels my profession. Whichever I'm working at, they both involve getting at the truth underneath the layers.

C. Granger offers a satisfied sigh as he pours all of the combined liquid, the mixing of which I've missed, into a buttered metal mold and moves on to how he analyzes his work. What he always does when he finishes writing for the evening is to get in bed and mentally revise what he's written.

That's how I work, too. After I finish my section I let it sit for a while, and I go over everything in my mind. It gives me something to do in bed. Although I might prefer other things, they aren't in the choice set right now. I've slept alone both literally and figuratively, even when I was married to Earle. For four years.

We met when we were paired in an accountants' charity golf tournament, both of us on partner tracks. He could hit the ball forever, but in unpredictable directions, and my short game wound up carrying the team, not unlike the marriage. Earle took off with an I.R.A. specialist who can't putt and chip worth spit. All I regret is not keeping his name, McIntire, unaware at the time of where my career was heading.

As an aside, C. Granger encourages us to write what we know. It's one of the things Aunt Arrow and I argue about. She thinks I should write a book about the decline and fall of corporate ethics, assuring me that there's ample steamy sex in that story to satisfy my penchant.

Where the hell is she, anyway? I'm really getting worried.

"Plotting," C. Granger begins again as he decides to add a pair of eyes to the back seat of the car traveling across the Indian reservation. Just the set of eyes. He doesn't know if they're human or animal. "When the driver is stopped for speeding, the policeman looks into the car, and that's where the other pair of eyes comes in. From the back seat of the guy's car, the eyes just stare out."

I'm thinking we're finally going to get through the plot and on to the spritzers, but C. Granger bends down to adjust the temperature on the portable oven prior to inserting his metal mold. Watching him purse his lips in anticipation, I expect him to connect the soufflé with his developing story, but instead, he tells us about a new computer software he's downloaded that allows him to perform some sort of incredible split-screen editing. My teeth clench.

I feel a poke on my shoulder. I turn around and there's my Aunt Arrow, finally, leaning in from the row behind me. Her face is red and blotchy. Before I can even whisper my concern, she motions for me to come with her.

I struggle past the re-annoyed row and nearly trip trying to keep up as Aunt Arrow rushes us toward the back of the room. By the time we reach the hallway, Aunt Arrow is sobbing.

"We have to leave," she manages to say. "It's terrible news. About Sally."

"What's happened?" I ask. Sally is Aunt Arrow's best friend. "Sally's dead. They found her body in the library."

~ Two ~
Deuces Wild

The Main Branch. Live Oak. Downtown. I drive us there as rapidly as our state of shock and traffic will allow. Austin's grown over not that many years from a medium-sized town to a small city with many of the streets and roadways still at town size. Drivers navigate otherwise.

On the way Aunt Arrow begins telling me what she knows and how she found out. "One of the *Times* reporters, Gates Stafford, heard it on the police band, death in a public building. Sarah T. Weathers." Aunt Arrow's voice cracks. "He called it in to Jake at the paper."

Jake and Aunt Arrow share most things intimate except housing, each preferring residential independence.

"Jake phoned me, and I had just turned on my cell phone to check messages between lunch with the other breakout leaders and meeting you for C. Granger."

I reach over and squeeze Aunt Arrow's hand.

"Somebody from the library staff found Sally in the basement stacks. She was supposed to be reshelving on the second floor. No one knows why she was in the basement. They suspect a stroke or heart attack but aren't sure what happened, because she was alone when she died."

"Alone?" I ask, incredulous that a major area of the public library could be so isolated.

"By herself. That's what they think," Aunt Arrow says, then adds in a barely audible tone, "I don't."

"We know that Sally was fine at 8:45 this morning," I finally say and immediately regret it, as Aunt Arrow breaks down crying.

Prior to the conference Aunt Arrow and Sally had met for their ritual Thursday breakfast, as they have for forty-plus years, and I picked Aunt Arrow up in front of the Bluebonnet Pharmacy Deli when they finished. Sally slipped me an egg, potato and sausage taco as she went off for her stint at the library, blowing kisses to us from the crosswalk.

I drive through my own mist. Sally and I shared a friendship too, not only through Aunt Arrow, but also as volunteers at the MLK Senior Center in the low income area out east of the freeway where I help seniors one afternoon a week with their tax returns. Sally's gig was calling Bingo, although I know she privately provided considerable support with personal problems.

"Was Sally having any heart trouble or high blood pressure?" I ask Aunt Arrow as gently as possible.

"No and no."

"Any family history that you're aware of?"

"She was healthy. Prime condition. Just had her annual physical. Boasted to me that her doctor made a comment about what good condition she was in for a woman of her age, then amended it to say a woman of any age. They had a laugh about it."

"Was she queasy or upset about anything at breakfast?"

"Only by the raise given to the university football coach by the Board of Regents," Aunt Arrow says, her voice strengthening.

The few spaces allotted to the library are filled, and I have to pull into the small parking lot between the library and the County Recreation and Parks building, taking a space marked For Public Officials Only, All Others Towed.

Aunt Arrow opts to wait in the car. Taking off the head scarf-turban, she releases her long braid, mostly gray with streaks of blondish red, and pushes the passenger seat back as far as it will go, urging me on to find out what I can. She'll come in after, if the situation warrants.

Yellow tape and an Austin patrolman block the library's entry. I notice a silver Calloway-Amherst Mortuary van parked in the drive-through where patrons drop off books after hours and hope Aunt Arrow can't see it. I thought hearses were always black.

I don't know why the police are involved with crime scene tape if Sally died of a stroke or heart attack. Sgt. Martinez doesn't enlighten me after mutual introductions and my request for entry.

"Library's closed for the remainder of the day, Ma'am. If you have books to return, you can use the book drop."

"I'm aware of what happened today to … I've come with my aunt, Aurora Edge of the *Austin Times*. We're personal friends of the deceased, Sarah Weathers. My aunt ate breakfast with her this morning before she came to the library for her volunteer duty. We'd like information about the death, and … we'd like to see her, if possible. Is Ms. Weathers' body still here?"

Sgt. Martinez turns around and steps away to speak into his shoulder. I can hear the cracklings of the shoulder speaking back.

"The body has been retrieved and taken to the county morgue," he tells me. "The van there," he points to the mortuary's vehicle, "we had an unfortunate mix-up about who was supposed to retrieve."

I gag, temporarily unable to take in air, bend over, then manage several deep breaths and wipe my eyes.

"I'm sorry, Ma'am. Do you want me to call someone for you?"

"We want to speak with someone inside the library who can tell us what happened." I sputter the demand.

Sergeant Martinez turns around, preparing to speak into his shoulder again, when a short, heavyset man gesturing wildly with a briefcase to his policewoman escort, emerges from the library's front door. "Your aunt's with the newspaper?" Sgt.

Martinez asks, and I nod. He motions me to wait where I am and goes over to the two of them on the steps, quickly returning with the stocky man in tow.

"I'm Gates Stafford, *Austin Times*. How can I help?" Sure enough, he's attired in regulation trench coat and fedora.

Gates walks around with me to where we're parked, speaks respectfully to Aunt Arrow, assesses the towing warning and suggests we move down the street a few blocks to Deep Eddy Ice House. Once there, he further prescribes draft pints all around, a suggestion that I suspect has come from Jake.

Aunt Arrow leaves for the ladies' room, and Gates says somewhat nervously, "The deceased, Ms. Weathers, I understand she's a good friend of Aurora's. How long have they known each other?"

Thinking Gates is seeking background for his story, I respond, "Since the late sixties. They met when my aunt was a reporter on your paper, her first job out of college. Anti-Vietnam War rally. My aunt was covering, Sally protesting."

"The library gave me personal data." Gates refers to an index card. "Five foot three, hundred and twenty pounds, brown eyes, grayish black hair, sixty-eight years old. One son, husband deceased." He looks to me as if for confirmation, and I nod.

"They allowed me to view the body, and it was something of a ... I mean, I didn't know she was black."

Now you do.

"Any problems with the biracial aspect?" He whispers the question.

Biracial aspect. Is he probing for something related to Sally's death, or is he just plain rude?

"I'm sorry even to ask, but there've been incidents in downtown, a skinhead gang harassing non-white ethnicities and the homeless. We've intentionally not given it much press, and no violence of the magnitude that ..."

Before Gates can say any more, Aunt Arrow returns to the table. We all take a few sips, partly homogenizing the atmosphere.

He tells us he's interviewed two members of the library staff: Todd LaJames, a reference librarian, and Delia Ingram-Kirksey, the library's Community Liaison Officer and Volunteer Coordinator. He'd also talked by phone with Detective Bertel Frederick, who's heading up the investigation for the Austin Police Department.

I remember Bertel Frederick vaguely from testifying in a case together three or four years ago. Attractive in a married policeman kind of way. Case involved a sales tax supervisor who stole $1.4 million by funneling tax revenues into accounts set up to benefit her boyfriend. Both are serving time, he in Huntsville and she in Gatesville. Ninety-two counts.

Gates tells us, "Ms. Weathers arrived promptly for her regular Thursday volunteer duty and exchanged only a brief good morning greeting with Delia Ingram-Kirksey. She picked a cart to reshelve and headed for the second floor. No one at the library is aware of anyone else talking with her."

I'm thinking that Aunt Arrow may have been the last person to have had a full conversation with Sally, unless she'd talked to a library patron who left before her body was found.

We learn from Gates that "the discovery occurred at 10:21, when Todd LaJames came down to the basement stacks to look for two books reported missing the previous afternoon. *English Pulpit Oratory* and *The Heeded Voice*. A patron could find no activity on them since 1937. The personnel assigned to that basement area weren't present, according to LaJames. One staff member was in a meeting, and a volunteer for the microfiche readers didn't show up."

Gates quotes LaJames as saying, "On the floor between the 100 and 200 holdings, I sighted the shape and attire of female body, not moving. Unable to detect pulse or respiration, I called 911 and notified the Director, Pernell Pearson."

I put an arm around Aunt Arrow's shoulders, slightly heaving.

"LaJames and Pearson stayed with the body until EMTs responded at 10:32, and shortly after, the police team arrived. Pernell called in the police because no one had observed the death, and whatever the circumstances, the cause of death can only be confirmed by autopsy. Ingram-Kirksey has no explanation for why Ms. Weathers was in the basement stacks instead of on the second floor."

"What's in the basement stacks?" I ask.

Gates consults his notes. "Religion, philosophy, psychology and generalities. And the microfiche collection."

"She must have gone down to look up something," I speculate.

"Or someone forced her to go," Aunt Arrow says.

"But why?" I ask.

"Detective Frederick stated that there is no evidence whatsoever to suggest that a crime has been committed, but the police won't release the area until cause is determined by autopsy." Gates flips to another page in his notebook. "Ms. Weathers' body was taken to the county morgue at 2:16 p.m."

I well remember what I was doing then.

"Unaware of the police procedures under way," Gates continues, "Ingram-Kirksey had spoken to Ms. Weathers' son and next-of-kin, Nathan Weathers." He looks at his notes. " He's an associate professor at the University of Virginia in Charlottesville, and Ingram-Kirksey contacted Calloway-Amherst, the Mortuary."

"Do you find these interviews reliable?" I ask.

"We're not running a story yet except for elemental facts in the Police Blotter," Gates says.

"So what's next?"

"The library reopens to the public tomorrow, but the basement stacks will remain closed."

"I meant with the investigation."

Gates' pager beeps, and he excuses himself.

Aunt Arrow and I wait in silence. We share a certain degree of comfort at Deep Eddy's, having come here together for many years, since I began visiting Aunt Arrow as a pre-teen from my hometown of Sublime. Her real name's Aurora, but I've always called her Aunt Arrow. She introduced me to the larger world of a university environment—art museums, films that didn't come to west Texas, live music in venues other than church, liberal political debate—and I eventually graduated from Dr. Pepper to Shiner Bock.

For a decade or so Uncle Richard kicked back with us, but somewhere along the way his arrow turned down. Now she has Jake, and I have to say it's not a bad exchange, except that Uncle Richard would sit for hours with me and play cribbage or seven card stud with deuces wild on aces, straights and flushes. Jake says he can't sit still long enough to finish a card game.

Gates returns with the announcement that Nathan Weathers is en route to Austin by air, which we already know because Aunt Arrow spoke with him on the phone from the conference.

Aunt Arrow, mostly uncommunicative with Gates until now, says, "Off the record, Gates, Nathan doesn't believe his mother died of natural causes, and I don't either."

Gates takes out his notepad.

"I mean off. That's all I can say for now."

~ Three ~
Gospel Music

Aunt Arrow tells me more on the ride back to her condo. "Three weeks ago Sally was out on the hike-and-bike trail for her morning walk, and a motorcyclist roared onto the trail through the trees. Took dead aim at Sally but missed. She jumped behind a metal bench, and a group of hikers came along. Barely missed."

"Did she report it?"

"Just to me. Wrote it off as an accident. Biker high on meth or some such."

"Why would anyone go after her like that?"

"You know better than I about Sally's involvements with people at your Center. All kinds of unsavory possibilities. Children in jail or should be. Drugs. Alcohol. Debts and loan sharks. Health problems. Family members out of work. She immersed herself in this underbelly, at least some of it illegal."

"What about racial tension?" I relate my conversation with Gates and his mention of the downtown gang violence.

Aunt Arrow says there haven't been any racially motivated incidents related to Sally and her in years. "And there's no skinhead gang. It's druggies. Based on the *Times* gossip machine, I think Gates was just trying to cover his bigoted ass."

I don't know what to think, other than I'm relieved Aunt Arrow's demonstrating a spark of her trademark fire. My favorite photo of her is one taken by my father with his Brownie when she was ten years old: her hands rest dauntingly on her hips with elbows pointing outward.

We don't look anything alike. I'm shorter and rounder with a soft plop of mostly brunette hair around my face, a few extra pounds and no freckles. What I've inherited besides the attitude are feet. We both wear size ten extra wide.

As I approach Aunt Arrow's building, she invites me in for beans and jalepeño cornbread. "We need comfort food."

I'm reluctant to leave her alone, but I want to be home. I need to regroup, and I'm also not up to Aunt Arrow's cornbread. Something we've never shared is her passion for pot. She says it settles her stomach, but it only makes me hungrier, an attribute I don't need to expand. Aunt Arrow doesn't smoke it. She bakes with it. I'm ever suspicious when she cheerfully pulls an oblong pan of something out of her oven.

But she's welcome to it tonight, and Jake will come as soon as he can get away from the paper.

A flurry of responsibilities and condolence-related activities consume Nathan after his arrival from Charlottesville. We don't have an opportunity to sit down with him, just the three of us, until Monday afternoon.

Nathan and I have an easy rapport, having spent a lot of time together during our own college years, his at Texas A&M and mine here in Austin at the University. He went to A&M on a basketball scholarship and came home *summa cum laude*. He was a tall, slender guy, mostly Adam's apple back then, and we got together during vacations when we would both wind up in Austin, usually to take in a movie with coffee or a beer afterward to discuss the film we'd seen.

On our last such outing we had been sharing a few draft Lone Stars and chewing on *Terms of Endearment* when Nathan told me he'd fallen in love. Not with me, obviously. I would have noticed. Then he showed me a picture of Perry Brownwell Lytle from Beaumont. They're still together, partners in every sense.

He affirms his belief that "Mother did not die of natural causes. Couldn't have." Alternating between angry defiance and grief-stricken breakdowns, he maintains, "Excellent health, walking at least three to five miles. Preparing. We had planned to hike a good chunk of the Appalachian Trail this spring."

Aunt Arrow confirms. Sally had asked her to join in the walks, but Aunt Arrow doesn't do 6:00 a.m. outdoor activities.

Nathan gives us the results of the autopsy, received that morning. "Cause of death, heart attack, and the police have found nothing suspicious in the circumstances." In communication with Sally's physician, Nathan has also seen the results of his mother's most recent physical examination, made less than a month ago. "She easily passed every conceivable test for heart risk. Blood. Echo. Stress. CT scan. And the only prescription medication she took was a low dose of antidepressant to help her sleep, prescribed after Daddy died two years ago."

Aunt Arrow nods agreement to that report.

"To top it off," Nathan says in disgust, "the medical examiner pointed out to me the number of athletes in top form who died of cardiac incidences in their twenties, thirties and forties."

Some persuasion.

Although reiterating his assurance that no crime had occurred, the investigating officer, Bertel Frederick, ordered a toxicology screen because of the public location of the fatality and, according to Nathan, "to relieve the anxiety that often occurs with sudden death. That means us. And it isn't just health related."

The police have again postponed releasing the death scene. With the lab backed up, full results won't be available for a week or so.

Aunt Arrow asks Nathan if he knows about the motorcycle incident, and he's well aware. "She was worried, Mother was. I think it was something at that Center, or someone. Did you see anything suspicious, Grace, when you were out there?"

"I didn't, because we had entirely different assignments, but I know she was involved well beyond B-14s and G-47s. I'll be going back on full alert."

Bingo regulars and others from the Center are among those packing the pews at Sally's memorial service, held a week after her death at St. Barnabas, an African-American Episcopal Church located east of the freeway near the MLK Senior Center. Aunt Arrow and I arrive early to take seats near the front, because Nathan's asked her to speak.

We sat together as well for the last two funerals I attended— my parents'. Dad died first, in a hunting accident. Eerie when I read several years ago about Vice President Cheney shooting his friend in that quail hunt. Same as Dad, only the shot penetrated his heart and lungs. Before he bagged his limit. I thought Mother would be lungs, too, because of the smoking, but it was bridge. Eleven months after Dad died, she had a cerebral hemorrhage in the middle of playing a small slam in no trump. Vulnerable. Her partner said she would have made it.

Choir members begin entering in ones and twos, moving to designated places on the riser behind the altar while softly humming an indefinite tune that I hear sometimes at the Center. The velocity of the humming grows gently, in harmony, while the church sanctuary fills and then overflows into the front hall. The gentle humming becomes the hymn, "How Great Thou Art" as the service begins, with a soprano solo and the choir's swaying refrain, "Then sings my soul ..." vibrating through the sanctuary.

Respect for Sally among friends in the African-American community becomes increasingly obvious as the service progresses. Worshippers weep openly, wail and stomp their feet. Some shout out, leaving no doubt about Sally's future.

"In the Lord's hands now."

"Praise God."

"Allelulia, sweet Jesus."

"Life and death, she's with you God."

"Jesus loves Bingo."

"Amen, Sister."

The Rev. Bertha Summerville from St. Barnabas does the liturgical prayers and introduces the eulogizer, Earnest Jiles, Pastor of Pine Grove Baptist, who helped found the MLK Center. Although I had been vaguely aware of Sally's religious faith through the years, I learn far more about its depth and style from Pastor Giles and responding congregants.

"… and after the good Lord made Sister Sally, God threw the mold away, threw it clean away."

"Praise the Lord!" comes from somewhere behind us.

"How she lived her life is a testament of faith. Giving to others, always giving. I felt in my heart that her death was a shock, but I felt like she'd lived her life right, just not enough of it. The sad part's leaving those of us who love her—family, friends."

"We love you!"

" I'll never forget the last time I saw Sally at a celebration to commemorate the twentieth anniversary of the Center. Her opening speech was powerful, powerful but simple. It was more like a prayer. And complete. Sister put God first, then family, friends, the world, the work of the Center. Some concentrate on themselves, but not Sister.

"Thinking of others!"

"We walked out together, Sister and me, after the ceremony. I told her that her talk was powerful. It moved me deep, way down deep in my soul. But not so much the words," he pauses before finishing in a quiet voice. "She inspired others, not by what she said but by her example."

"Amen!"

It takes quite a while for the congregation to settle, and Aunt Arrow, scheduled to speak next, whispers to me that she feels like a *non sequitur.* I assure her she'll be fine.

Aunt Arrow walks to the front and begins by saying that she has another kind of story to tell about Sally's religious faith.

Murmurs of assent.

The two of them had taken a trip to Italy together the summer after they met, and one of the major sites Sally wanted to see was the Basilica of St. Peter in Vatican City. "When we walked eagerly up to the gates, the guard told us not only did our legs have to be covered, which ours were in jeans, but our shoulders also had to be covered, which ours weren't because we were both wearing sleeveless blouses. The guard wouldn't let us through the gates."

"Gates to the kingdom!"

"We had to think quickly because we were leaving Rome the next day, and this trip would be a huge disappointment if we didn't get into St. Peter's. Our hostel was too far across the city to go back to change. Ever the innovator, Sally pulled a trusty packet of Wet Wipes out of her bag and made us sleeves from the damp tissues. Four sleeves, a set for each of us, plastered against our upper arms. Did we look cool, or what?"

The sanctuary erupts in laughter.

"The guard allowed us to enter. Sally knelt, prayed and lit a candle. And we shot two rolls of film, documenting Sally's ingenuity as well as the young boys who tried to pick us up on the way to the bus." Aunt Arrow sits down to thunderous applause, and the service ends with the recessional, "It Is Well with My Soul."

When peace, like a river, attendeth my way,
When sorrows like sea billows roll;
Whatever my lot, thou hast taught me to say,
It is well, it is well with my soul.

Aunt Arrow and Pastor Jiles hold joint court at the reception at nearby Piney Creek Tavern.

On Friday morning, the day after Sally's service, Nathan returns home to Charlottesville with the understanding that Aunt Arrow will monitor the situation and keep him informed.

Aunt Arrow sucks in her breath, clutches my arm, and informs me that we are going to the library to view the stacks where Sally died. We are referred to Delia Ingram-Kirksey, who refuses our request, explaining, "We have the basement still sealed. No one is allowed in except the police and vetted members of the library staff."

"What if I want a book from down there?" Aunt Arrow demands. "I'd have to go down there to get it."

"No. You fill out a request form with the title, author and call number," Delia says, "from the online catalog. If it shows that it's available, we send someone down for it, but you may have to wait. Our staff is busy, busy, busy."

"What about my niece, Grace Edna Edge?" I step forward from behind Recent Acquisitions—Nonfiction. "Grace Edna is a forensic accountant. Would you allow her to view the scene?" Aunt Arrow asks.

"In which area of forensics do you work, Ms. Edge, the county morgue or the crime lab?" Delia asks.

"Neither," I say. "I'm a forensic accountant. My work involves helping companies and schools and nonprofits detect illegal financial activity."

"As a public institution we have an outside audit every year. Clean as a whistle," Delia says. "You're way off base if you think anything's amiss here."

"No, I'm not accusing, I'm just explaining …"

"So you're with the police?" Delia interrupts.

"No, I'm self-employed."

"But she's testified for the police in some of their cases," Aunt Arrow breaks in. "I'm sure they'd vouch for her."

"She's the general public, then," Delia says.

I've been accused of many things in my life, but never that.

Aunt Arrow doesn't respond.

"Nope," Delia pronounces. "No one from the general public is going into those stacks on my watch."

Except me.

I agree with Aunt Arrow about having access to the scene where Sally died. A subsequent telephone call to Detective Bertel Frederick yields the same response as Delia's to our request to view the scene, although he is more polite, rejecting the request in a deep, resonant voice with no reference to our status as lay or professional, general or specific.

"No dice," I say to Aunt Arrow. "Detective Frederick won't grant permission to view the scene."

Aunt Arrow pinches her lips together. "Then we'll have to grant our own permission, won't we?"

~ Four ~
Burping Strawberries

From my lookout position between 581.5264 *Deciduous Forests of North America* and 581.65 *Just Weeds,* I see the library activity beginning to dwindle. My visible clothing is muted—a mauve and gray soft suit with elastic waist pants and a matching overshirt—but underneath I wear boldly striped purple, pink and green socks with dancing kokopellis. I circle behind 614.317 *Textbook of Meat Hygiene* and head toward the stairwell leading up to the second floor. It's the Tuesday after Sally's service, and I'm staying the night.

At exactly 4:40 p.m. I enter the large walk-in closet that serves as the library's lost-and-found center, located in a far back corner of the building's second floor. I have no problem blending myself and my supplies among the lost-and-found array. In a large maroon bag I've brought the necessities: wallet, toiletries, notebook, pens, calculator, cell phone, two small flashlights, mace, change of underwear, two t-shirts, a pair of running shorts and six pairs of socks in a variety of color/shape combinations. Having enough socks is essential to overnight stake-out.

I sit at the back of the closet, enveloped by a left-behind jumble of jackets, caps, umbrellas, tote bags and sweater vests, as well as a few surprises, such as a pith helmet, bowling ball, *Book of Common Prayer* and a wicker basket filled with styrofoam fruit. I employ one of the exercises I've learned, which is to make imaginative use of props found in the natural landscape.

From concentrated reconnaissance over the past two days, I know that the closet will be part of the security patrol prior to the library's closing at 5:00 p.m. The patrol consists of a rapid open and shutting of the closet door. Sure enough, it occurs right on schedule today at 4:52. Whish, whoosh.

I stay hidden a few minutes beyond 5:00 to ensure that all of the staff members have left before emerging from my cocoon, spontaneously confiscating the pith helmet. Softly, I walk downstairs to the main floor, avoiding the elevator so as not to risk breakdown, and check for lights in the staff office and staff kitchen. None. Assured that I'm alone, I take the stairs to the basement.

The library keeps low-level lights on throughout the building for security, but has no human guards or security cameras after five o'clock. The security system relies on alarms, which sound in the downtown police precinct if anyone attempts to enter the library once the code is set at the end of the day.

I learned all about this system with surprising ease during my reconnaissance by asking a volunteer at the Information Desk if anyone had ever gotten locked in by mistake after hours. The volunteer, who introduced himself as Henry Schmidt, explained solicitously that he had once wondered about the same thing. Henry went into an office and efficiently returned with a laminated card showing diagrams and a description of the library's security system.

"You see," he had said, pointing, "the premises are all protected by these invisible rays that go across the doors and windows. That's what would set things off, crossing one of those rays. No one's going to get closed in here, because the entire building is thoroughly patrolled before closing. All the nooks and crannies are checked. You know, to protect against the derelicts that spend much of the day in here."

"Uh huh," I had said to Henry.

The first thing I see in the basement is yellow Police Area— Do Not Enter tape across the pathways to every aisle, across the entry to the microfiche area of files and readers, and across a sitting area between the stacks and microfiche section. Through the tape barrier, next to a table, I notice the outline of Sally's barely five-foot body chalked on the floor. Beside the tape is an overturned cart stamped with 300-400, designating the Science and Language book stacks. Sally's cart.

Ducking under the tape, I walk over to the table and find a photocopied page containing a list of the fifty most prescribed drugs in the United States and two books: 338.47 *Generation RX: How Prescription Drugs are Altering American Lives and Bodies* and 615.11 *The Prescription and Over-the-Counter Drug Guide for Seniors*. I sit, subdued for a few moments, to compose myself, thinking of Sally's spirit, wherever it now resides, possibly right here with me, observing supportively, although I fully agree with the assessment made by her friends from the MLK Senior Center concerning the ultimate prospects for her afterlife.

I pace slowly through the basement stacks. Not seeing anything else that appears related to Sally's death, I walk over to the microfiche area, curious about why that is taped off, too. Next to Microfiche Reader #4, labeled Check with Microfiche Staff before Onputting, is a fiche. I slip the fiche into the machine and onput without permission.

The title comes up on the screen: "The high cost of prescription drugs; hearings before the special Committee on Aging, U.S. Senate." Scanning through, I read testimony and see tables documenting the effect of escalating drug costs on seniors, the confusion caused by the Medicare prescription drug plan, the specific problems related to drug use by seniors in low-income, multi-racial areas.

I visualize a scenario. Sally picked up her cart, rode to the second floor and reshelved her books. She must have retrieved the two books from the stacks after reshelving the one from where she worked and the 600 from another part of the library. Then she came back down on the elevator, bringing the now-empty cart, to look up the microfiche. I wonder why she didn't drop the cart off on the first floor before coming to the basement.

Another question puzzles me. The library has computer monitors on every floor. Sally might have done a search while she was on the second floor and found the microfiche and books that way. Or she could have searched the online catalog before she came in and already knew what she wanted. Or she could have had a conversation with someone in the library. Or any one of countless other possibilities and combinations.

Why was Sally so interested in prescription drugs for seniors and their costs? Which drugs, and why the hearings? Was it something connected with her husband's death? Maybe she read about these hearings and followed up because she cared about the seniors at the MLK Center. East Austin is a low-income, multi-racial area relative to the rest of the city. Then what? Did she find something? Did something or someone scare her? Had she really been by herself in this basement?

Am I?

I make extensive notes and a long list of questions for Aunt Arrow, including whether she and Sally discussed prescription drugs the morning Sally died. I don't call Aunt Arrow from the library on my cell phone because, barring an emergency, we agreed to wait until I come out, not wanting to take any more risks than the marathon one I'm already running by being in the library at night by myself.

Marathon running reminds me that I need exercise. I return to the station I've established in the stacks and change into the running shorts and T-shirt from my maroon bag. Running up and down every aisle in the 700-900 stacks four times takes twenty-three minutes and elevates my heartbeat to the desired one hundred forty-five beats per minute level.

Next I take a sponge bath, using the double sink in the staff kitchen, one side for soapy water and one side for clean. I climb up on the counter so I can dip myself into each side, singing from 784.4 *Swedish Emigrant Ballads*. I boldly use seventeen of the staff's clean dish cloths to towel myself off.

Clean and dry, I dress in a pristine, long-sleeved t-shirt, the pants to my mauve soft suit, and a pair of yellow socks with an array of blue spirals. That afternoon I stashed dinner rations, picked up at Threadbelle's Takeaway, in the library's staff refrigerator. Twenty-one staff and a rotation of volunteers generated plenty of activity in and around the staff kitchen to camouflage my storage.

Most of my favorites don't work for library smuggling because of smells and bulk, so I'd brought in a chicken and green chili quesadilla with a side of salsa for an efficient, non-odiferous one-dish dinner to complement fresh strawberry pie, even though strawberries make me burp. Sitting at the table in the staff break room, I bless my evening meal. "Thank God for white wine," I pray, having found a container of Chardonnay-in-a-box at the rear of the staff refrigerator. Every now and then, it's worth it to burp strawberries.

While I eat I read from 808.352 *How To Write a Romance Novel from Smolder to Sizzle*, and I can see that I have some major revision ahead, because according to the author, I'm supposed to finish with a satisfying and optimistic ending. I'm also supposed to reward good people and punish bad ones. None of that came up at the writers' festival.

In spite of my thorough preparations the library presents one remaining obstacle: where to sleep. I don't like Current Periodicals because of the cold Formica floor. The offices have carpets, but they're locked. Too much open space in Reference. The area behind the circulation counter is cramped, and that's the first place the staff comes in the morning. If I accidentally oversleep, which isn't likely, since I'm going to set the alarm on my watch as well as those on my cell phone and calculator, they'd find me first thing. I'd be booked for misdemeanor at a minimum. How I know that is that I called a police precinct in Austin, explained that I was a writer and had a character who was discovered living in the Bob Bullock Museum. What would be the charge, I'd asked, for being caught residing in a public building?

I finally settle on the Children's area, which is isolated and cozy, enclosed by bean bag chairs and yellow plastic crates and a stuffed cloth family whose members are leaning against the Youth Readers' Reference Desk, watching me. Mother, father, pubescent girl, toddler boy and curled-up yellow cloth tabby. I persuade the curled-up yellow tabby to leave the group and join me on the sofa. We are grateful to the Live Oak Library's Celebration of Quilting Heritage this month for our bedding and settle in underneath the oil painting of Davy Crockett and James Bowie.

My alarms never have a chance to ring because I don't sleep a wink after 2:14 a.m, which is when I'm awakened by the sound of a toilet flush. That I can hear it means the flusher is on the ground floor with the restroom door open. Ground floor, where I am, and close enough for me to hear.

As rapidly as panic will allow I abandon the tabby and scoot behind the Young Readers Reference Desk. Have I been under observation the entire time, naked in the sink?

The low level lights reveal that he's fully attired. Jeans, flannel shirt, running shoes and an Astros baseball cap, near enough to me I can read the letters on his cap as he enters the Children's Library area and sits down nonchalantly in a maroon bean bag chair. It squishes as he plops. He doesn't look around for me or anyone else. Out of his front shirt pocket comes a baggie. Finger dips into baggie, finger goes into mouth. He's wearing a head set under the cap, and he taps his foot. Must be listening to music, which could have blocked the sounds of my movements. All of them.

So maybe he doesn't know I'm here, if he came from somewhere upstairs in the library, having figured a way to hide and now, like me, seeking the cozy comforts of this space. For what?

For sleep. He stands, mashes the bean bag as flat as possible, re-plops and stretches out his legs. Soon he's snoring.

I don't leave my post until he abandons his at 7:42 a.m., about the time my heartbeat returns to normal. I watch as he stands, stretches, clutches, scratches, leaves the area, enters the men's restroom near the main reference desk and closes the door. Within seconds I'm in the stairwell leading to the second floor. After making a quick and unflushed stop for my own relief, I'm in the lost-and-found closet again, this time with questions about the night visitor. Who is he? How did he get in? What was in the baggie? Is there a connection with Sally? Was he in the stacks that morning?

Enid Slack, the library's main branch assistant director, opens the door promptly at 9:00 a.m. I am dressed in my complete soft suit and the pith helmet, perusing 598.2734 *Birds of the Peloponnesus*. Several patrons follow Enid through the door, so there's enough activity to cover my entering from the stacks as the regulars settle into their places, one in the seat east of Recent Acquisitions—Large Type; two anchoring either end of the table between Telephone Books, U.S. Cities, and Telephone Books, Texas Only, and an assortment on the sofas by Current Periodicals, D-F. He's nowhere in sight.

I walk by Recent Acquisitions—Fiction, with distaste for the markers they put on the Romance novels. Their Westerns here have cute little icons with a lasso looped around a pair of boots, and mysteries a clever-looking Sherlock Holmes type character with a pipe. But the romances have lips. Big red lips. My maidens don't wear lipstick.

I move on to the computer bank and search "Prescription Drugs," finding all of Sally's items, plus more than a hundred additional ones. I trip slightly going down the library's front steps as I dial Aunt Arrow's number on my cell phone.

~ Five ~
Hiccups

Aunt Arrow and I agree to meet at the downtown police precinct. We talk only briefly about my library findings, because she's heard from Detective Frederick, and he now has the toxicology report on Sally. He can see us at eleven o'clock.

When I reclaim my car from the parking garage, I study the payment scale on the sign posted at the garage entrance and decide to pay for a full week of parking. The weekly rate is less than the charge for the eighteen hours and twelve minutes my car was actually in the garage, even though this makes no sense. I suggest to the attendant in the pay station that people should be encouraged to use parking garages less, not more. The attendant is noncommittal but doesn't argue with me about the payment, which he could have, since the computer ticket shows that I owe for nineteen hours, not a week.

What I don't discuss with the attendant is my opposition to parking structures as a philosophical and aesthetic concept. I have opted to use this one in spite of that stance, because my Legacy faced an uncertain future when I entered the library.

I make it back to the police precinct at 10:55 a.m., clean and pressed into a gray, calf-length, flared skirt, yellow turtleneck shirt, gray vest sprinkled with tiny daisies, green and yellow polka dot anklet socks and shiny black Mary Jane shoes. I park my car on the street at a meter. In the police station I literally bump into Kira Mattingly, who is walking across the entry with a clipboard and stack of folders. She doesn't see me until she hits me, sending the folders scattering.

As I help pick them up we talk about golf. We're members of the Friday morning ladies league at Penick Park. We play in the same flight but don't know each other well, because she's in one of the cliques. They drink cocktails at each other's houses. I'm not a party to this and don't want to be, although I wouldn't mind being asked. Plus, she always beats me. Kira has a crinkly smile that lulls her opponents into thinking she's going to be a pushover. Hah.

"I'm here to see Detective Frederick about the Weathers case," I explain calmly. "Sally Weathers. She died in the public library. It's a personal connection with my aunt."

"I'm sorry for your loss," she says in a perfunctory tone. "I remember the report and thought there was only the son. Didn't know the victim was related to you."

"No, it's not my aunt who died, it's a friend of my aunt," I explain. Her superior attitude causes me to babble on. "I'm helping my aunt. Well, really helping my aunt help the son, because he's gone back to Virginia. He teaches at the university and has barely started the spring semester. That's when the wisteria bloom up there."

"And you are involved how, exactly?" Kira asks.

"The lab reports weren't all back yet when he had to leave. Aunt Arrow is sort of standing in for him, trying to determine how she died—Sally, that's what everyone called her even though her real name is Sarah. Was, I guess I should say. We're meeting with Detective Frederick about the toxicology report. That's why I'm here."

"Third floor, room 342. Turn left from the elevators, right if you take the stairs. Much quicker," she says, "and the stairs are good for the big muscles." Kira swings the clipboard like a driver, crisply launching a paper wad off the police intake counter. "That's where you get your power," she says, strutting away down the corridor.

Massaging my thighs at the top of the stairs, I find Aunt Arrow waiting for me on a long hallway bench similar to a church pew. Attired in a floor-length purple and gold caftan, she stands up, gives me a hug and pats my cheeks between her hands. "I'm so glad to see your face sweet and safe," she says, squeezing my cheeks again.

Detective Bertel Frederick comes out into the hallway before there's a chance to say any more about anything. I'm guessing mid-to-late forties. Thinning and frizzy brown hair beginning to gray. Taller than me but shorter than Aunt Arrow, he bulges slightly in a midsection that rides over a thick brown leather belt. He's dressed in a long-sleeved checked wool shirt with rolled-up sleeves, blue knit tie and gray wool slacks. No wedding ring or visible tattoos.

I memorize the relevant details of his appearance. On one of the cases I'd worked with the police, the investigating officer had turned to me with no warning, right in the middle of a conversation, and asked me to close my eyes and describe him as a sort of test of my attention to detail. I passed.

Detective Frederick greets us politely and motions us into his office. When we are seated in the police-issue metal chairs with gray vinyl seats, he says with no preliminaries, "Zoloft and Thorazine."

We wait for more.

He picks up some papers. "Those are the pertinent elements from the tox screen. The victim's heart attack could have occurred naturally but was probably propelled by the interaction of Zoloft and Thorazine. They were the drugs found in her system and can lead to cardiac arrest."

I expect a who-what-where-when-why response from Aunt Arrow, but she says nothing, so I ask, "How?"

"They affect something called the QT interval. Knowing how important these questions are to the victim's son, I had an extensive discussion about the cause of death with Dr. Wheatcliff at the crime lab," says Detective Frederick. He nods to assure us. "I kept at it until I was fully satisfied relative to the conclusions regarding this victim. I know you'll be relieved, too, that there is nothing in the toxicology report to suggest the need for any further investigation, and we can put the matter to rest."

Aunt Arrow still sits surprisingly mute. "What's the QT interval?" I ask, "and what do the drugs have to do with it?"

"QTs measure how long it takes the heart to recharge after each beat," Detective Frederick says. "Thump, thump again. Between thump and thump again, that's the QT interval. When certain drugs interact, such as Zoloft and Thorazine, the new research shows they create something called the LQTS, the Long QT Syndrome, which means the interval is prolonged."

Detective Frederick consults his notes. "With the LQTS it takes more and more time to get from thump to thump again, sometimes resulting in cardiac arrest. There's no thump again at all following the thump. That is what apparently happened to the victim. Victim's heart just stopped beating."

"Her name is Sarah Helen Weathers," Aunt Arrow finally speaks up, "not victim. We are talking about a person here, a human being, not some body in a laboratory muddled up with alphabet letters. A human being named Sarah Helen Weathers, who goes by Sally. An actual woman who could walk parallelograms around people half her age, whose heart condition was excellent." Aunt Arrow is now flushed and shouting. "Sally, who was living and breathing, not goddamn thumping and thumping again."

"Sorry," Detective Frederick puts the papers down and leans back in his chair. "It is Ms. Weathers who experienced the cardiac arrest. No disrespect intended. I know this is difficult for her family and friends."

"For her son Nathan. He's her only family, not some big group of relations, and for Grace Edna and me, who represent him today. Yes, it is difficult to make any sense out of what you are saying because Sally took only one prescription medication, Zoloft, in the lowest possible dose, prescribed after her husband's death. Nathan confirmed that with her physician."

"Our search of Ms. Weathers' premises turned up both medications present in her home," he says, leafing through a notebook. "I conducted the search personally with Sergeant Willhaver. That's what her son thought, too, just the Zoloft tablets, one each day. It's an antidepressant, often prescribed for the elderly. My mother's on it, adjusting to a move into assisted living in Minnesota."

For some reason I'm surprised to learn Detective Frederick has a mother.

Aunt Arrow says angrily, leaning over with her hands on the desk, "She's sixty-eight years old, not elderly. Grief. Her husband died. That's why Sally took the Zoloft, grieving the death of her husband. When someone you love dies, that's what you do, grieve. It's a human response, but I'm sure you wouldn't have a thing about that in your police notebook lab interrogation pile of ..." She stops, because Detective Frederick has tears in his eyes, green above rectangular, rimless reading glasses.

No one speaks. Detective Frederick takes off his glasses, pulls a handkerchief out of his pants pocket and wipes his eyes. Aunt Arrow begins to sob softly, and he pushes a box of tissue across the desk toward her. I reach across and rub her back.

"My wife died two years ago. Lymphoma. She was forty-four," he says in a voice that is barely audible. "It's different for everyone. I can't say I know what you're suffering or her son, or what Ms. Weathers went through after her husband's death. But I understand how hard it is to lose someone you care about very, very much." He wipes his eyes again and puts the glasses back on.

I'm now sniffling, and he pushes the box toward me. I take a tissue, wipe my eyes and sit quietly with my hands in my lap. Suddenly I am very tired from the sleepless night.

"I'm sorry, Detective Frederick," Aunt Arrow says.

"Bertel," he says.

"Aurora," Aunt Arrow says.

"Grace."

"I'd like to explain what I learned about the Thorazine," he says.

"Isn't Thorazine an antipsychotic?" I ask. I remembered that one of the partners at the firm where I had my first job had been on Thorazine after he heard clients' voices in his head telling him that old accountants never die, they just lose their balance.

Bertel picks up a stack of papers, leafs through them and pulls out a sheet. "Dr. Wheatcliff gave me quite a bit of info on Thorazine. It comes in tablets, liquid concentrate, injectables, and, um, suppositories. You're right, uh, Grace, it is an antipsychotic, used in treating schizophrenia, but it's also prescribed for some other conditions such as uncontrolled hiccups. That's what the vic ...uh, Ms. Weathers had. I have the instructions from her label: For severe hiccups, one tablet three times a day. Her tablets were fifty milligrams. Both prescriptions were filled at Bluebonnet Pharmacy, the Zoloft recently and the Thorazine about a year and a half ago." He rocks back and forth in his chair.

"The hiccups were a temporary problem," Aunt Arrow says. "Her system was out of whack after Thomas died, food and drink not digesting normally. On Thanksgiving Day she and Nathan were eating with me. The hiccups started during the second quarter of the Cowboys game. We tried everything. Drinking water out of the wrong side of the glass, holding her breath, sugar, finger at the back of her tongue. Wouldn't stop. Nathan finally took her to the ER, and that's what they gave her. A shot of Thorazine at the hospital, then the tablets for after. She doesn't need them anymore."

"Thirty tablets prescribed. Eighteen left in the bottle," Bertel says. "She took them more than just a day or two."

"She took them for several days after the attack as a preventative," Aunt Arrow says.

"She must have taken a dose that morning," Bertel says.

"I ate with her. She didn't have hiccups."

"It would have been before she left the house—either had an attack or felt one coming on and, like you say, as a preventative. What did she eat for breakfast?"

"Two tacos. Potato, egg, and cheese. Pork and green chili. Pico. Orange juice. And she didn't have any hiccups."

"I don't think she would have eaten pork and green chili," I say supportively, "if she'd felt hiccups coming on." I would have had trouble digesting the pork and green chili that early, I think, although I can handle them after five o'clock.

"For some reason she took the Thorazine, because there's no other way it could have gotten into her system," Bertel says, his tone edging back to abrupt.

"She would have said something," Aunt Arrow insists.

"I agree that there are things about the death that are bewildering, but that's not uncommon when the death is sudden and unexpected, and we're left with many unanswered questions. I have to admit, Aurora, that from a law enforcement perspective we just don't have anything to investigate." He looks down at papers on his desk.

"She was almost run down on the bike trail about three weeks ago by a motorcyclist. Motorized vehicles aren't allowed on the trail," Aunt Arrow says.

Bertel's head snaps up. "Did she report it?"

"No, she was scared witless at first but then decided she'd overreacted, just some guy high on drugs."

"Was there any reason to think someone would want to run over her intentionally?" he asks.

"She's always involved at the Center, helping people and such, and some of the circumstances aren't exactly tidy," Aunt Arrow says.

"Do you have any names?" Bertel picks up his pen to write. "Or any specific untidy circumstances?"

Aunt Arrow admits we don't.

"What about the books and the microfiche about drugs with her body and the cart in the wrong place?" I say too quickly to stop myself.

"How do you know what was found with the body?" Bertel asks.

"Heard it from one of the library staff," I lie.

Bertel frowns. "She was obviously interested in prescription drugs," he says after looking at his notes. "Ms. Weathers and about half the population. She did volunteer work in a senior center. I've interviewed the director. He didn't mention any untidy relationships. Ms. Weathers obviously had reason for concerns about the cost of drugs—for herself and others. There's nothing else suggested by the materials she was reading."

I want to ask more about what I saw in the library, like why she would go downstairs in such a hurry that she didn't return her empty cart. And what about the vagrant? But I hesitate to reveal what I'm not supposed to know.

"My conclusion—and I've consulted with our staff and the lab on this—is that Ms. Weathers died of cardiac arrest, probably effected by the interaction of the two prescription medications she ingested, the Zoloft the evening before and the Thorazine the morning of her death." He shifts forward in his chair as if wishing we would now go away quietly.

"I have a call in for Ms. Weathers' son," Bertel says. "I'll go over the toxicology report with him. In light of what you told me about the incident on the bike trail, I'll keep the file open for a while."

Aunt Arrow pulls herself up from the chair and stretches to her full five feet, nine inches. "We will be in touch, Bertel," she says. "You can expect to hear from us."

Bertel. That would be a great name for a wounded warrior. But I'm not sure about the hair. A warrior should have flowing locks. He's cute, though, even with the bare patches. Does he notice I have no wedding ring or tattoos?

He stands up.

Yes, I think Bertel could work, but not the Frederick. He'll need another last name if I'm going to put him in tartan. And if he wears a kilt we'll lose some of the butt, which would be unfortunate, I notice, as he walks toward the door.

He turns to us and says, "Aurora. Grace. Thank you for coming in today. I'm so very sorry that the circumstance of our meeting is the death of your good friend, Ms. Weathers."

Aunt Arrow doesn't suggest that he call her Sally.

"I also regret that my report doesn't answer all of your questions," Bertel adds. "Sad as it is, I believe that what's in the report is all we're going to know with any certainty."

That's what he thinks.

~ Six ~
Wild Geese

Aunt Arrow and I pick up chicken salad sandwiches from Whole Grains Market and take them across the street to Live Oak Park. We crave sunlight and warmth after the dimness of the police station. While eating, we watch the park worker next to our picnic table, watering an oak designated by a brass marker as the oldest tree in the park.

Walter, whose name is stitched on his shirt, explains that he's hand-watering "because these sweet old ones want a long, slow soaking. The fandangle sprinkling systems just can't manage it. They're always in a hurry to finish and get on to the next station."

It's not until he's moved slowly and rhythmically on to another tree that we talk of Sally—what the police think, what Aunt Arrow knows and what I found in the library. She clucks over my nighttime companion, pronouncing him a dangerous, homeless junkie. I don't disagree and point out that, given his degree of comfort with the library's ambience, he could be well aware of Sally, and possibly she of him. But like me, she doesn't think we can discuss him with the police yet.

Aunt Arrow asks me to read through everything I recorded from the scene and then to repeat the portions about the book titles and microfiche. Sally was well provided for in her husband's will, so she was under no financial pressure. Aunt Arrow speculates that the drug cost concern relates not to Sally's situation but to seniors from the MLK Center, many of whom she cared about on a personal level, something I can attest to from observing her before, during and after her Bingo sessions.

According to Aunt Arrow, Sally said nothing at breakfast about drugs, prescription or otherwise. She did express concern over one or two of her seniors' increasing problems with finances. "I recall Sally's saying they were seeking relief in what she strongly suspected as a troublesome place," which Aunt Arrow assumed might mean loan sharking. More than once Sally had bailed out someone with financial problems, but Aunt Arrow didn't get the impression that was a solution for these two.

Aunt Arrow tells me what Sally said about the motorcyclist on the trail. "She was out for her morning walk, which she took about the same time every day. In an isolated area of the trail she saw the motorcycle coming toward her. She moved off to the side, but as the cyclist approached, he picked up speed and came directly at her. Sally avoided being hit only because she jumped behind a metal bench. The motorcyclist nearly hit the bench, almost turned over, but managed to stay on the vehicle. Then he rode away before Sally could catch her breath and stand up. No chance of getting a description or plate number."

"Sally must have been terrified," I state the obvious. "I wish she had reported it."

"She changed her route after that morning and didn't have any more trouble."

We have no answers for the questions of what she was researching in the library and why.

The Thorazine in Sally's system completely baffles Aunt Arrow. She knows Sally had no hiccups that morning by the time she came to Bluebonnet Pharmacy. Having monitored Sally thoroughly through the previous year's episode, she's sure Sally would have talked about any need to take the Thorazine.

I suggest the possibility that Sally took the Thorazine by mistake. Sleepy in the morning. Just picked up the wrong bottle of pills.

Aunt Arrow has a key to Sally's condo. We decide our next step is to search it, including a survey of the medicine cabinet. We wave goodbye to Walter.

Sally's modestly high-rise condo is near Aunt Arrow's in downtown Austin. Aunt Arrow's has a view west toward the Texas Hill Country, while Sally's overlooks the town lake trail she so vigorously walked. Aunt Arrow recommends that we begin with the view. We pass quickly through the entry hall and dining area to Sally's balcony, where we stand, looking down on kayakers, bikers, walkers, redbud in bloom and a couple of black labs swimming eagerly, leads attached, away from their owner, who runs after them along the shore. We look up to see a flock of wild geese.

"This was Sally's favorite perspective on the universe," Aunt Arrow says and doesn't need to explain why.

We work our way back through the living room, furnished simply with an eclectic blend of family heirlooms and contemporary comfort pieces. Bookshelves line the room on three sides, filled with Sally's lifetime of reading treasures, including a collection of first editions. We find Sally's Thorazine in the medicine cabinet of the bathroom but not the Zoloft, which is on the kitchen counter. That shoots my theory about the accidental dosage. With the drugs in two different places, Sally would have had to have taken the two drugs separately and intentionally.

From Aunt Arrow's ongoing and frequent contact, as well as my own observations of Sally's behavior at the MLK Center, we reject the notion that Sally might have taken the Thorazine as a supplement to Zoloft to combat psychological problems. So that leaves us exactly where?

In Sally's study I leaf through a small notebook on her desk, feeling invasive. Sally's photo gallery distracts Aunt Arrow, who appears in a fair number of the pictures. She holds one up showing the two of them standing proudly in front of San Pietro in Rome, Sally barely reaching Aunt Arrow's shoulder. I'd never before appreciated the sleeves.

We need to explore these records in Sally's study more carefully, but not now. I sense that Aunt Arrow would benefit

from some time on her own. I drift back to Sally's balcony and
sit for a while, thinking about loss, my own as well as Aunt
Arrow's. I've lost both my parents, leaving Aunt Arrow as my
only living relative. I wonder if I should count the dissolved
relationship with Earle as a loss but decide that was a gain.

Aunt Arrow didn't exactly lose Uncle Richard, since it was
her choice, but she's never had children, and I know she has a
sense of loss because of that, even though she has me. For many
years she's been with Jake, but not living together and not
married. That's always made me feel all right about not marrying
again because of Aunt Arrow's semi-single status as my model.
Unlike me, Aunt Arrow's never been much of a feeling sharer,
so don't know what she needs to help with her grief. I walk back
into Sally's office and find Aunt Arrow, crying softly on
Memory Lane.

~ Seven ~
Coming Up Roses

Jared Stanley intercepts me as I rush toward my table next to the Foot Care Station in the MLK Center. Jared directs the Center and has his hand in other social support programs for seniors in this low-income neighborhood. Ours are the only two white faces in the facility on Thursday afternoon.

Still exhausted in spite of a nap at home, I'm running late but don't want to disappoint any of my clients or the spirit of Sally Weathers by failing to show up for my tax assistance session. And I've agreed with Aunt Arrow that I am our highest and best hope for finding a drug connection at the Center.

Jared offers a perfunctory lament for Sally's death and moves on to the revelation, "I've been contacted by the police for background information about Sally. They wanted to know what she did here as a volunteer, how often, how well she got along with the clients." Pulling on his chin he asks, "Have you heard anything about the investigation of her death?" His dyed hair, shoepolish brown, has a bangs-like patch riding across the front of his forehead that seems to rise and fall as a barometer of his moods. Right now the patch kicks out at about forty-five degrees.

Since Bertel's told Aunt Arrow and me that he interviewed Jared, I see no reason not to say the police didn't find anything suspicious about Sally's death. "There may have been some drug interaction from prescription meds, but they're not even sure about that," I tell him.

"You just never know, in spite of all the warning labels," he says. "It's such a relief to have closure." He pats down his wayward strands. "For our people here."

Jared doesn't know Aunt Arrow, so I don't offer Aunt Arrow's evaluation of closure, its lack or my own. I notice the quiet in the Center. No one is dancing, because nothing is playing on the jukebox. The only noise I hear comes from the clicking of dominos at the games tables along with a few conversations drifting in from the arts and crafts area. Even the afternoon coffee drinkers around the snack bar are quiet. It hits me then what's missing: Bingo.

My station's quiet as well. At least three or four people normally await my arrival at the tax table. Today there's only Aldeen Wilson, who's already mailed in her 1040 and awaits a refund of forty-seven dollars.

"How you doin,' Grace Edna?" Aldeen helps me unload my calculator, books and laptop from my briefcase onto a large Formica table. Sassy brass earrings jangle a string of stars, moons and planets-in-their-orbs as Aldeen bends. Her daughter is a jewelry maker who donates a share of profits to the Center.

"I'm sad not to hear Bingo and not to see Sally," I say.

Aldeen nods agreement.

"Is there something you'd like me to go over again with your income tax return?" Aldeen's form was a straightforward preparation, income from her part-time job at Hilltop Assisted Living and interest from a savings account I encouraged her to establish by expounding on the security my own savings provide. It gives me such a sense of comfort to know I have enough to live another eighty-two years, when I'll be one hundred twenty-seven years old, adjusting for inflation at a five percent annual rate.

"Nope. We're done with mine," she says.

"Why don't you and some of the others get a Bingo game started?" I suggest.

"No one but Sally's gonna call it. We don't want any more Bingo."

The podiatrist comes on Mondays, so I know Aldeen's not hanging around for foot care. "Is there anything else I can do for you?"

"We're sad. All of us. We need something else in here. Not Bingo, something special. For Sally."

"A memorial of some kind," I quickly agree. "Let me think." I know that Sally regularly donated books to the Center, her own and others she collected from friends. I gave her some, and Aunt Arrow did, as well. There are stacks of books all around this work area on tables like the one I use. "We could set up a library," I suggest, "have all the books organized in a special way. Put up some shelves."

"Instead of hodgepodge," Aldeen says enthusiastically. We could call it the Sally Weathers Memorial Library."

"Do you know who she was close to especially? Maybe someone she was helping who might want to work with us on this?"

"Dahlia and Eddie. Jamail. She talked to all of them after Bingo last week and Suella on the phone, but they're not here."

It must be someone from that group that Sally told Aunt Arrow about, someone she was trying to help. "If you give me their phone numbers, I'll get in touch with them," I say.

"Yeah, I will. I already asked Jared about a memorial. He says we don't have money for anything, but Eddie's good with his hands. He'll help. Sally worked with him on his reading. She was always talking about reading and writing but not arithmetic. She never said anything about arithmetic. Can you do stuff besides add up taxes?"

"You know, Aldeen, now that you ask, there is something I do that would fit this project, something besides accounting. We could write a book for the library," I say in a brilliant burst of bravado.

"Write about what?"

"Anything you want, stories, and collect them as part of the memorial. You make it up as you go," I say, gaining momentum. "You can even make up who's doing the writing. I do it. I'm a writer. I make up stories, and when I do, I use another name."

"You're not Grace Edna?"

"I'm still Grace Edna, but when I write, I call myself Jasmine McPherson. I'm pretending to be someone else to help me develop the story ideas, the plot and the characters, how they dress, and the scenery and the period in history when it's all supposed to be happening."

"That way no one knows who's really telling it. Uh huh. So it doesn't sound like some list of itemized deductions."

"You got it," I say, laughing.

" Jasmine. I like that. I might be Tiger Lily. Or Avocado. My daughter gave me a seed, and that plant's growin' all the way up to the ceiling in my bedroom. I keep addin' wires for it to climb. Avocado."

Rosella and Dewayne Franklin walk up to the table. We started on their tax return last week, and I asked them to bring in some more documents. Rosella carries a large manila envelope and sets it down on the table.

"You got customers now. I'll go ask around," Aldeen says. "Jasmine."

"Good," I say encouragingly. "Talk to some others, see about interest, and I'll run it by Jared."

"Yeah, Jasmine."

Dewayne looks at me, head at an angle, and asks, "What your name anyway, girl?"

As I'm finishing the Franklins' return and calculating the schedule of estimated payments, I hear Fats Domino singing "Blueberry Hill" from the jukebox. Then Shirley Sipora asks for help interpreting her W-2 as "Baby Love" comes on. I look up to see Aldeen, a la Diana Ross, whom she resembles, and a supporting cast of Supremes dancing, lip-synching and waving thumbs up. I interpret their communication as the signal that our proposal is officially off the ground.

With no one else in line I go across to Jared's office and wait for him to finish a telephone call. I tell him what Aldeen has said about the request for a memorial and what we've come up with, the library and writing project.

"We've tried these classes before," he responds. "They never last."

"We haven't tried this one."

"I can hardly hear. They've got that thing turned up so loud."

"The regulars here are in shock from Sally's death. Building a library and working on a writing project would be a healthy step toward healing and give us all an outlet for our feelings."

"Sex and violence. We don't want to encourage that." His patch is at half-staff. "The Columbine shootings in Colorado started with creative writing, and you know what came out of that."

I decide to try a different approach. "The project wouldn't cost the Center anything. Aldeen would get Eddie to build whatever we need to put the library together, and I'd volunteer to lead the writing group. We don't need anything from your budget."

Bingo.

Ten minutes later Aldeen and I have a plan. She's already signed up five participants for the writing group, and I agree to come an hour earlier than usual. I begin to make a mental list of writing triggers. She gives me phone numbers for Eddie, Dahlia, Jamail and Suella. I'll contact Eddie about building shelves, and Aldeen will work on donations for lumber.

"I think I'll be Tea Rose," Aldeen says.

~ Eight ~
Hullabaloo

It's Ladies' Friday at Penick Park Golf Course, a balmy
early spring day, unseasonably warm. I practice on the putting
green while I wait for my tee-time and watch others drift in. Kira
arrives wearing sea mist Capri pants and matching polo shirt. I
know the outfit because I tried it on at Dillard's, regrettably not
styled for my shape. She's round, too, but in the right places.
Those pants used to work for me when they were called pedal
pushers and came with shirts that weren't meant for Q-tips. I'm
in a Penick Park pale blue golf shirt, navy blue shorts with a ten-
inch inseam that cover lower thigh flab, and blue anklet socks
spattered with tiny pineapples. Kira and I don't often play
together because they try to make up foursomes from mixed
flights, but they moved me up today because someone canceled
at the last minute.

Ruth Ranigan and Della Williams, both in their seventies
and fully capable of beating the pineapples off my socks, fill out
our group. Ruth always manages to find something kind and
positive to say, no matter how bad the situation. If I hit a shot
sideways into the rough, she comes up with something like,
"What a good angle into the green." I haven't played much with
Della, but she looks natty in a pink print ensemble.

As the starter calls our foursome up to the tee box, Kira
whispers that she's heard the case is essentially closed, and I
made something of "an impression" on Frederick, which I want
to watch "because he's emotionally vulnerable." I'm not sure
how I'd go about watching an impression. Rumors had floated

around the ladies league a few months ago that Kira was dating someone from the station, and I'm wondering if that was Bertel. I decide to stick to business, and Kira learns from me that my aunt and I aren't totally persuaded by Frederick's reports and are continuing "with our attempts to resolve unanswered questions."

Kira puts a finger up to her lips and makes a hushing sound, which I assume is a warning not to discuss the case during our round, which I have no intention of doing anyway. She's playing mind games already, and I'm not going to let it affect my round.

I set up carefully on the tee box for my first drive. The set up is key to the golf swing, according to my most recent instructor. The one before that said it was all in the elbow, and before that the wrist hinge, and before that the take-away. I'm going with the set-up. Before the putting green I practiced on the range for about half an hour to ensure a correct and consistent stance.

The variable is what Kira meant by "impression on Frederick." I'd had no knowledge of that when I was out on the range. Now I do, causing my drive to ricochet off three trees like a pinball machine, about forty-five degrees northeast of the tee box. Pecans scatter in the rough.

Ruth says, "Looks like a good day for the squirrels."

I offer my total-humiliation-but-good-sport smile and pull out my five-wood with the intention of rocketing my second shot down the center of the fairway, well out of their vision. Instead I top the ball, and it travels about seventy yards in the rough.

The rest of the round goes somewhat better except for a minor water-logged seventh and a putting-disaster fifteenth. I thoroughly enjoy the two older women and discover that Della tells the best jokes in the league. Golf generally helps my writing vocabulary by introducing new and creative ways to use four-letter words, combinations that never would have occurred to me.

For a few hours the golf takes my mind off Sally and Aunt Arrow. Coming into the clubhouse, I consider the specials:

turkey wrap and fresh fruit, blueberry smoothie, or tuna melt
with French fries. I see Kira at the scorer's table, confirming her
win for our flight, but I feel encouraged since she beat me by
only seven strokes today.

She turns toward me with a patronizing smile, which I
decide to wipe off her face. "What did you mean, by the way,
when you said I made an impression on Frederick?" I ask.

But once again she takes the match.

"Your intellect, of course," she says, backing away from the
scorer's table, then winks before joining her social group.
Whatever the hell that means.

I'm still not persuaded Sally was murdered, but I wouldn't
want Aunt Arrow to know I'm ambivalent. Sally may have taken
the meds together of her own choice for health reasons, like a
case of morning hiccups that she didn't care to mention, and died
from the fluke drug interaction. She may have died of a heart
attack unrelated to the interaction, or she may have been the
victim of a sinister plot because of something criminal she
uncovered in connection with drugs. It seems a stretch. I suspect
it's Aunt Arrow's grief and Nathan's that won't allow them to let
the death go as natural causes.

I've spoken to Nathan on the phone and exchanged several
e-mails, the most recent about Bertel's report. Nathan's not
planning to come back to Austin for a few weeks, he's told me,
when he'll meet with the lawyer to begin settling his mother's
estate. Unless we need him. "If you do, I'll be here quicker than
you can say hullabaloo caneck caneck," he quotes from the
Texas Aggie fight song.

Nathan isn't wavering one iota from his suspicions,
especially after hearing my library discoveries, excluding my
companion. "Something triggered that drug research," he said as
we ended our phone conversation, "and there's no way she
would have taken those drugs together. Mom hated the
Thorazine, even when she needed it to stop the hiccups. You and
Aurora should contact the police guy, Frederick, if you discover

anything at all—and watch it. Mom found out something dangerous, and look what happened. Please be careful."

That's one of the topics I take when I go over to Aunt Arrow's Friday night for a casserole of spinach and tomatillo enchiladas, a pitcher of sangria, and guacamole salad, which means, regrettably, that she serves it with without any salted chips. In preparation for coming I fortified myself with Pringles, intending to eat just nine, but I don't believe it's possible to eat less than a half-can.

As we're sitting at the table Aunt Arrow rushes over to the oven and pulls out her pan of cornbread with its distinctive smell of home-grown weed that I pretend not to notice. Oh, what the hell, I take a couple of squares just to be sociable. We finish with Aunt Arrow's special flan and vanilla-almond sauce, while discussing the case and making specific plans about who's going to do what, as if we know what we're doing.

I'll continue to pursue the connections at the MLK Center. Aunt Arrow will return to Sally's condo to look more carefully through the contents of her office. Nathan has Sally's cell phone records and will send us a list of calls, though he believes she just used the cell for long distance. He's also reviewing the last six months of check and credit card payments. They want me to analyze the contents of the library resources, once they're returned to circulation, and I need to follow up in some way about the man and baggie.

I pass along Nathan's warning. "We're taking some risks just by looking around. If we get close to something, Nathan thinks we might be in danger." I'm hoping she'll begin to back off.

"Reading the letters will be the hardest," Aunt Arrow says, ignoring the warning. "Sally kept up with so many people from all parts of her life."

"How are you doing without Sally?" I ask, sensing the opening to shift the discussion to her grief.

"It's hit me hard, really hard. Makes me sad about everyone I've lost," she says, sighing. "Sally, but others, too. My parents. Your dad, my brother Bill. The divorce. Even though I wanted the split, it was the end of a dream to have my own family. Children."

Aunt Arrow speaks quickly, as if she can block out the emotion if only she can talk fast enough. Whoa. I can't remember ever hearing Aunt Arrow speak like this, reflectively and about herself. It must be the cornbread. Aunt Arrow's face is pale.

We walk back out on her balcony, and I carefully avoid tripping over her "herb" garden, one large section of which has two plants growing three feet apart, staked to posts. They're located to receive the requisite eight hours of sun.

Having not yet consumed my recommended daily allotment of fruit and vegetable servings, I take the sangria pitcher, now empty of liquid, and munch on the wine-laced oranges. I look at the night sky, stars muted by city lights but still visible, like Aunt Arrow's freckles through her pallor.

Aunt Arrow sits down and says quietly, "As I get older my losses accumulate, and I grieve more and more people and things that are gone forever."

She says it without a single bit of cynicism, so I know she's not herself yet. And in spite of the difference in our ages, what she says resonates with me.

Much of Saturday I devote to catching up on my paying work, some of which I can now do by computer, thanks to software programs capable of expediting the detection of the financial fraud. In go the debits and credits, out pops the sinister credit card scheme or whatever.

Later in the day I take an hour or so to telephone the MLK Center people whom Aldeen suggested, concentrating on those Sally had helped in some way.

Eddie agrees to work on the shelves for the memorial library. "Anything for Sally," he says. "She got help for our little Katy, my son's youngest. Teachers said Katy wasn't smart like the other kids in her class, so Sally had her tested by a specialist. Turns out that Katy's dialectic. Reads backwards. Now we have a tutor for her, and she's making A's and B's. Wouldn't have happened without Sally. You betcha I'll build all the shelves you want in that library."

Suella thanks me for calling. She's the primary caregiver for an older sister with severe osteoarthritis and C.O.P.D. It's not possible for Suella to come to the Center as much as she'd like, but she will do something for the library project if I have a specific job she can work on at home, such as crocheting runners for the library tables.

"Ruth Ann's in so much pain" Suella says. "I just hate to leave her for very long. Never know when she's gonna need me. Wants to do things herself, but she's crippled with the hurt. We can't afford to pay someone to come in, but I can sit and sew for Sally. I can do that. She was so sweet, that lady. Every Thursday night after her Bingo, bringing us ribs from Bud's Barbecue. You tasted those? Ummm-ummm."

I make a note to pick up ribs for them and for me next Thursday.

Jamail says he's busy with a new job that Sally helped him find at Lester's Diner as a short order cook to supplement his social security check, "measly because my first thirty years of employers didn't have to pay in." If he works the breakfast-lunch shift on Thursday, he can make it to the writing group.

"Would it be all right to work on menus for the writing project?" he asks. "Lester's could use some up-do."

I assure him that restaurant food would be a most appropriate creative writing topic.

Mark and Annie will try the group, but neither has time to talk for very long on the phone with me.

The conversation with Dahlia, though, offers some promise of criminal connection.

"I've always wanted to do something like that story-writing stuff. I make 'em up for my grandchildren, and I'd like to get them set down on paper," Dahlia says, "the stories, not the grandchildren. They don't set."

"That would be very special for them," I say. "Do your grandchildren live far from you?"

"No, they live with me. Amos and Esther. Their mother's in and out."

"In and out?"

"She's addicted. We've tried everything. Sally helped us get her into treatment. She almost made it, but now she's back in the big house. Gatesville. Dealing."

Gatesville, the women's prison.

~ Nine ~
Show, Not Tell

A tall African-American man and a shorter Hispanic woman greet me when I enter the St. Barnabas narthex on Sunday morning. The woman says, "Good morning, welcome to St. B's. I'm Rosa Gonzalez, and this is Ben Jackson. Are you visiting?"

"I'm Grace Edge, and this is my first time for a Sunday service, but I love your jazz." I've been to St. Barnabas' annual jazz festival in the spring but have never attended a service here except for Sally's memorial. Partly in response to my conversation with Aunt Arrow about grief, I've decided to try attending church again.

Ben bends up and down, playing an imaginary saxophone.

"Please fill out a name tag," Rosa says, shaking her head at Ben and handing me a paper tag and magic marker. "As a newcomer, we'd like you to use a blue tag."

After writing my name I peel off the back, stick it on my blouse and wad up the sticky backing, which Rosa takes. I'm grateful, because usually you have to put it in your pocket and find it weeks later in the washing machine, the wadded paper permanently smushed into a corner of the pocket.

"Welcome, Grace," Ben says, then repeats my name more slowly. "Now, Grace. Is that irony or metaphor?"

Amused, I don't know how to respond.

"Metaphor, I'm sure," he answers for me with a big smile.

"We'll want to give you some cookies," Rosa says.

"Thank you just the same, but I don't want any cookies. I'm here for the ten o'clock Eucharist."

"Our cookies are for the newcomers to the church. We give all the first-timers a packet to say welcome," Rosa explains, "on your way out after the service. That's why we have you in a blue name tag, so we know who gets the cookies and also to introduce you to our congregation. Are you new to Austin?"

"Oh, no," I say but offer no further information.

"Uh huh," Ben says. "Next time you come, you'll get a green name tag. This is your only shot at the cookies."

I like the reference to next time, as if they've already decided they want me to return. I quickly find the way to my usual church seat preference, three-quarters of the way back from the altar, right side, and glance around. The diversity among the worshippers impresses me, as I estimate about fifty percent African-American and the remainder a mix of Caucasian, Asian, Hispanic and assorted other. Elderly to newborn. Families. Singles. Couples in combinations of same and opposite sex.

We stand for the processional, a robust rendition of "Mine Eyes Have Seen the Glory." As the choir rolls in I'm pleased to see Aldeen and several others from the Center, singing and clapping their way up the aisle, "Glory, glory hallelujah. God's truth is marching on."

The priest, Bertha, whom I recognize from Sally's service, greets us with kind eyes and short-cropped gray hair. She announces the celebration of Martin Luther King, Jr.'s birthday this morning, even though his actual birthday was a couple of months before. "You'll find out why shortly," she promises.

Following the reading of the Gospel, which today is the story of Jesus' cleansing the temple, Bertha walks to the pulpit but does not preach. She introduces Madeline Lewis, a dean from Howard University, as the guest preacher. "This is the day Madeline could be with us, so this is the day we are having our birthday party for Dr. King. I can assure you that she is very much worth waiting for."

I'm quickly caught up by Madeline's sermon when she says that one of the main things Jesus and Martin Luther King, Jr. had in common was a ministry of showing, not telling. Madeline pauses briefly, then holds up a Bible. "In the Gospel for today Jesus confronts the money-changers and the dove-sellers," Madeline says, slinging her hands, "He disrupts everything, tossing coins, releasing birds from cages, shouting at the sellers, turning the tables upside down."

A young girl near the front shouts, "You go, guy," to nods and smiles.

"King's house was bombed, and how do you think King responded to that attack?" Madeline asks.

"Meet hate with love," comes a voice from the choir.

"You know these stories and what they mean," Madeline nods. "We don't have to be told that God has a powerful impact on the lives of Jesus and King because they showed us that impact through their actions," Madeline says.

"No one has to tell us they were compassionate human beings—they showed us in how they treated others. No one has to tell us that they valued diversity and equality. They showed us in every step they took."

I want to say, "Me too, me too," because that's exactly what I try to do in my stories. I don't tell my readers a character is feeling brave or lonely or lustful. I show that through action, dialogue and apparel.

When I tune back in to the sermon, Madeline is saying, "They dreamed big, Jesus and Dr. King."

A man in the row behind me shouts, "I have a dream." Others join in, and voices repeating the familiar refrain echo all around the sanctuary.

Madeline nods emphatically. "We all have a dream, but it's up to us to make the dream come true. In how we treat each other. In how we treat our friends, but also our enemies. That's what we're here to celebrate, but also to carry out their models in the world. Dr. King and Jesus showed us how to love one another as God loves us. All are equal."

Usually preachers get really loud during the big important points, especially as they're winding down. That's how we know they're getting to the end, but Madeline's voice gets quieter. She almost whispers, "Look around you. Front, back, side to side. We are equal in God's sight."

She sits down somberly, and the congregation responds with respectful silence and stillness.

The lull is only temporary, however, because after a reverential creed, confession and absolution, Bertha opens her palms and says, "The peace of God be always with you," apparently the signal for pandemonium.

With these words everyone but me begins to move boisterously around the sanctuary with one objective in mind: hugging. I'm used to the "passing of the peace" ritual at St. Jude's, my former church, that involved greeting with a handshake persons seated in the immediate vicinity, but this St. Barnabas version is well beyond my experience. Although I fear I'll hyperventilate, I begin tentatively exchanging a few hugs, gradually building momentum. Aldeen, Sam, Rosa and Bertha all come up along with about fifty or so others. I turn out to be quite the hug-ee with my blue nametag.

The remainder of the service is relatively familiar to me until we near the finish. That's when the choir rises up from behind the altar, a sea of chocolate and white and black faces. Instead of a recessional, with service leaders and choir leaving the sanctuary down the center aisle, choir members move out into all three aisles and along either side, as the pianist plays the opening notes to, "We Shall Overcome."

The congregation stands to sing, holding hands and swaying to the music. My mother taught me never to cry in public, an admonition I ignore along with most everyone else in the sanctuary. "We'll walk hand in hand, we are not afraid, we shall live in peace someday ... Deep in my heart, I do believe ..."

I'm still sniffling when Rosa and Ben bring me a packet of cookies. Ben says, "It's a rare Sunday, missy, when you get the sugar cookies with sprinkles along with the raisin-oatmeal-chocolate chip. We're celebratin' today."

I thank them for the cookies and the celebration as Aldeen walks up with her granddaughter in tow. I meet Kelley, who soon dances off with her girlfriends, all of them, regardless of race, sporting cornrows with brightly colored barrettes flapping at the ends of their braids.

Aldeen motions me over to the refreshment table where she begins setting up the coffee urn and a punch bowl with lemonade. I tell her how much I liked the music. She introduces me to Tilly, a soprano from the choir.

"We do have fun with our singing," Tilly says.

"It's obvious," I say.

"You been able to get hold of Eddie and Suella and them about the library for Sally?" Aldeen asks. "Tilly here's interested. She'll be our token white student."

Tilly makes a curtsey.

"Mark's white, but he's our token jock, and you can't be in more than one category." Aldeen tastes the punch, makes a face and adds more sugar.

"That's great. We'd love to have Tilly." I give them a brief rundown. "Eddie's ready to start work on the shelves. Suella will do what she can from home. She's offered to make something for the tables, but she doesn't think she can come to the group. She seems pretty homebound, caring for her sister."

"So she says." Aldeen rolls her eyes.

"Isn't her sister suffering from arthritis?" I ask.

"They're just suffering over there, period."

"I'll meet them this week when I take some food over to continue Sally's barbecue tradition. Guess I'll see for myself."

"Guess you will."

Aldeen doesn't elaborate.

"Dahlia and Jamail both plan to come," I tell her. "Do you know anything about Dahlia's daughter? The one in prison."

"Crystal meth the latest. Drugs since she was twelve. First an addict, then a dealer. Probably cooked it, too, and whatever else necessary to finance her habit. It's just about broken Dahlia's heart. Tries to rehab, then lapses. Those kids keep her going."

Aldeen begins cutting and serving slices of a giant birthday cake. "How about some of this cake?" she offers, and I accept, quickly hiding the packet of cookies. I notice there's a message from Aunt Arrow on my cell phone, which I'd turned off during the service, and I wave goodbye to Aldeen and Tilly.

Aunt Arrow can hardly get it out fast enough that she believes she's discovered how Sally got the Thorazine. She wants me to come over to Sally's condo right away, and she'll wait for me there.

~ Ten ~
Fruitcake

Aunt Arrow asks if I'd like some soup for lunch. She'll find some for me in Sally's well-stocked larder. I explain that I've already had lunch, birthday cake.

"Whose birthday?" she wants to know.

"Martin Luther King, Jr."

"The cake must be pretty stale by now," Aunt Arrow says, "since his birthday was in January."

"St. Barnabas celebrated today to accommodate a speaker from Howard University. Just terrific. So was the service."

"I thought we'd broken you of that."

"Broken?"

"Going to church."

"I missed the potlucks," I offer as defense.

Aunt Arrow's Sunday morning concentrates on mourning doves, newspapers, cinnamon rolls and Jake—a combination, I concede, that could feed a spiritual center.

"I'm anxious to see what you found with the Thorazine."

Aunt Arrow motions me over to the kitchen counter. She holds up a Collin Street Bakery tin. I'm familiar with the Corsicana, Texas, fruitcakes that sell all over the world. She opens the lid, and I see about a third of a cake inside.

"Apricot Pecan," Aunt Arrow says, holding the cake up for me to smell. "That's the only kind Sally liked. She kept one around to nibble on. Said the nut and fruit combination made a good start to her day."

I read the description on the side of the tin: Australian apricots, native Texas pecans, glazed golden crust. "It sounds pretty good, but what does it have to do with Thorazine?"

Aunt Arrow dumps out some of the orange-colored Thorazine pills onto the countertop and waits for me to respond. I must be missing something.

"You think the cake gave her the hiccups after she ate it that morning," I finally guess, "and that's why she took the Thorazine?"

"No, that's not what I think at all. Look at the pills, and then look at the color of that crust and the apricots in the cake."

I see the similarity, but I'm not sure where this takes us, unless … "Are you thinking that someone put Thorazine in the cake, and it was disguised because of its color and texture?"

"That's exactly what I'm thinking. There could be pills packed into the remainder of the cake, and Sally wouldn't have noticed. "

I look more closely at the cake and at the medicine. "You may be right. This cake could hide a variety."

"And the taste. The fruit in the cake would have covered up the citrusy flavor of the Thorazine pills," Aunt Arrow says. "Someone packed this cake with the meds, knowing Sally would eventually eat it. If she didn't or served it to someone else, nothing would be lost."

"But who? "

"All sorts of people work in, on and around this building for the condo association, for individual owners. Real estate companies show units for sale and lease. We have dozens of possibilities."

"Yes, but who among all of the possibilities would know about Sally's cake habits and that she took another med and even the unlikely drug interaction?" My voice rises in direct proportion to how far off base I believe Aunt Arrow is.

"Well, to begin with, I agree with Nathan that she had to ingest the Thorazine without knowing it. If she were onto some criminals involving drugs—which is what I think, based on what you found in the library—they would have wanted her out of the picture and would go to whatever lengths necessary to accomplish that."

"This is sounding bizarre," I say.

"As to the interaction potential, there have been stories in the press and on television about such drug interactions. I checked the archives of my paper, and we've recently run a series of articles about studies linking different combinations. One specifically focuses on these two classes of drugs and that interval effect Bertel talked about. The story in the paper reported the likelihood of problems, especially for persons over sixty years old. Whoever did this already knew something about drugs."

"What about fingerprints?" I notice Aunt Arrow isn't wearing any gloves when she handles the tin.

"There would already have been so many prints from the factory processing that fingerprints aren't relevant, but the remaining contents of the cake tin certainly are."

"Why not just kill her in a drive-by shooting or some kind of accident, like when she was out for her morning walk? Ah, the motorcyclist's attempt. I see where you're coming from. But this way, with the drugs, it depends on so many variables. Getting in and out of her condo without being seen. Putting enough pills in the cake. Her eating. The drugs' impact. There are so many other ways to do this."

"But too suspicious or difficult to accomplish," Aunt Arrow reasons. "That one effort failed. Then Sally shifted her routine to be on the trail when there were lots of other walkers. The last thing whoever did this would want would be to stir up so much attention that the police would get involved in investigating a crime."

Certainly not.

"We need to bring in the police on this fruitcake discovery," Aunt Arrow continues. "They have the lab."

"So, you'll contact Detective Frederick?"

"No, sweetie, I'd like you to do it. We had that emotional thing, he and I, when I got angry about his insensitivity, and he talked about his wife. I think if you take in the cake, we're more likely to keep this whole thing focused on the facts essential to solving the case."

Right. The fruitcake theory.

Back in the police department hallway on Monday afternoon, I wait in the pew-like seats. Fortunately, I didn't see Kira on my way in and have to explain why I was bringing Detective Frederick a Collin Street Bakery tin containing a partial portion of apricot pecan cake. I sit, holding the tin and planning for the twenty-seventh time what I am going to say.

Bertel's head appears in his office doorway, and he motions for me to come in.

He's dressed in crisply creased khaki slacks, a light blue dress shirt with rolled up sleeves, a blue knit tie, grey sweater vest, navy blue socks and loafers. I have on the khaki slacks but without the crisp crease, blue sweater vest, white mock turtle neck shirt, blue socks speckled with gold scales of justice, and the now slightly scuffed Mary Janes.

We exchange critical information about the weather and airborne allergens. Bertel inquires politely about Aurora.

"It's actually her investigative work that has brought me in today," I begin.

"Uh huh," he says, loosening his blue knit tie and immediately retightening the knot. His cheeks flush slightly.

"As I mentioned on the phone we think we've discovered how Sally ingested the Thorazine," I say.

"Yes, proceed."

I set the cake tin, now encased in plastic wrap, on Bertel's desk and slide it toward the center.

He looks but doesn't move to touch it. The cake tin sits marooned, halfway between us on his desk.

"It's from the Collin Street Bakery," I say, "in Corsicana."

He rubs his hand over his chin, seemingly deep in thought.

"They're famous for their fruitcakes, but this is a different kind of cake. It's apricot pecan."

"Yes, I can see that on the side of the tin from here."

"Aunt Arrow found it on Sally's kitchen counter. Sally ate a slice most mornings."

"And the relationship between the cake and Sally's taking the Thorazine is what?" Bertel hones right in without my having to explain Sally's motive for the early morning cake eating.

I open my purse and take out a Thorazine tablet, also encased in plastic wrap. I shove the pill across Bertel's desk to the cake island.

"To show you, I'll have to take this wrap off," I say, and he nods. Just as I'm introducing the final piece of my evidence presentation, the phone rings. "Sorry," he says. "I have to take care of something, but I won't be gone long. If you could just hang in here for a bit, I'll be right back."

I tell him I can wait for a few minutes and always have some work with me, pointing to the file folders peeking out of the side pocket to my bag.

"Would you like some coffee to go with that cake?" He asks. It takes me a few seconds to realize he's made a joke. Right here in the police department with all this evidence between us. I'm laughing slightly as I shake my head, and he leaves the office.

I take out my laptop and begin writing.

In pursuit of a security leak Captain Bertel climbs the stairs to Lady Jane's quarters because he suspects her of duplicity, on the one hand playing the long-suffering fiancée of Major Chesterton, while on the other stealing secrets from the Major during their love trysts. The good Captain raps lightly at the chamber door, which is opened not by Lady Jane but by her lady's maid, Constance-in-Waiting.

"Your Constance, might I beg your favor to grant me a few brief words with M'lady?" Captain Bertel asks, bowing.

"You cannot, oh sire," Constance-in-Waiting replies, giggling. "My Lady is absent, not to return for hours, because she's all the way across the glen."

"I see," Captain Bertel says. "What's in there?" he asks, pointing through a portal.

"My Lady's sleeping chamber," Constance-in-Waiting replies, blushing as she twists the tassels of her bodice laces. "Come, sire. You may enter."

"Again, sorry for the interruption, Grace," Bertel says as he walks briskly across his office, and I bolt up in my chair, sensing heat spreading across my cheeks and down my neck.

He sits back down, leans forward, rubs his hands together and puts them both on his desk. "Now let's have a look at what you've brought."

"It's possibly contaminated," I say quickly, closing the lid of my laptop.

"How's that?"

"Aunt Arrow and I. Fingerprints. We contaminated it somewhat by handling these items, but we figured they'd already collected so many prints in the processing that a few more wouldn't matter."

"Go ahead and unwrap them," he says abruptly, "and explain to me what you're getting at here."

I pull everything back to my side of the desk, unwrap the plastic from the pill and cake tin, then carefully remove the lid. "See?" I hold up the pill. "The Thorazine tablet looks like some of the contents in the cake." I turn the cake tin sideways for him to see inside.

"Aunt Arrow believes someone searched Sally's condo and found the two kinds of medicine," I continue. "They put the Thorazine pills, probably broken up, into Sally's cake, and she unknowingly consumed the Thorazine that way. A lot of people have access to the condo building where Sally lives."

"Why would this someone want to do that?" Bertel asks, his tone skeptical.

"Because Sally was onto some kind of crime being committed, probably some drug-related ring," I suggest. "We know she was researching prescription drugs and think she uncovered evidence through her contacts in the MLK Center, people she was helping. Sally did things, like take meals to shut-ins, help them find jobs, find resources for their families. She must have discovered something so big that the criminals wanted her out of the picture, so to speak, because of what she'd uncovered."

"Drug-related ring?" he says in the same skeptical voice.

"That's what we think," I say and sit back in my chair, feeling the blush spread out to my ears. "The *Austin Times* has recently run a series on dangerous drug interactions that include these two drugs."

"Let me be sure I understand this correctly." Bertel writes a list of several items on a notepad and speaks as if he's reading out the list.

"Ms. Weathers volunteered at the MLK Center. She had contact with persons from the Center outside of her volunteer time. One or more of these persons was involved in illegal activity or knew of the illegal activity. The illegal activity was related to drugs in some way. We know that her discovery was related to illegal drug activity because she was conducting research for unknown reasons about drugs."

I nod.

"Ms. Weathers learned of the illegal activity through communication with, or observation of, this person or persons with whom she had contact through the MLK Center."

"Uh huh."

"The perpetrators or potential perpetrators learned that Ms. Weathers had knowledge of this illegal activity," he says. "One of them or one of their representatives entered Ms. Weathers' premises, determined that she took Zoloft as well as having on hand a prescription for Thorazine, and decided the best way to eliminate her was to put Thorazine in her granola."

"No, it was fruitcake."

"Sorry, fruitcake," Bertel makes a note on his pad. "Someone who knew about the minuscule possibility that these drugs would combine to cause her death because they read an article in the *Austin Times*."

It would be difficult for Bertel to make this theory sound any more improbable than he already has, just by listing out what I've told him. I guess that's his objective, to underline how unrealistic we are.

"The taste of the Thorazine would be disguised by the cake," I say anyway.

Bertel looks up from his notepad and puts down the pen.

"I told you and your aunt when you were here before, as well as Ms. Weathers' son on the phone, to let me know if you had other questions or findings, and I would follow up as appropriate," he says. "To honor that commitment, I'm willing to take this one step further. I'll have the lab check the cake and tin for traces of Thorazine."

"You will?" I say, in mild astonishment.

Bertel puts the cake tin, Thorazine tablet and plastic wrap into what must be an evidence bag.

"Does that meet with your satisfaction, Grace?"

"Well, yeah, and I know that Aunt Arrow and Nathan will appreciate your efforts, as well, in following up on this."

And I know you don't believe a word I've said, I added to myself, and you are doing the lab work to get rid of us once and for all. But even if you know all that, you don't know everything.

"Umm," Bertel says, standing up and looking at his watch as I gather my bag and folders. "Again, I apologize for the interruption that's kept you so late," he says. "Could I make it up to you by taking us out for a bite to eat?" he asks, putting both hands in his pockets, then taking them out and retightening his already taut tie knot. "I have to eat anyway."

If the Thorazine weren't in the evidence bag, I might take one.

By the time I leave his office, what's evolved is an agreement to meet Bertel for dinner, not tonight because I'm going to Aunt Arrow's from here, but a Tuesday night of next week, when he thinks the lab report will be back. It will be an opportunity to discuss the findings without so many distractions. He'll call me to set the time and place.

It's certainly not a date with him, because I don't do dating. After the divorce I went through that period where you're fresh meat in the marketplace, a few one nighters and a couple of three or four monthers. Then it dwindled to the occasional, with rarely shared nights, and finally to the I-like-living-alone-so-why bother stage.

It's also not a date, because we're meeting to discuss the case, and we're not going together to the restaurant in the same car. Is it?

~ Eleven ~
Lone Star

Aldeen has everyone chattering and mostly seated when I arrive on Thursday afternoon. She slides a name card over to me that reads, "Grace Edna Edge, a.k.a. Jasmine McPherson." Apparently she's already told them something about my pen name, because they immediately want to know about Jasmine.

"Does she write hot stuff?" Eddie asks.

Although I'm flattered by the attention, I don't know what to say about the temperature of Jasmine's writing. Instead of answering I promise to talk about my own work another day so we can devote all of our class time to their writing.

Jamail says he has a question. "We might have some writing with stuff like the S and F words, is that a problem? Jared's told us we have to keep our language clean in this center, no profanity, and he doesn't allow rap on the juke box. Treats us like children."

Everyone seems eager for my response, which is to explain the approach I take with my own writing. "Let's say a character in my story walks out the back of her house and accidentally locks her keys inside the house just as a wasp stings her neck, and she cries out so loudly that it scares the dog, who jumps over the fence and runs out into the street, trampling her neighbor's newly producing tomato plants. What do you think the character says?"

They hoot with laughter, and Tilly says, "So you're telling us it's OK as long as it's appropriate to the situation."

Aldeen adds, "Or describes what a character does," and everyone laughs some more.

"I think you've got it," I say. " Let's get started. I'll bring in a topic each week, and you can write on that, or you can work on something you choose for yourself. Today's topic is to introduce yourself to the group. Write anything about yourself you'd like us to know about you, who you are and what you're about."

"Writing about ourselves," Jamail says, "a subject dear to our hearts."

Annie shakes her head. "Speak for yourself."

"Keep your hands moving for the next twenty minutes, and I'll let you know when the time is up." I show them my watch. "That'll be when the big hand gets to the green tulip." It impresses no one.

I'd planned to write along with them, but as they begin I see Jared across the room, waving at me to come over to his office. I consider pretending I haven't seen him but decide to get whatever he wants over with now rather than postponing it until after class.

Patting down his hair patch, Jared says, "You have a pretty good-sized group to start, but I doubt that it'll hold up. They never do." He hands me a stack of forms and spends several minutes going over the instructions for filling them out and maintaining records on who participates how many times and notifying him in writing of any expected costs outside of the initial budget, which for this project are nil.

"I appreciate your support, Jared," I say.

"How's the investigation?" he asks with his hair bristling at about one-quarter staff. "Anything else surface on Sally's death, or have they put that to rest, so to speak?"

"No, it's ongoing," I say, ignoring his tactlessness.

"Going where?"

"The police are looking into several unresolved issues."

"What issues?'

"I don't know what specifically, just that the case is still open."

"I'm surprised. I thought they'd decided it was a drug interaction that killed her. Why's it still open?" His hair is now at close to ninety degrees.

"You can contact Detective Frederick if you have questions." I sense the escalation in Jared's interest for no apparent reason. "I really don't know anything more," I say, "except that the police have not completed their work."

"What about your aunt? Sally's friend?"

Why is he bringing Aunt Arrow into this? How does he even know about Aunt Arrow? I remember seeing him at the memorial service. "She doesn't know anything else, and she's staying completely out of it," I say protectively. "I have to get back to the group. The big hand has gone by the bluebonnet and is approaching the tulip."

"Don't forget to bring me those forms next week."

When I call time, almost everyone seems surprised that twenty minutes have passed. I explain the plan for the rest of the class is for everyone who wants to share from their writing to read out loud, but no one should feel obligated to do so.

Six hands shoot up for sharing, all except Annie, who keeps her eyes down. Jamail goes first.

"I'm introducing myself with what I do at work. It's a poem called 'Scraping the Grease.' He reads in rap rhythm about his life as a short-order cook, the endless blackened aftermath on the grill of bacon rashers, doilies of eggs, slabs of ham, bubbling burgers, johnnycakes flippin', and whatnot hash. He has us tapping our toes until he gets to the final verse about the residue on his inner grill, now scraped clean. "But that ol' Black Tar and alcohol can ignite the fire any time." Several in the group nod.

Inspired by Jamail, Tilly proposes singing what she's written. She stands up and bursts forth with an aria in a strong soprano voice, a tribute to Sally, who encouraged her to go back to singing after treatment for cancer. "Alleluia, alleluia," she finishes on notes so high the window panes rattle.

By then the others in the Center have stopped whatever they were doing to listen, and when Tilly sits down, there is a ripple of applause that begins at the table and spreads throughout the building. I see Jared in the office doorway, his hair in total disarray.

Dahlia reads a story she's written for her granddaughters, "A Shoe Returns from Winnie," about a car trip she took with her own grandparents, Mac and Momma. Her grandfather sold twine to hardware and lumber yards, traveling all over East Texas, and one summer Dahlia accompanied them, wearing a new pair of patent leather pumps with rhinestones around the toes. Oh, how she loved those shoes! After Mac had called on Hobson's Lumber in Winnie, Dahlia looked for her shoes and discovered one was missing, apparently having fallen out of the car while she and Momma were waiting for Mac. At the first filling station, Mac called Bert Hobson, who found the shoe outside and said he'd mail it back. Four days later the doorbell rang, and when Momma opened it, the postal carrier was bent over laughing. He handed Momma Dahlia's patent leather shoe with the rhinestones, unadorned by any packaging, just tied around several times in some of Mac's twine, with a mailing tag attached.

As we're all laughing at that image of the shoe coming through the mail, Eddie announces he's writing about how to take care of a car, "practical things you can't find in the manual that comes with the car." He reads to us about how to clean the front windshield without leaving streaks, something I've never known how to do. His writing includes illustrations, which he holds up for us to see, and he promises a fascinating follow-up next week on checking fluid levels under the hood.

"Ladies and gentlemen, our next author," Aldeen begins, offering a humorous bio of growing up in East Austin, just six blocks from the MLK Center, where she still lives, and all the trouble she stirred up in the neighborhood, her schools and church. "Not much has changed," the chorus around the table agrees.

Mark shows us a map his teenage grandson Casey drew when he was serving time in the juvenile detention center "for a convenience store thing—running with a bad crowd. He got his head on straight at juvie with good counseling." Casey lives with him and his wife Ella, and Sally helped him get a job when he was released, delivering and setting up oxygen tanks. The map has Mark's house in the center with roads going out in several different directions, leading to a branch of Austin Community College, Belle Computer Solutions, a graffiti-painted fence near the East Austin High School, an alley behind a strip mall and the highway to Huntsville State Prison. "Casey is coming to the crossroads. He knows that computer stuff and could get himself a good job at Belle with the right kind of schooling. I'm writing stories about each of those possible directions on his map."

After murmurs of support for Mark, I turn to Annie and ask if she'd like to read anything. She looks at the pages in her lap, shaking her head. Aldeen rubs her hand across Annie's shoulders, telling her in a voice loud enough for all of us to hear, "Go ahead, honey, you're safe in here."

Annie is quiet for a time, then slowly starts to read about her struggle with domestic violence, being overwhelmed with fear of her husband Jimmy, who had punched and kicked her so many times, always ensuring that the bruises would be hidden by her clothes when she went to work the next day. He'd held a gun to her head more than once, punched holes in the sheetrock. "That night he pinned me down and tried to strangle me, a neighbor called the police, and Jimmy was arrested. But I was more terrified than ever because his furious looks always said it was my fault, and I knew he wouldn't be in jail forever."

Annie reads about spending time in a shelter, getting group help and counseling. "I was finally able to admit how angry I was. They helped me learn to use the energy of my anger for good stuff like my own protection and building a new life. It took three years, but that's what I'm doing." Now divorced, her former husband Jimmy still lives in the area, in and out of trouble. "I'm sorry to finish us on a such a downer," Annie says, "but I'm following the guidelines, writing about what hurts."

"Right on, Sister," from the chorus.

I tell Annie her piece is not a downer at all, quite the opposite, and thank her for her courage and everyone at the table for their participation. I don't know what I was expecting from this class, but along with some well-written, honest stories, they've certainly provided fodder for Sally's case: drugs, alcohol, family members with criminal pasts and presents, all aided in some way by Sally.

"I look forward to seeing you all next week," I say. "Sally would have been totally impressed by the creative spirit reflected here."

"Correction," Tilly says. "Sally is impressed."

No one's waiting for tax help, and I leave the Center quickly to avoid any further conversation with Jared. I head straight for Bud's Bar-b-cue. Loaded with take-out orders, I call Suella on my cell phone to tell her I'm on my way with the ribs, but the line is busy. When I arrive at the address she'd given me earlier, I park and walk up the sidewalk, cluttered with rusted yard implements, motor parts, a bicycle with one tire and several broken flower pots. A handwritten sign next to the front door says "Knock hard," so I do several times. I can hear voices inside and a television playing loudly.

When a woman finally answers the door, I say, "I'm Grace Edge with the ribs. Are you Suella? I tried to call, but the line was busy, so I just came on over with the food."

She wipes her hands on an apron, looks back into the living room, then at me and says, "Come on in. Ruth Ann'll be happy you made it."

I see a woman across the living room in a recliner, covered with a quilt, watching the television. She waves. "This is Sally's friend," Suella tells her.

Two Caucasian teenage boys stand by a table near Ruth Ann's chair and fidget, seemingly annoyed by the interruption. They're dressed in the standard male youth attire, loose jeans with the waistband a continent below their midsections, brightly colored boxer shorts, heavy chains connecting their wallets to something in the vicinity of belt loops, ears wired and pierced.

Suella backs up slightly, and I step inside, handing her the bag.

"She's brought us ribs from Bud's." Suella says, looking and sniffing in the bag. "And beans, potato salad and that good toast." She sets it down on a table spread with several empty beer bottles.

"If that's what you like, I'll bring it again next week," I say, "but I'm not sure I have enough for all of you.'

"Are you planning to eat with us?" Suella asks me.

"Oh, no, I've got an order of my own and have to get home."

"These boys aren't eating. They just come by to see if they can help with anything. So nice, uh huh." The boys continue to shift restlessly. "This here's my sister, Ruth Ann." Ruth Ann smiles and waves again.

"That's all right then," Suella says, putting her hand on my shoulder and pressing me toward the door. "Another time you stay. We keep cold ones iced." Ruth Ann smiles and waves again.

"It's sad about Ruth Ann," Suella whispers to me once I'm back outside on the front porch. "Used to be so active. Now needs the pain pills round the clock, oxygen for her breathing, can hardly get out of her chair, tied to that tube. Ties me down, too. That's why I can't come to the Center. I'll fix her a plate. She loves those ribs."

I see through the open door that Ruth Ann has already walked over to the table and begun fixing her own plate. While

I'm sitting in my car, checking cell phone messages, the teenagers come out of Suella's house, one of them carrying a sack, and I think that Suella's given them some food after all. I could bring more next week.

They boys climb into a taxi-yellow Hummer parked across the street, drive four houses down and stop. A middle-aged woman emerges from the side yard. She says something to them, gets into a black Silverado, and they all drive away.

~ Twelve ~
Pain Killers

Delia Ingram-Kirksey must have nothing to do on Fridays but look at the library passers-by, because she intercepts me as I walk by the Circulation Desk and asks me how to get in touch with Nathan, needing to contact him "right away before they go elsewhere with Sally's extensive collection of first editions."

I dictate his snail- and e-mail addresses, then mill around the seating areas. I notice a number of apparently homeless persons hanging out but see no sign of my nighttime companion.

Moving on to the stacks I secure *Generation RX: How Prescription Drugs Are Altering American Lives and Bodies* and *The Prescription & Over-the-Counter Drug Guide for Seniors*, the books Sally had used that morning in the library.

Generation RX documents the overmedication of the American public. Aggressive drug marketing by pharmaceutical companies creates its own increasing demand. With both supply and demand skyrocketing, the price goes way up, too. Interesting, but there's nothing really revolutionary.

The Prescription Guide for Seniors offers a list of brand name prescription drugs with the actual drug name in parenthesis, such as Advil (ibuprofen) and Aleve (naproxen). It gives reference information about the drug, such as the form available for use, whether it can be purchased over the counter, if a generic form is available, the main uses for the drug, recommended doses for seniors, special instructions for taking the drug, how soon it will start working and whether it's all right to drive while taking the drug. This doesn't tell me much either.

Flipping back to the page on one of Sally's own drugs, Zoloft (setraline), I read about its purpose and doses, then begin paging back to her other drug, Thorazine (chlorpromazine). Stuck between pages I find a thin strip of paper like a short cash register receipt. I recognize it as the printout the library gives at checkout with the book title, barcode and due date.

Sally hadn't checked these books out yet, according to library records, so this receipt must have been left by a previous customer, unnoticed by library staff when reshelving, as well as the police. I've often found those slips in books I've checked out and have probably abandoned some myself when returning books.

On the back side of the receipt there's a handwritten list of drugs: Dilaudid (hydromorphone), MS Contin (morphine), OxyContin (oxycodone) and Darvon (propoxyphene). I recognize Sally's handwriting and signature green ink. Excited about my finding, but not wanting to take any chances with losing or mishandling, evidence, I officially check out the book from the circulation desk.

Unsuccessful in reaching Aunt Arrow, I leave a message on her cell and head home myself. While waiting for Aunt Arrow's return call, I busy myself attempting to calculate if and how much the assistant principal has embezzled from employee withholding funds at Morning's Minion Day School.

Aunt Arrow finally calls back a little after 9:00 p.m. from the Front Porch, where she's sitting in on a set of Carrie Rodriguez singing from her new album *Seven Angels on a Bicycle.* Aunt Arrow's followed and supported Carrie's career since she began as a classical violinist, switched over to back-up pop singing with a composer friend, and more recently moved on to develop her own sound, the current version of which Aunt Arrow now tells me is sweet, soulful and sassy.

I readily discern from the texture of the oral review that Aunt Arrow is sipping, as well as sitting and possibly smoking, with Jake and a few friends I can hear in the background, and this might not be the best time to report my latest findings in living color. We agree to meet for breakfast the next day at Bluebonnet Pharmacy. I don't know if what's left of my waistline will survive this case.

I've suggested Bluebonnet as I need to pick up a med. When Aunt Arrow comes into the pharmacy, I'm waiting at the counter, and she walks over to wait with me. She says, "This is the last place I stood next to Sally. She picked up a Zoloft refill and commented she wasn't sure she still needed to be taking it."

The pharmacist's aide, Simone on her nametag, steps up, hands me the prescription and runs my credit card. She looks familiar to me in the way that some people do when you see them out of context. You know them from somewhere, like the continuing education class for C.P.A. credits or the Democratic caucus, but you don't recognize them in their current setting. I've had people who know me from golf come up in restaurants and say, "I didn't recognize you in your clothes."

I'm about to ask Simone for a life review when another customer walks up, and Simone is able to do only a bare minimum of Bluebonnet homey chitchat. I like their chatter, which is one of the reasons I use this pharmacy in spite of its higher prices. The staff makes you feel almost good about being sick.

This is Aunt Arrow's first time back to eat at Bluebonnet Deli since Sally died. She thought she was ready but breaks down as soon as she begins ordering "a breakfast taco with …" and I have to step up to the counter and fill in with "egg, green chili and chorizo."

"I'm sorry I'm so teary," she says.

"You needn't apologize. Research shows that the tears of grief are healing," I quote from overnight library research.

Aunt Arrow continues to cry and apologize as she chews, sniffles and complains about the mildness of today's batch of green chili.

Over a second cup of coffee she reports on her latest communication from Nathan, that he's found nothing suspicious in Sally's records from her credit card or cell phone. As a child of depression era parents, Sally apparently didn't use either product extensively. Under a mutual pledge of confidentiality I outline key elements of the writing group as well as the conversations with Jared Phillips.

Aunt Arrow and I develop a list of Sally's potentially dangerous connections and circle Jared Phillips as a person of interest. She doesn't know what to make of the ribs-delivery story but agrees we should explore the background of Annie's former husband, Jimmy Joplinson, possibly Mark's grandson Casey and Jamail, even though he seems in recovery. We should also find out more about the drug history of Dahlia's daughter Ophelia before she entered prison, as well as who her connections outside of prison might be.

I offer to contact Kira to ask her to do a background check on our potentials but will have to make her think it's her idea.

Although she's fascinated with the discovery, Aunt Arrow has another twinge of sadness upon seeing Sally's handwriting in the green ink on the slip of paper from the library book. "I've seen a sea of that ink through the years."

Aunt Arrow has brought along some of the items she's retrieved while going through Sally's desk and records, including a file folder of articles from newspapers and the web. She looks through the folder and pulls several that discuss the drugs Sally has listed, most prominently OxyContin.

"It's a pain killer, right?"

"Yes, effective as a time-release pain med," Aunt Arrow says, consulting the file, "but abusers crush the tablets, destroying its time-release aspect. Then they ingest it, snort it and chew it to get a quick and powerful high, like heroin. It's highly addictive, and illegal use has grown steadily," Aunt Arrow reads, "but here's the kicker. The pills sell for ten or more times their prescription price on the black market, depending on the area of the country. That's what Sally was onto. I'm sure of it." I, too, am beginning to concur that Sally's notes and articles confirm Aunt Arrow's suspicions.

As the next step we agree that I should show Bertel the library list when I meet with him. We cross our collective fingers on the fruitcake test as conclusive evidence to get the police fully engaged.

I wave supportively while driving away and almost immediately have to change lanes to avoid an aggressive motorcyclist at my right fender. I can't lose him until I turn onto my home street, when he finally peels away.

~ Thirteen ~
Ready Mix

I spend much of what's left of the weekend in my yard, which accomplishes two purposes. It's an opportunity to process my work mentally and to placate the neighbors, especially Gladys Marks, who lives next door. She thoughtfully left a note in my mailbox, offering me the phone number of her "yard guy who does excellent work, as you can see from looking at our place, and his charges are reasonably reasonable—Ha! Ha! Just in case you need some backup. We know how busy you are." Smiley face. All of that translates to, "You'd better get the hell outside, mow your yard, edge along the curb, sidewalk and driveway, and clear out all the branches that fell in last week's hail storm."

The neighbors have been thoroughly confused by my approach to lawn, garden and home maintenance, primarily because I have my own cement mixer. Initially they thought it was a high-tech planter, because Gladys asked me what I was planning to grow in there. When I responded with, "Ready Mix and water, nothing complicated about the formula," she retreated, only to return an hour later with her husband Joe Ray. Accommodatingly I demonstrated how the motor turns and hums.

"And you use that for what?" Joe Ray asked, looking sideways into the barrel.

"Oh, patching things, like cracks in the sidewalk. Making the foundation for a patio. Hiding body parts. Setting fence posts. Would you and Gladys like to put in your handprints and initials the next time I patch?"

Gladys suggested we get together sometime soon for a glass of iced tea so we can get to know each other better, but so far we haven't drunk or mingled. I'm something of an anomaly as a native Texan in that I don't actually like iced tea, although I haven't confessed that to Gladys and Joe Ray. Nor have I ever told them I don't take the Bible literally, in spite of instructions on their various bumper stickers.

My philosophy is that there are certain facts and opinions one withholds in order to get along in this world, just as there are certain fallen branches one needs to pick up, certain edges one needs to trim, certain leaves one needs to rake, certain weeds one needs to pull. Where I draw the line is my back yard.

I take a break from picking up branches and edging edges for another celebratory round at St. Barnabas on Sunday morning.

At coffee hour Aldeen invites me to "come over and see the jangles." Next to the coffee, punch and cookies is a table spread with beautiful jewelry in stunning geometric patterns, shapes and dangle-lengths, being sold by Aldeen's daughter with the proceeds benefitting the women's shelter.

I carefully select a concentric circles pin for myself and a dangle of hexagon earrings for Aunt Arrow; then it's back to the yard foliage.

My cell phone rings late Sunday afternoon as I'm trimming the last branch into the correct size for city pick-up. If you leave them too long the city truck drives right on by as if they're not sitting at the driveway in tied bundles.

On the phone is Bertel, confirming, "Tuesday evening's still OK for a bite."

"It is, and I have some new information about the case I'd like to discuss with you when we get together."

"And I'll have the labs."

We agree to meet at six-thirty, and Bertel offers me a choice of Mama Rosa's or Tula's Serape.

I'm well familiar with Mama Rosa's but haven't heard of Tula's Serape. "It's a welcome new face for Mexican," Bertel explains, "according to the review in today's paper."

"Could I read about it and let you know? I haven't gotten to the paper yet today."

"Talk to you later."

I rush inside and grab the Entertainment section. Three and a half stars. That's somewhere between very good and great. The review starts out appealingly enough, with "a tasteful, subdued, subtly lit main dining room; huge, free parking lot adjacent to the restaurant; and plenty of ice cold Dos Equis, Tequiza and Corona."

Unfortunately it goes on to describe the food. "Your taste buds won't soon forget the ahi tuna-avocado-cilantro mousse: tasty and sweet flaked tuna with lightly dressed slivers of avocado topped with pressed cilantro; slivered cod nachos: buttery cod playing musical chairs with gently fried rice noodles; mustard-elk tamale with an addictive, invigorating overlay of mole; tangy vinaigrette-slathered tangelos; and a bombastic flan glazed with freshly picked and pickled mountain berry compote.

Musical Chairs. Elk in tamale. Bombastic flan. Is that a misprint? The article shows a photograph of Serape's tuna-avocado-cilantro mousse, which resembles a bird's nest stacked on top of mashed potatoes. That's the deal-breaker.

I leave a message on Bertel's work phone that I'll see him at Mama Rosa's on Tuesday.

My back is sore from all the yard work, so I get out my Body Alive Personal Massager by Pollenex and experiment with several different attachments, using both speeds, depending upon body location. "Ummmmmmm."

The exercise and its aftermath inspire me to spend a couple of hours working on my new novel, *Gersalina's Dilemma*.

~ **Fourteen** ~
Pigweed

After uncounted but multiple outfit try-ons, I leave the house
to meet Bertel at six-fifteen on Tuesday night, armed with Aunt
Arrow's mandate to find Sally's killer. I'm attired in jeans, a
university sweatshirt and coordinating blue-and-burnt-orange
argyle socks. Raucously popular with university students, current
and former, Mama Rosa's parking lot is already jammed.

I finally find a place four blocks over, making me about
three or four minutes early, which I can't precisely determine
because it's hard to read my petals in the dim light. Parking may
have been the one advantage for Tula Serape's, but that is
already offset by Mama Rosa's impressive entry, the large purple
neon sign and bright pink stucco facade.

I note thankfully that Mama Rosa's main dining room is not
tasteful, subdued or subtly lit. The yellow ceiling is covered with
brightly painted purple, yellow, orange and blue wooden parrots,
flowered rope swings and pink fans, with a continuous blue
plastic wave around the ceiling's ledge. Fish of all types and
sizes swim in and out of the undulating waves. The center of the
room is dominated by a six-foot aquarium filled with an aqua
and yellow striped ferris wheel, salmon pink castle, verdant
green forest and three tiny goldfish.

A major scenic attraction adorns each of the four walls: Gold
sequined Elvis on velvet painting above an altar shrine to the
north. Large fire-spitting green and orange dragons, east and
west, and a neon turquoise and silver '55 Chevy, south. The
booths offer a variety of red, blue and orange plastic seats with

gray Formica tables. The lighting is garish, the live mariachi music loud and brassy.

I spot Bertel in a blue booth across the room, anchored between one of the spitting dragons and the '55 Chevy. He appears to be chatting up the female server, festively attired in a flowered skirt and peasant blouse and exposing I'm not sure how much or what as she's bending over to hand him the menus.

As I drift away mentally in a haze of possible plot lines with relevant scenarios that include Gersalina in a low-cut peasant blouse and Captain Bertel in tightly fitting officer pants, a voice at my side startles me. "Grace, I just spotted you standing over here. Have you been waiting long? I already grabbed us a booth."

Bertel suggests a pitcher of margaritas when we settle in.

"How much is in a pitcher?"

"They're mostly ice."

It takes us a glass each for Bertel to decide on the comida deluxe with two blue corn enchiladas, chili con carne, crispy beef taco, chalupa, beans, and rice; and me the pork enchiladas with spicy verde and a side order of refried black beans. We agree to share the grande chili con queso with chips as a starter, a basket of sopapillas with, and to postpone our business conversation until after we eat.

"To our cholesterol," I say when the food arrives, assessing the contents of the fat-laden dishes.

"I've found a way to lower mine," Bertel says, raising his glass in toast.

"Your cholesterol?" I'm curious, eyeing his dinner selections.

"Yeah, I'm participating in a nutrition study a grad student is conducting at the university. She asked for volunteers from the police department, studying the effects of a special diet on cholesterol. We have plenty to offer up in the department. With the diet I can only have certain things, such as beef, three times a week, but the real kicker is eating three amaranth muffins a day."

"Amaranth?" Now I think he's teasing me. "I haven't heard of that one."

"It's a weed," he says seriously, "grows wild out east of here, especially near cotton plants. A cheap source of fiber."

"How does it taste?"

"Doesn't really have much taste, maybe a little bitter like turnip greens, but the recipe allows for plenty of brown sugar. It's sometimes called pigweed. You've probably seen it growing with reddish-purple flowers."

"All these years, and I never knew." Our hands, sticky from honey, touch briefly as we both reach for a second sopapilla, and Bertel makes mock sounds of Velcro pulling apart.

"My cholesterol is already lower after only six weeks," he says, loading butter and honey into a second sopapilla.

I think he overestimated on the ice.

We order coffee, and at mid-refill I ask about the lab report.

Bertel leans over the table and puts his hands together, barely avoiding the remnants of the chili con queso.

"There was nothing in the cake but cake ingredients. I'm sorry. You were partly right, though. Ms. Weathers' stomach contents did show she'd consumed some of it that morning, and the lab checked those partially digested particles, as well. Ms. Weathers didn't get the Thorazine that way, Grace. Not from the apricot cake."

"Apricot pecan," I correct weakly. What I can't correct are the lab results. The doubts creep in.

"As I said before we'll hold the file open, but we don't see anywhere else to go with this case for now."

"I do have somewhere else to go." I show Bertel the slip from Sally's library book. "This came out of one of the books Sally had with her when she died. I went back to the library and looked through the books that were found with the body to get an idea of their contents, and I found the list in the *Drug Guide for Seniors*. Just stuck in there, so thin the staff missed it—your people, too, I guess. The list is in Sally's handwriting and ink.

She wrote with this green ink. Aunt Arrow's positive about the writing, but you can check out the ink. It's hers."

"How do you know what books she had with her when she died?"

"Library staff told me," I say quickly.

"I see that she's written the names of some opiates. That's interesting, but it doesn't really suggest any lead we can follow."

"She was tracking prescription drugs that sell illegally all over the country at highly inflated prices. There's big money in those drugs."

"What do you mean, tracking?"

"Sally Weathers helped several people at the Center on personal matters, and we now know she was researching drugs that often sell illegally. This slip confirms her interest. That's what I know for sure from the list, but what it also suggests is that she may have stumbled onto some of this illegal activity through someone she was involved with at the Center. Several have criminal backgrounds or connections. "

"But there's no known connection between Ms. Weathers and anyone selling these drugs illegally in the area."

"Except that she's dead."

"From what we believe is a drug combination that she ingested. By accident, I'll grant you, but also by her own hand and free choice. If the lab had turned up Thorazine traces in the cake, we'd have something concrete, but they didn't."

"Aunt Arrow won't accept this as a final result. I'm sure she won't."

"I feel for your aunt. She's sincere, but I believe grief may be making her somewhat irrational. Grief can do that."

"Aunt Arrow is the sanest person I know," I say.

"If something else develops, as I said before, let me know. I'm out of town the rest of the week for a conference in L.A. and spending some time with my son, but I'm here otherwise."

I didn't know he had a son. First a mother, now a son. Sweet.

"I'd like to stay in touch with you anyway, maybe get together for another one of these health-conscious meals?" He waves his hand over the congealing remnants. "For sustenance during our business discussions."

"But not at Tula's Serape."

"No tuna nachos for the young lady," he pretends to write on his napkin. Bertel leaves cash on the table to cover the check and tip, disallowing my offer to contribute.

As he walks me to my car I say, "I'd like to know something—where does the Bertel come from? It's such an unusual name."

"I'm descended from the Danish sculptor, Bertel Thorvaldsen. Famous in Europe during the late eighteenth and early nineteenth centuries. Neoclassical stuff."

"Oh, an artist." My mind races with revision.

"Yeah, I have some prints of his work, if you'd like to see them, but I'm warning you up front, most are nudes. Adonis. Jason and the Golden Fleece. Venus. Shepherd Boy with Dog. Hylas and the Nymphs. There's a statue of him in New York City's Central Park. Handsome dude."

Bertel smiles, his already ruddy cheeks reddening.

"I've enjoyed this evening with you, Grace," he says, reaching out to say goodbye with a gentle pat between my shoulders, just as I turn to shake hands with him. Mine lands on his belt buckle and his on my left breast. We both back off rapidly.

"Want to try again?" Bertel recovers first. "It's a left hook to the midriff, followed by a right to the jaw, and the winner is in the blue trunks with the orange topping." He bends over, kisses my cheek and raises my left hand in victory. "I'd better get out of here while I'm still in one piece."

The kiss isn't a peck like the one Jake gives me. I feel moisture with it.

My drive home is cautious. As I'm walking into my house I spot an oversize envelope protruding from my mailbox. Since I already collected the mail earlier today, I assume I've received more marching orders from Gladys and Joe Ray. Dammit. My yard is immaculate. What is their problem?

I drink a large glass of water, hoping to dilute the tequila into submission. It's too late to call Aunt Arrow. I turn on the set and catch a Lyle Lovett concert on public television.

Lyle bolsters my spirits enough to deal with Gladys and Joe Ray. I'm thinking cement mixer options as I tear open the envelope. I extract a single 8-1/2" by 11" white sheet with a message in computer printing that looks like Times New Roman, about forty-eight points: M.Y.O.B., Bitch.

It's odd, the reactions you have when you're in a state of complete panic. The first thing that occurs to me is that the note is correctly punctuated.

~ Fifteen ~
People of Darkness

On the phone minutes later with Aunt Arrow, I manage, "If it's related to Sally, not only do they know I'm digging into her murder, but they know where I live." Which can't have come from the phone book, because I'm unlisted. I have an ad in the Yellow Pages but no address. "Walking right up to my mailbox when I wasn't home means they were watching my movements."

I think of the motorcyclist from the night before.

Still quivering slightly, I've wrapped myself in the big quilt I inherited as a child from my great-grandmother, one that she made of ships at sea while living in Galveston. I'd like to be sailing on one of them now.

"Calm down, sweetie, we'll figure this out," Aunt Arrow says sleepily. "Think about who knows what we've been doing."

"Did you get anything at all like this?" I'd been so focused on myself, I hadn't thought to ask.

"No. No, I didn't. I haven't received a thing."

That's a relief. Whoever it is could know about Aunt Arrow, too, but I hope not the extent of her involvement. I relax slightly. Possibly it's something related to my accounting work. It wouldn't be the first time I've received hate mail.

"Let's take it back through our steps," I say to Aunt Arrow. "We had the conversations with Nathan. Someone at the memorial service could have overheard something, and at the library they're certainly aware that we wanted in to see the stacks where Sally died. No one there knows the whole story. At least, I don't think anyone does, but they know I've been back in the stacks. Several staff members have seen me."

"Delia Ingram-Kirksey fits both of those categories," Aunt Arrow says, beginning to wake up.

"She has plenty of obnoxious traits," I say, "but behavior with malicious intent isn't one that stands out."

"Don't be so quick to dismiss her. She attended the memorial service, we talked to her to make our request to view the stacks where Sally died, and you saw her again when you went back in to look at the books Sally had used."

"But she has no motive." In my wildest imagination I don't think wanting Sally's first editions donated to the library qualifies.

"We'll pencil her in lightly," Aunt Arrow says.

"It could be someone else in the library, like that man who found the body. But again, why? The big can of worms has to be the Center. Jared knows there's an ongoing investigation. He keeps talking to me about it, asking questions. Aldeen, and now others in the writing group and the library memorial project, all know I've been asking around about who Sally helped, who she spent time with from the Center. And the police. Bertel knows. An entire review committee of officers meet to discuss the status of cases, so they all know." Kira Mattingly knows, I think. I wrap myself up more tightly in the sea of ships quilt.

"I think you should come right over here and stay with me for tonight," Aunt Arrow insists. "My building is much better protected than your house."

"The note's just to warn me off. I'm not concerned about anyone breaking in here," I say more confidently than I feel. "Besides, I have mace, and I know where to direct a blow with my elbow."

"Have you contacted the police yet?"

"Yeah, before I called you, I left messages on Bertel's cell and his office phone that I'd received a warning to back off, but he's probably not checking messages in the middle of the night."

"I'm coming over there." Aunt Arrow says. "I want to hear what he said at dinner anyway, and I'd feel a lot better if you're not alone."

"Not now. I don't want you out driving. I didn't call you when I came in because I thought it was already too late. Now it really is."

"So give me the report about the cake, and let's see how this incident tonight fits in with all of that." Aunt Arrow rises to full alert.

"It doesn't. Bertel said the lab didn't find any Thorazine in the cake, not in the cake from inside the tin or the cake Sally had begun to digest. She had eaten some that morning. I'm sorry, I know that sounds morbid, but it's what Bertel said. Neither tin nor stomach contents."

"I'm really surprised. And disappointed."

"He was definite about the lab results."

"What about that list of drugs you found?"

"I showed Bertel the slip from the library book, and that didn't impress him either. Just some notes on opiates, he said, confirming Sally's interest but leading to nothing else. That was it, he's shutting this thing down, the whole case except lip service to us. Whoever left me this note is really stupid. They've managed to bring the police into the case, or will when they hear. Finally."

Guess scaring the shit out of me is good for something.

"Oh, honey."

"I'll be all right."

"Do you want me to call Jake and have him come over?" Aunt Arrow offers. "He's probably still up."

"No, not tonight. I've been all over the house carefully and have everything sealed tightly—doors, windows, psyche."

"Let's talk first thing tomorrow."

The phone rings about five minutes later, and I'm expecting to hear Bertel's voice, but it's Jake's. "Hi, there, G.E., Aurora's just phoned to let me know about your love note. I'm coming over right now to bring you Babe."

"I can't take your dog."

"Sophie and Shorty will still be here to keep me company." Jake has three dogs, all animal shelter breeds. "Babe's the ideal one for you—she's a fierce protector, vicious-sounding barking and growling when anyone strange approaches her territory, but your all-time basic sweetheart as a companion."

I've never had a dog, only cats. I don't know how to take care of a dog, and the middle of the night probably isn't a good time to start learning. "I appreciate the offer," I tell Jake. "Could we do it tomorrow, try Babe out over here in the daytime? I'm OK for tonight. Promise."

"Will you call if that changes?"

"Cross my heart."

I dawdle a few minutes getting ready for bed, still not sleepy, and cast about for something else to occupy my mind, such as it is. Golf does that for me. When I'm playing golf, I concentrate on golf. But a round of golf isn't an option at 1:17 a.m., and I don't want Kira Mattingly in bed with me.

Second best is a crossword puzzle, and I haven't worked Sunday's.

The *Austin Times* carries Premier Crosswords in its Sunday edition, and those always have something lengthy running all the way through, like riddles with answers or clever plays on word combinations, linking to a theme. This week's offers "Notables with Something Extra." I get a couple of the big ones right away: the "dexterous artist" is HandyWarhol, and "SPamShriver" works out to Send cyber-ads to a tennis player. This crossword is doing it for me. Filling in a six-letter word for gnawing critter (rodent) gives me the help I need to solve frustrate a politician as CRossPerot. Working through other clues, I decide that "spirited pop singer" is GAmyGrant, "Songwriter with silver hair" is GRayStevens, and "Nourished a variety show host," "FEdSullivan."

I'm stumped on the bottom right corner, though, until I realize the five letters across for "hysteria" spell panic, which should have been immediately obvious to me tonight. A few others offer letters for "Unfeeling detective novelist": S _ _ _ Y _ _ _ L _ _ R _ _ _ .

Then I get it: STonyHillerman. The rest of the puzzle's a breeze.

A famous mystery writer, my companion in the middle of a terrifying night. Could this signal a trail to follow? Threatening note, crossword puzzle as balm, and now Tony Hillerman. I remember I have some of his books in a big box I've been collecting to take to the MLK Center's library.

Sure enough, I discover a cache with *A Thief of Time, People of Darkness, Hunting Badger* and *The Wailing Wind*. I look for a sign of where to begin and find it almost immediately in *People of Darkness,* because that story's opening sentence relates immediately to Sally's death. It's set in a laboratory. "It was a job which required waiting for cultures to grow, for toxins to develop, for antibodies to form and for reagents to react." I keep reading for Tony to tell me where to go next.

~ Sixteen ~
Security Systems

I must have dozed off finally because I'm awakened by the simultaneous ringing of the front door bell and the telephone. Yikes. Who's at the door? I grab my robe, the mobile, and peek through the miniblind slat at the front window.

"What's happened?" from Bertel on the phone. "I've just picked up your message on my cell."

It's Jake and a medium-sized black dog on the front porch, the dog wearing a red bandana and sitting alertly at attention beside Jake. As I unlock the door and wave them in, I point to the phone and mouth, "Police."

"Babe," he points and mouths.

Jake hands me a coffee from the Coffee Traders around the corner, uncaps the lid to his own and gives Babe a biscuit while she sits again at attention. Her bandana has a cowgirl on a horse, roping a calf, and reads, "Welcome to Montana." Jake points toward the back of the house and mouths, "Outside." He walks Babe through to the kitchen and out the back door to the patio as he makes hand-rolling motions for me to continue my phone conversation and pointing fingers to join them when I finish.

I tell Bertel about finding the note and read it to him. He has me read it again, then asks a few questions about paper, packaging and the location of my mailbox. Am I sure it wasn't already there when I went out for dinner? I am, because I swept the front porch as an aerobic break between trying on outfits before I left to meet him, and I'd earlier picked up my day's mail delivery.

"I'm absolutely positive whoever brought the note came while I was eating with you," I say as if it's at least partly his fault. "I'm guessing the person had been watching and knew when I left. Although I don't know that for a fact," I add, and it gives me the creeps.

Surprised by this development, Bertel utters words that are calmly professional, intended to reassure me, but I can sense the element of alarm in his tone. "Do you have other enemies, and by other I mean other than if whoever did this is connected to Ms. Weathers in some way? Cases you're working on, that kind of thing."

I tell him about my current case, the suspected embezzlement at a day school, with the suspected embezzler a long-term, elderly female employee.

He says, "Uh huh," and implies that with this development, the case will obviously remain open. Although he won't go so far as to call the note "the proverbial smoking gun, it's a hell of a lot more volatile than the blanks I thought were being fired."

As soon as he can call into the department, he'll arrange for an officer to come to my house to take a report and pick up the note "unless you want me to come over. I'm leaving for the airport and can stop by on my way if you're feeling unsteady or unsafe."

"No, but thanks for the offer. The cavalry has just arrived."

"Calvary?"

"Her name is Babe, and she belongs to Jake Young, who's managing editor of the *Times* and my aunt's boyfriend. From the look of how efficiently Babe retrieves the tennis ball Jake is throwing for her across my back yard, I believe I'm in good paws."

"Oh, a dog," Bertel says perceptively.

"She's on loan for the duration."

"Okeedokey, we'll be in touch."

I take my coffee outside and sit on the edge of the deck. Jake puts the tennis ball back in his pocket. That leaves Babe with the difficult choice between chasing a squirrel up the pecan tree or investigating me. Quickly sensing the squirrel has climbed beyond her reach, Babe runs over to the deck and licks around my ankle, which is about all the skin that's available between my robe and slipper. Apparently satisfied with the taste, she starts in on the other one.

Rubbing Babe's head and ears as she laps, I guess aloud, "Spaniel, lab, shepherd and collie?"

"That's about right, maybe some English sheepdog thrown into the mix. They didn't know at the animal shelter when I adopted her as a puppy two Decembers ago. She'd been picked up from a mostly empty student housing complex, probably abandoned at the end of the semester, scrawny and barely alive. They think she was beaten. She's still leery of a rolled-up newspaper."

"She's certainly thriving now. Are you sure you can do without her?"

"Sophie and Shorty will miss her. Me, too. But they're plenty of canine companionship for now. What's important is providing some for you."

Babe has stopped licking long enough to nestle into the folds of my terry cloth robe, drowsing as Jake and I talk and drink our coffee. Suddenly her ears perk up, and she races to the fence gate, barking sharply. The barking deepens and intensifies, vicious sounds becoming louder, as we hear the delivery guy bringing the newspaper to the front porch. Babe continues barking relentlessly and bangs up against the fence gate until he has moved on down the street well beyond my house.

"That's the kind of protection you'll get from Babe," Jake says. "If anyone she doesn't know approaches the property, whether she's inside the house or out here in the back yard, she'll scare the bejesus out of 'em."

"What would she do if a stranger actually tried to enter the house?"

"Babe's not really an aggressive dog, in spite of those sounds and movements, but she'll keep up the growling and snarling, bare her teeth and likely turn anyone away before they get very far. I've got some Beware of Dog signs in the car we can post on the front of the house and the fence gate. If you'd like her to stay, that is."

Babe has returned to the deck, her bandana askew. Jake takes it off, saying, "You don't need your dress suit any longer, Missy." He fills an empty plant dish base with water from the hose, which Babe enthusiastically laps while Jake slips me a stash of biscuits in a plastic bag. "Make her sit first," he instructs, which I do, and she takes the biscuit eagerly.

"What else should I know about taking care of her?"

Babe squats, as if on cue. "She needs to be let out periodically but can hold it overnight for twelve hours," Jake says. "I've brought a bag of food and biscuits for treats. She needs exercise—walking, which she does well on the lead, chasing the ball, and she loves to swim. The main thing, though, is what you're doing now, and you might have to live in that robe."

Babe has resettled with her head in my lap. "Yes, I'd like her to stay, in case we haven't made that obvious."

"Think of it as a gift for Aurora so she doesn't worry so much about you."

Up go the ears again, a deep growl, and back to the fence for barking. I see a City of Austin Police car pulling into my driveway.

"I'll be off after I put up the signs and leave the food in the garage." Jake attaches Babe's lead, rubs her ears and neck, and hands her off.

I bring Babe, now barking furiously, in through the back door. When the doorbell rings, I confirm that it's a police person from the uniform and the patrol car, make Babe sit and open the door. Babe leaps up onto the man, who says, "Good dog," exactly what I'm thinking. I pull her down, make her sit and give her a biscuit. She doesn't budge from the front entrance until she hears my tone of voice inviting Officer Boyd Dunbar into the living room after he's introduced himself and shown me his credentials.

He's pleasant looking, crisply polite, about my height but with double wide shoulders and a strawberry blond crewcut. I retrieve the note and packaging from my office, and after we both sit down, Babe lies protectively in front of me.

"That's quite a security system you have, Ms. Edge. I use a similar service myself, a three-year-old black lab. I think they're plenty competitive with Brinks and ProtectAmerica, but don't quote me on that." His smile produces dimples.

I relax slightly as I respond to his questions about when and where I found the note and whether I've seen any unknown persons hanging around or approaching the house, which I haven't. He places the note and mailing envelope in an evidence bag. Explaining that he's been briefed by Detective Frederick about the case, he asks me to name the people with whom I've had conversations about "your suspicions regarding Ms. Weathers' death."

He's limited the question only to people with whom I've discussed suspicions. That would be Nathan, Aunt Arrow, Bertel and Kira. While he writes down names and telephone numbers, I try to decide whether to tell him more about connections with the library and the MLK Center.

"You're referring to Officer Mattingly?" he asks. "Kira Mattingly from the Department?"

"Yes, that Kira."

"Where did you talk to her?"

"We were walking across the fairway at ...."

His pager beeps. Officer Dunbar checks the page and excuses himself, "just real quick, be right back," to go out to his patrol car.

In spite of myself I go right ahead and dress him mentally in the Dunbar tartan kilt with the punchy red and green squares and a handsome pair of epaulets on those shoulders, charging through the field of heather.

"I have to go out on another call, but we'll be following up on all of this, Ms. Edge," Officer Dunbar says politely, having miraculously reappeared from the Battle of Otterburn, waving an arm across my living room like a magic wand. "Before I head out I'll talk to the neighbors on either side and across the street, but not to get them stirred up. I'll say it's a routine check for vagrants."

"They'll appreciate the tact," I say.

Officer Dunbar pauses and stands stiffly by the front door, hat in his hand, with Babe in a similar posture at his side. "Then I'm on my way to meet with your aunt. Detective Frederick, that was him on the page, is leaving on a trip, but he wants to get with you and your aunt as soon as he's back. He says there are a few things he wants to pull together before he meets with you."

I'll bet there are.

~ Seventeen ~
Digging for Moles

Tony Hillerman's proddings remain on hold while work keeps me busy through the day. I fax over the preliminary report on my investigation of Morning Minion Day School and wouldn't be surprised to read about an arrest in tomorrow morning's *Austin Times.* An employee for thirty-seven years at church day school caught with her hand in the withholding funds till. That's what she did, helped herself quietly over the years to thousands in payroll deductions.

I'd met with her. Snow white hair in a bun, gentle voice and demeanor, floral print dress, impeccable manners. She said regretfully, "What I'll miss most is having my chats through the day with the little darlings. They slip in and out, know I'm always good for a piece of hard candy from the glass heart I keep on my desk. I like to give them something to suck on." Just the one flaw in her character. "Won't you have a piece?"

By e-mail I respond to pending requests from several parties for my accounting services, business I'll need more now that I'm supporting a family of two. I begin work right away on a new case for a client who wants me to advise her about some odd conversations she's overheard regarding financial dealings at the company where she works in Houston.

The prospective client, a Registered Nurse, runs the health clinic where employees come in for screenings, flu shots, weigh-ins and allergy injections. They apparently assume they can talk about most anything they want concerning finances with no danger of being understood by a health care worker. Among other things, such as the continuation of her job, she's concerned about her 401K and considerable family funds she'd planned to invest in the firm, a high-flying company called QuadRay Energy.

She contacted me, not for investment advice but rather to dig into the company's performance records and evaluate the existence and potential seriousness of any financial problems. The client writes, "You come recommended by Bernie Schwartz, who says you know how to get underneath the gloss and find the sludge." A former colleague at Coopers & Lybrand, Bernie's thrown quite a bit of business my way. QuadRay's stock has almost doubled in the last year, and Wall Street analysts predict that's only the bullish beginning. I go online and print out annual and quarterly financial statements.

Babe takes me for a long walk to and through the Rosewood neighborhood park, where we meet Aunt Arrow for a picnic lunch and lengthy debriefing. She's brought her hamper packed with pimiento cheese sandwiches and a batch of oatmeal raisin cookies she baked while waiting for the arrival of Officer Dunbar, to whom she now refers as "that nice Boyd." She tells me with a smile that he ate four cookies while conducting the interview with her.

Babe eats the two biscuits I've brought, and I'm hoping Aunt Arrow doesn't slip her any of the cookies when I leave briefly to walk over and read the park entry sign, confirming the changes our neighborhood association has approved for the weekend curfew hours. I pull several poop bags from the container by the sign, nicely designed and provided by the city for sanitary, efficient scooping.

Aunt Arrow will ask Jake to run a check from his newspaper archives on the same group of library and Center people that we want Kira to screen in the police files: Delia Ingram-Kirksey and Todd LaJames from the library; Jared Phillips, Ofelia Taylor, Casey Guthrie, James "Jimmy" Joplinson and Jamail Davis from the MLK Center group.

Having had approximately nil social life since Sally died, unless you count the dinner with Bertel, I welcome the invite from my friend Janna to stop by for a late Wednesday afternoon drink with her and her partner, Daisy Harrelson. Jana and I grew up together in Sublime, where we won first place in the Halloween parade four years running in the pair category—Alice and the Mad Hatter, Buffalo Bob and Howdy Doody, Jack and the Beanstalk, vanilla ice cream and hot fudge sauce.

Daisy is a defense attorney whom I've recommended to several of my criminals, and Jana teaches anthropology at the university, specializing in bones. Janna offered several enticements when she telephoned: "books that Daisy and I want to donate to the MLK Center library in response to your e-mail request, a new creation for Daisy's Dairy Daiquiris, and the *piece de resistance* that can only be delivered in person."

The latter turns out to be an announcement. While we sip, Jana shows me the invitations she and Daisy picked up that very afternoon from the printer for the Blessing of Union ceremony to be held next month. "Mother's coming, can you believe it?"

"The Sublime Ladies Bridge Club will probably disband," I respond, along with hugs and a toast, spilling my mostly whipped cream cocktail.

"I think Daddy persuaded her," Jana says. "They're doing the reception. Full deal. Napkins printed with our names and the date and two rings. We'll keep the refreshments casual. I'd like you to be there, of course, but no chiffon."

I accept and agree to all terms readily, since I don't own any chiffon except for some curtains. They invite me to stay for dinner, and I'm temporarily tempted until I find out the entrée is veggie-burgers. It's hard to recognize Jana as a vegetarian. Our favorite meal out ever since we both landed in Austin has been the sixteen ounce T-bone at Roy's Ritz that comes dripping in butter from the grill along with chunky home fries and washed down, after we were legal age, with a draft and whisky shot. Anything for love, I guess, watching Daisy spread hummus on baked pita crackers. Babe, who's accompanied me, abandons the face-off she's having with Jana's cat Small Change to sample a few.

When I finally get around to Tony Hillerman late in the evening, I approach him with an entirely fresh weapon that's going to knock his socks off: forensic accounting. What I've figured out is that getting help from his mystery novel requires the same three steps I apply to the QuadRay Energy financial statements for my client.

In analyzing the financial statements, I first make a pass through all the material, noting any items of significance that stand out for whatever reason. Second, I determine the significance of anything I've marked as noteworthy in step one. Finally, I draw conclusions from steps one and two. That's where the intuition kicks in, because as Tony would surely agree, rational thought can take us only so far.

Step One. What jumps out of the financial morass with QuadRay? Right away, I spot several signals blinking in my pass-through: Revenue growing faster than net income. Credit sales rising even faster. QuadRay manages to show profit but not always a positive cash flow from its operations. And the notes to the financial statements, which are supposed to explain and clarify, seem unnecessarily obtuse. One would need a combined Ph.D. in math, finance and rhetoric to interpret them with any confidence.

Step Two. QuadRay is losing control of expenses, overstating earnings and failing to generate cash. The company may be hiding potentially unscrupulous dealings by intentionally confusing the reader.

Step Three. Wall Street aside, I'll be advising my client to invest her family funds elsewhere, to cease and desist from putting any more of her 401K into QuadRay and to shore up her resumé.

Next up are the *People of Darkness*, using the same steps to seek Tony's advice on how to proceed with Sally's case. It's as simple as one, two, three.

Step One. The People of Darkness are a religious group, the members of which use moles as an amulet, a sort of charm they wear as protection from evil and injury.

Step Two. Moles symbolize the dark underground.

I begin to shiver when I reach Step Three, even though the thermostat's kicked in, the heat's come on and the windows are closed. The message is as clear as the skies over Navajo Nation: find the mole.

~ Eighteen ~
Hen and Egg

I must be the right track, because looking for Kira in the Police Department feels a bit like stepping into the dark underground. She eventually surfaces at the counter in response to my request via the Officer on Duty and beckons me to a cubicle. I explain that I've come to see Detective Frederick but was told he was unavailable.

"He's out of town," Kira says.

"Oh," I say in a faux receiving-new-information tone.

"Attending a training session on community liaising, you know, working with the general public, which we have to do more and more of these days."

"Umm," I nod.

"It's a part of the job that unfortunately can take time away from our real work, you know, like solving crimes."

"It's the real work I've come about, actually, and I'd be glad to minimize the liaison and press on with the solving, if we can ..."

"But it's more and more part of our in-box," Kira says, ignoring my offer. "The simple things some officers apparently don't know, like learning to listen when we're interacting with the public. They manage to put things in the wrong bucket, and I suppose the department powers-that-be assessed Bertel's need for improvement in this area."

Or sent him because he's a detective and you're a line officer.

"While he's out there, he's seeing his son, who supposedly attends UCLA," she adds, "but mostly he's surfing Laguna, from what I hear. It's been a rough patch for Bertel, not altogether his fault that he has trouble with bucket contents allocation. Wife died a couple of years ago, on his own as a single parent."

"I'm sorry for his loss."

Kira sits up in the chair, hugs herself and sighs. "Over the months he's turned to me, and we've grown to be, how should I say it, more personally involved. Yes, I'm owning that we have a personal relationship as well as a professional one, but there's no conflict. He's not my superior."

Of course not.

"I'm sure you're a great comfort for Detective Frederick in his time of need," I say, "and that compassion is why I asked for you. I'm scared, and I don't know what to do." I fold my hands meekly in my lap. "After finding that threatening note in my mailbox."

"I heard about the note. We're on it. What else?"

"My aunt and I have a strong sense, and it's now backed up by reality, that Sally Weathers' death was no accident. I don't think I can wait until Detective Frederick gets back. I need help now from someone who can understand and support what we think." I look around.

"Yes, well, that's one of my jobs, to help the public."

"See, we believe Sally uncovered a drug ring or something related to illegal drugs through her volunteer work, probably at the MLK Center but possibly at the public library. That may have led to her death. At the Center, at least, I know we have recovering addicts, family members in prison, potential gang activity, victims of domestic violence, something of an undertow in the Center's periphery. My aunt and I have drawn up a list of people that, uh, we have some reason to think might be connected to the drugs and Sally's death, or we have questions about. I was going to tell Detective Frederick who they are so that possibly ..."

Kira interrupts with, "We all work together here whether we're specifically assigned to the case or not. You should go ahead and give me your list. This can't wait for Bertel's return. Detective Frederick. I can see how difficult this is for you. It's really scary to have a possible perp hanging around, literally on your doorstep."

And you'd just love to get credit for solving this case. In the meantime, knowledge is power.

"Give me your list of names. I'll run them through the computer and let you know what I find and where that might lead, follow-up-wise."

Bingo.

I tell her first about the library, the ongoing contact with Delia Ingram-Kirksey, and that one of the reference librarians found the body, but he was alone in the stacks. I turn my palms up in a gesture of questioning innocence. For Sally's contacts at the MLK Center, I reveal as little as possible beyond that they are known to have been aided in their personal lives by Sally or are related to someone who was.

"How did you learn of these connections?"

"I do their income tax returns," I say, "as a volunteer at the Center."

This apparently satisfies Kira, because she records all the names without further comment. She calls someone on the phone and says, "There's an Edge in my office."

Quite the understatement.

"We'll want you to wait just a minute," she tells me, banging the eraser end of her pencil on the tablet where she's written the names, "and I'll start in on the computer search. You stay here." Kira goes across the hall to another cubicle. I take out my laptop to begin making a character outline for *Gersalina's Dilemma*, with just a hint of action.

Gersalina, a Commoner from the High Country who's come to Regal City to earn money for the family, impoverished by her father's inability to work because he broke a leg when a horse cart turned over on him while he, too, was digging a trough for the new country-wide irrigation system

Lady-in-Waiting-to-the-Queen Kira has learned to trust few. When she needs information, her only reliable course is to head for the trenches. She learns that Gersalina is staying at the Hen and Egg and found out about the job over pints from a good Captain in the royal service.

"That two-timing bastard," thinks Lady Kira. She decides to take care of the wench, swinging her shovel toward Gersalina's head just as Gersalina bends down to retrieve a kerchief she's dropped. Missing the target entirely, the shovel swings around and wallops Lady Kira's own head, knocking her senseless.

"… important to keep going on about your life normally, Ms. Edge, but immediately report anything or anyone that impresses us in any way to be related to Sally Weathers."

I look up from my tablet to hear a man speaking to me while bending toward my chair. Must be the senior detective in the department, because he's wearing dress slacks, tie, shirt with sleeves rolled down and a waistline suggesting he should be participating in the amaranth study.

"We're taking this one step at a time," he continues, "but you can count on all of us, like Officer Mattingly here, to pull out all the stops and move full speed ahead on this one now and leave no stones unturned with the kind of team that will take us all the way to the finish line. You have my personal guarantee on that."

I'm impressed by his mixing of metaphorical clichés.

~ Nineteen ~
Warm Spit

Upon entering the MLK Center Thursday afternoon, I begin searching right away, based on what I've learned from Tony Hillerman. I don't especially like doing this kind of survey with these sweet and vulnerable people, but the message was clear. Find the mole.

I begin by appraising appearances of the suspects, and it would be impossible not to notice that Jared Stanley looks like a mole. He's small with a thickset body; his hair is light brown and graying; his eyes are rudimentary; and his fat hands would be perfect for digging. The reason I get such a good look at Jared is that he's sitting at the table where the class has gathered for today's session, writing on a thick stack of papers.

"I'm observing today," he tells us. "Just pretend I'm not here."

Right. Everyone from the previous week is back except Eddie, who's sent a diagram in with Dahlia, showing what's under a car hood and providing a numbered list matching caps on various fluid locations with smiley faces.

"This week's assignment," I announce with no preliminary banter, "is to pick a person relating to the story you wrote last week, your intro bio, someone living or dead, and write them a letter expressing anything you'd like to tell them." I wait for questions or protest, but none come. Class members start to work, writing intently for twenty minutes. I whisper to Jared that he can write an introduction of himself, which was last week's assignment, but he continues working on his stack.

At the end of the twenty minutes I ask, "Who would like to share?"

Aldeen starts us off with a letter she's written to her grandmother, expressing regret at not being able to say goodbye before her grandmother died. "It's all the things I would have said to her if I could have, what she did for me, what she taught me, the pieces of her I carry. I'm going to tie it to a balloon filled with helium and mail it."

Jamail reads a rap song he's written on his ongoing theme of igniting the flame of desire, only this week, in place of grill grease and alcohol addiction, its object is Wilhema, one of the waitresses he works with at the diner.

Dahlia writes to her daughter about unconditional love and God's grace.

Mark introduces his map with a letter to the teenage grandson Casey that pleads with him to stay off the two so-called mean streets, one leading to the graffiti-painted fence, where the gang members congregate, and the other to the alley behind the strip mall, where drugs are sold. "Those two streets run together to form the Highway to Huntsville." He concludes with practical, as well as alluring, reasons for taking the streets that lead to the community college and computer jobs: money and girls.

I nod encouragingly and breathe a deep sigh as we move around the table, still wishing Jared wasn't here but beginning to think it'll be OK with these relatively benign pieces. I'm surprised that Annie volunteers next without any prompting. She tells us she's written a letter to her former husband, the one who brutally abused her.

"Dear Jimmy," she reads, "fuck you." The tirade goes on from there, integrating richly drawn passages about the spawn of Satan with "fucking asshole" and "shit" used in brilliantly creative combinations that I haven't heard even on the golf course.

The table explodes in applause with one notable exception. Jared doesn't know about our class rule allowing profanity when it fits the circumstance. I decide Annie's letter is a fine note on which to end my career teaching creative writing at the MLK Center as Jared stands and says he would like to speak with me privately.

"But I haven't read yet," Tilly says, "and we haven't heard what Eddie sent in."

"Go ahead, and I'll talk to Ms. Edge after," Jared says. His hair patch bristles with ions.

"McPherson," Aldeen corrects.

I say nervously, "If you're upset about language, I want to explain that as a class, we've adopted a …"

"We have certain rules in the facility, Ms. Edge, and your class is violating them. I'm going to allow it, however, because this is a class where those words serve a certain function, but I don't want them spilling over anywhere else." His eyes form tiny slits before he turns and slinks away.

"Power of the pen," Jamail says when I sit back down at the table.

After class Jared interrogates me about my lesson plans and pumps me for new information regarding Sally's demise. I provide little other than that I've heard the police are keeping the file open but don't know any details. Before Jared can rend his garments, Kelly Jackson comes up to ask me for help with a withholding issue.

Later I drive the four blocks to Bud's and pick up the barbecue for Suella and Ruth Ann but opt not to get any for the boys, having checked the value of a Hummer H3 in the Kelly Blue Book as thirty thousand dollars plus. They should buy my dinner. On a more ominous note I think about the loitering that must have taken place prior to the note-leaving at my house. Loitering, as in watching my movements. Suella said the boys came to her house to help, but help how? They would have seen Sally deliver the barbecue like I am.

Again I'm not able to get through to Suella by phone, so I pick up the same order as last week and head the half-mile over to Suella's house with it. As I pull up, sure enough, one of the teenagers from last week leaves the house, walks down the driveway, carrying a bag similar to last week's, sits on the curb and begins talking on his cell phone. Definitely loitering and not to eat barbecue.

Suella opens the front door before I can knock. "Hideedoo, Miz Friend-of-Sally. I'm sorry, I can't remember your name."

"Grace Edna Edge."

"Grace Edna Edge. Yeah, that's it. Now I remember. We tried to get that oxygen all fixed before you got here. That young man who came, he's with the oxygen company."

That's a relief. Not loitering, helping with Ruth Ann's oxygen tank and its tubal connection. Must be Mark's son Casey.

"Would you like me to take that?" She reaches out for the bags of food I'm holding.

"Oh, I'll bring them in for you and say hello to Ruth Ann."

Suella doesn't budge from the doorway. "We don't want to cause you any trouble, don't you see?" She's holding a sealed, unaddressed, padded envelope.

"It's no trouble. I'd like to see Ruth Ann." I move forward with the food, now determined to get inside the house.

"She's poorly today," Suella says and puts the envelope on the coffee table. "It's the new instructions for the oxygen. We're having some trouble. That boy comes whenever we need him, so nice."

"Is his name Casey? I think I know his father."

"I don't remember his name," Suella says.

"Casey," Ruth Ann shouts, leaning back in the same reclining chair as last week, covered with a quilt, watching television. "Like at the bat, when the outlook wasn't brilliant for the Mudville Nine." She reaches for a sip of beer from the bottle on her TV tray. "Hi there, Miz Grace. You're so kindly to bring us this good food. Woncha sit?" Ruth Ann laughs at something on television.

I can hear now that she's watching "Jeopardy."

"Who's Wilma Rudolph?" she says loudly. "They all missed that one, but I got it. Can you believe none of those three panelists knew the first American woman to win three gold medals in the Olympics? Two thousand dollars."

"That's just fine there," Suella says, following me into the kitchen. "You're so nice to do this, like Sally. It means a lot to Ruth Ann. She just doesn't have much she can look forward to in this life. With all her pain she's talking more and more about the hereafter, if you know what I mean." Suella points toward the ceiling.

"She seems pretty comfortable tonight," I say.

"Oh, she hides it in front of company. Before you came she was talking to that boy working with her oxygen tank. Ruth Ann told him she's getting ready to meet her Jesus. She says she'll be sitting at the table with Jesus, and she's gonna hold her dog in her lap, hide him under the napkin so he can be at the table, too. She used to have a miniature poodle. Lives in the past. Says that little dog gonna stick his head out and say hidee."

I hear Ruth Ann clapping.

"Sorry we can't ask you to stay," Suella says. "Ruth Ann just isn't up to it. Maybe next time. It's her breathing, don't you know." The telephone rings.

"Who's John Nance Garner?" Ruth Ann shouts.

"Gasping for her next breath, don't you know," Suella says as she goes to the back of the house to answer the phone.

"Who said the vice presidency isn't worth more than a bucket of warm spit?" comes from Ruth Ann.

I peek around the door to the living room. "How are you feeling tonight, Ruth Ann, are you hungry?"

"Am I ready for some ribs? Mmm, mmm. From Uvalde, Texas, John Nance Garner. You ever been out there? There's a café on the highway, the Amber Sky, serves a fine slice of chocolate meringue pie."

"Yes, matter of fact I have been to Uvalde. It's near where I grew up in Sublime."

"Where they have that sign that says, "This is God's country, don't drive through it like hell.""

I nod. "You're right, we're known for that sign. Is there anything else I can do for you?"

"Do you know how to try out for 'Jeopardy'?" Ruth Ann asks.

"Yeah, there's a quiz you take online. They have a schedule and announce it on the program. I tried out once, wasn't accepted. But you're just full of relevant 'Jeopardy' material. Do you have computer access?"

"No, ma'am. We have an old IBM Selectric, but it's broken down."

"You could go to the library. Do you have portable oxygen?"

"I don't need it. Suella go on and on about the oxygen. I'm just fine." She takes a deep breath and exhales to show me.

"I'll check the schedule for tryouts and take you to the branch by the MLK Center or the main library downtown."

"Ruth Ann can't travel." Suella walks back into the kitchen. "She's limited because of the oxygen and her pain. "

"I'll look into it for you," I tell Ruth Ann.

"You want to go out this side door? You can slip right on around to your vehicle." Suella pushes me toward a screen porch off the kitchen with an outside door. "We thank you for coming, but you don't need to go to this trouble for us."

"It's not a problem for me to bring the barbecue," I say through the screen reassuringly. "I'm nearby, and I like to pick up the food for myself anyway. It's a treat on the nights I volunteer at the Center."

"Sure do appreciate what you're doing, like Sally. Maybe I'll see you at the Center. It's just hard for me to get away now or even do the sewing with Ruth Ann slipping down. She's getting delusional, too, as you can probably see."

What I did see was an oxygen tank in the corner with the tubes attached, but nothing was connected to Ruth Ann's nose.

In spite of what Suella's claims, Ruth Ann obviously doesn't need it all the time.

~ Twenty ~
Undertow

For this Friday's rendition of ladies' day, I arrive in a meadow green mesh polo shirt, desert khaki easy care crops by Lands' End, classic wing buckle shoes by Ecco, wrap sports style, polarized gloss black frame eyewear with unigrip temple pads by Texas State Optical, and a chartreuse visor from the Penick Park Golf Club sales rack. Unfortunately I'm flying my shots long on the driving range but pulling everything way left of my target.

To correct the pull I need to realign my shoulders, hips, knees and feet, like my two instructors-before-last said, or put the ball farther back in my stance so I don't pick it up too quickly. Then I remember what Judy Rankin, the analyst and commentator, said on television about the problem with amateur swings, which is that we take it back inside and come out over the top, although I have absolutely no idea what that means. Whatever. I'm out of range balls.

After checking in with the pro shop, I sign up at the ladies' table for my flight. We used to put in a few bucks each week and divvy up the antes to the first, second and third place winners in each of four flights, but all that changed when it turned out that Thelma Lewis, who ran the table every week, was dipping into the pot. I never could understand how my second or third place finish yielded less than what I'd contributed.

Now we award the winner of each place a golf ball that comes out of club dues. One of the members dresses them up in fancy little sock-like packets you can reuse to hold your golf tees or quarters for chip-ins. That is, I could reuse it if I ever won one.

Kira only beats me by an average of four stokes. I sit down on a bench near the putting green to complete preparations for my round—mentally by spending ten minutes in deep meditation and physically by eating a raspberry and cream croissant—while I visualize my future putts. Sixteen foot left-breaker curls in. Next, a deceptive downhill three-footer catches the right edge.

As I send a thirty-footer up a slight incline, breaking toward the river and dropping into the cup, I hear, "Are you OK to play?" from Kira. "You look a little logy."

I return from my victory on the eighteenth hole of the LPGA championship as Kira hands me a computer printout, saying, "I ran the info you wanted."

"Thanks, Kira. You're efficient." I hadn't expected anything so quickly. "And such a natty delivery service."

Kira's attired in the off-aqua, head-to-toe, fully coordinated set from TaylorMade and Footjoy.

"It's because there's nothing there to follow up on." She turns on her heel and begins walking rapidly toward the tee box.

Rushing after her, I knock over my clubs and cart, causing my leg to bleed, which I sop with the printer papers. I'm having quite a round, and I haven't even teed off yet.

As curious as I am to see what's on the printout beside my A positive blood sample, I have to tee off in Kira's group again.

Everyone in the foursome is walking today, so there is blessedly little opportunity for any private conversation with Kira. I hold my own with her until we arrive at Number Eleven, a one-hundred-twenty-two-yard uphill par three over a lake. Approaching the tee box, I visualize the water as a field of grass. Madison Mueller, who's in her early eighties, hits a Calloway Big Bertha driver, and the ball lands on the collar of the green. I know from experience she'll get up and down for par. Gladys Brockton barely clears with a nine wood. Kira goes next and puts her ball within four inches of the cup, using a seven iron.

I usually use a six iron here, just to be sure, but we have a slight head wind, and I really don't want to be short. It's a lot of club, but I'm thinking four-hybrid, uphill and against the wind, and so what if I'm over the green slightly. On the other hand, I don't want Kira to think I'm a wimp, which she will if I use anything but an iron. Better to use a longer iron with the same enough-distance theory. She's standing over by the tree, talking to Gladys, and won't know it's a five iron.

No, that's silly. Go with my gut. The essential matter is to carry the water, not to impress Kira.

My compromise is nine wood, but Gladys barely cleared with that, and she usually hits farther than I do with the same equipment. I pull out my seven wood. Normally I hit that club one hundred forty-five yards. There is trouble lurking behind the green if I go too far over. I put the seven wood back in my bag and pull out the nine wood.

Not wanting to tee up the ball too high, I pound a tee into the ground so the head is barely at the surface and place my ball on it with the logo lined up in the direction of my shot. I step back and take a couple of practice swings. The club just doesn't feel right, so I put it back in the bag and quickly take out the five iron.

With no practice swings at all, I let it rip. And ripple. That's what I see next, ripples. Damn. With all the energy I put into club selection, I forgot my visualization of the pathway to the green as grass, not water.

Kira walks over and reminds me I can either re-tee, hitting three, or go to the drop zone, also hitting three but much closer and on the right side of the lake. Madison nods encouragement.

I choose to re-tee and wallop my four iron. The ball travels across the surface of the lake like a skipped rock and falls in the water about six yards short of the far shore.

"You can use the drop zone, honey," Madison says.

I re-tee and set up with my seven wood.

"Hitting five," Kira says.

I put the ball in the bunker behind the green. "Made it over, I say," my polarized eyewear askew.

We cross the bridge and set up for our next shots, second for the other three and sixth for me. I try an explosion shot with my sand wedge, completely miss the sand, and send the ball over the green and into the lake. Gladys has to duck.

"It's a lateral hazard," Kira says, "so you can either …"

My ball has landed just inside the hazard, in the mud but not in the water. "I'll hit it from here," I announce, because my other choices are to drop behind the lake where I started or from the trap I just left.

"You can't ground your club, Kira shouts, adding "hitting eight," as I smack the ball to the edge of the green, leaving a trail of flying mud in its path. My right Ecco classic wing buckle is sopping wet.

"You can have a little breather now, honey," Madison says. "It's my turn."

Gladys and Madison both make pars, Kira a birdie, and me an eleven. Gladys calls my score a quadruple buffalo in an effort to cheer me up and assures me she once had an octo-buffalo, which I doubt but appreciate. Kira thoughtfully offers a few suggestions on the benefits of course management.

By the time we turn in our cards, my leg is bleeding again, and I've convinced myself that it's only golf. Mary Lou Watkins at the scorer's table asks me what happened to my shoe. But I do have the printout to look forward to, thanks to Kira.

"Nice round," I say to her as she claims her new Titleist DT So Lo for Feel-Good-Distance. As if she needed it. We move away from the table conversation and tallying flow. "Thanks again for running those computer checks."

"As I already said, you won't find anything relevant to your drug ring theories," she tells me in a near-whisper. "Only narcotics violations are long ago and incarcerated. Detective Frederick or I will be in touch if there are any developments. I'll confer with him just as soon as he gets back. We stay in close communication, if you get my drift. Meanwhile, I'd advise you and your aunt to stay out of the undertow."

"Uh huh," I nod dutifully as my cell phone rings. It's Aunt Arrow, asking me to meet her at Sally's condo.

"I have a sad mission," she tells me on the phone, her voice breaking. "Sally's personal effects were released to me this morning with Nathan's authorization. I'm taking them home."

I'm curious as to what they are but don't press.

"I also have Jake's archive searches," Aunt Arrow says, "which we can look at together."

"Kira Mattingly, the officer I contacted for help, gave me the police data this morning as well. We'll compare results. I'm still at golf but welcome an escape," I say, regretting that Aunt Arrow didn't call me five hours earlier. "Be there in about forty-five."

~ Twenty-One ~
Police Records

On the way to Sally's condo I make two stops, the first to salve my ego with a double meat and cheese Whataburger; the other at Bluebonnet Pharmacy to salve the oozing gash on my leg.

At the pharmacy counter Simone is holding forth with a customer about side effects. Again I try to recall how I know her but can't come up with a connection by the time she finishes her lecture on rashes, sleeplessness and diarrhea.

With no preamble, I request peroxide, first aid cream and bandages large enough to cover the cut on my leg, which I lift up to show Simone. As I'm lifting Simone bends partially over the counter to view the gash, and makes sympathetic murmurs. Her earrings jangle, an attractive chain of multi-sized quadrilaterals, which I recognize as the distinctive work of Aldeen's daughter.

Church. That must be where I've seen Simone.

"Do you go to St. Barnabas?" I ask in my Christian-love-and-fellowship voice. "Episcopal."

She looks somewhat puzzled and shakes her head.

"I know you from somewhere, and I've been racking my brain, trying to remember where. Do you know what I mean?"

Simone looks sideways at one of the pharmacists, who's waving at her, and provides me with an even better view of the earrings.

"The reason I thought St. Barnabas is the jewelry, because they had a sale of them at the church last week. I know the artist, or I should say the artist's mother, and that prompted me to think church. Your lovely earrings."

"Oh, thanks, but I bought them at a street fair in East Austin. I remember a little card in the box with info about the artist. I agree, they're sweet, but they didn't come from any church."

She probably thinks I'm one of those people who knock on doors with salvation leaflets.

"I wasn't trying to evangelize you. Quite frankly, I don't believe in that missionary sort of thing, and I apologize if ..."

"You'll find the peroxide on aisle three. The bandages and the cream you'll want for that ooze are on five." Simone walks to the far end of the counter and takes a stack of receipts from the waving pharmacist.

"Well, that went well," I say to the counter display of seasonal cold remedies. She now thinks I'm an evangelical pervert.

When I'm paying for my purchases, I see Simone behind the deli counter, drawing a drink from the fountain dispenser. I consider sidling over and trying again with a companionable lemonade or cranberry juice, thinking it might be useful to have an ally behind the Bluebonnet prescription counter. Before I can make up my mind, she's already back in her side-effects pulpit with another customer.

Next up is Aunt Arrow, who opens the door to my knock, which is helpful because my hands are full of first aid products, and I'm walking with a slight limp.

"Oh, honey, what have you done to yourself now? Come sit, and let's get that cleaned up." She ministers to my wound with compassionate efficiency and finds a dry pair of socks in Sally's drawer. I welcome them in spite of their not matching anything else I'm wearing.

Cleansed, creamed and bandaged, I ask how she's doing with Sally's effects. It sounds so sterile to call them that, as if they were on one of my balance sheets as assets rather than something warm and human.

Aunt Arrow insists I keep my leg elevated and brings over Sally's pea coat that belonged to her husband when he served in the Navy. "She loved wearing that coat, felt his arms wrapped around her." And her purse, black leather. "Carried it for years. Believed in classic, never out of style."

Aunt Arrow reverently takes out the contents. Lipstick. Blusher. Needlepoint eyeglass case with gold-rimmed half-glasses. Plastic case with travel-size toothbrush and toothpaste. Folding hairbrush. Wallet with driver's license, Medicare card, supplemental insurance card, one credit card, AAA card, library card, Randall's supermarket card, blood donor card, twenty-seven dollars in bills and forty-four cents in coin. Checkbook. Fountain pen, real, that Aunt Arrow demonstrates by uncapping and writing Sally's name in green ink. Bluebonnet Pharmacy bag, inside of which is a drug information sheet, the prescription bottle of Zoloft and some tortilla crumbs.

Aunt Arrow rattles the prescription bottle and hands it over to me, as if it's contaminated. I read the label: Weathers, Sally. Sertraline Hydrochloride. Take one tablet by mouth daily. 50 MG Tab. Pr. Ellison, Daniel R. Refill 2 times.

Continuing to give Aunt Arrow space to weep, I scan the drug sheet. When I get to dose, I learn that Zoloft is available in twenty-five and fifty milligram tablets. Why, I wonder, if she's on the lowest dose possible, according to Nathan, Aunt Arrow and Sally herself, is she taking fifty milligrams instead of twenty-five?

I mention this gently to Aunt Arrow, who dries her face with the linen handkerchief she's found in one of the pea coat pockets. "Sally insisted on cloth, never used paper tissues." But she has no idea why the pills are fifty milligrams unless it's a mistake. "Sally couldn't see anything close without her reading glasses," Aunt Arrow says.

We go into Sally's bathroom and look at the bottle she'd been using. The pills in it are also fifty milligrams, light blue. Aunt Arrow remembers Sally had a travel case with cosmetics and other necessities she kept packed for trips, in her bedroom closet. We find the travel case, and in it is a prescription bottle with Zoloft. Light green twenty-five milligram tablets with a fill date six months earlier than the bathroom bottle.

"Sally's dose was increased in the last year," I conclude.

"No, it wasn't. She was considering going off the Zoloft altogether."

"Apparently the doctor didn't agree. All three are prescribed by Dr. Ellison," I point out.

"Daniel was receptive to taking her off. She'd just had that appointment and was going to every other day in spite of what the instructions said." Aunt Arrow raises her voice. "They'd agreed to try the reduced dose."

"Well, something's off here. Either he changed the dose and Sally didn't notice, if she took the pills without her glasses, or maybe she didn't want you to know she needed a bit more help."

"Less, not more." Aunt Arrow shakes her head, vigorously.

"I'll call Nathan and have him confer with Ellison. The doctor won't release her records to us."

Aunt Arrow nods agreement to that proposal and resumes wiping her eyes and nose with the handkerchief.

"I'll just get the police printout now." I lower my leg and limp over to the table to retrieve my maroon vinyl case. Aunt Arrow doesn't have to budge to remove a spiral bound steno tablet from her red pepper cotton carry-all.

We spread our respective paper products on the coffee table. I've memorized mine with perusals at respective Penick Park, Whataburger and Bluebonnet parking lots as well as four backed-up signal lights along 17th Avenue, and I don't agree with Kira. They may not be overtly drug related, but the suspects offer a plethora of possibility.

Ever the reporter, Aunt Arrow offers to cumulate the results from our separate sources. "Delia Ingram-Kirksey," she rings out and raises Sally's pen in readiness.

Delia Ingram-Kirksey. From the newspaper archives we learn that she has served on myriad committees to support charitable galas and silent auctions. We are surprised to note that she is also cited in both newspaper and police records for a Failure to Appear. Ms. Ingram-Kirksey backed out of her driveway and into a neighbor's brick planter, demolishing the front and one side of the planter. The neighbor filed against her in small claims court, which is where she failed to appear. The *Austin Times* archives article reveals that she beat the claim because the City of Austin had widened her street, making the planter closer to the curb even though its geographic location was unchanged. According to the neighbor, Harold Steblich, Ms. Ingram-Kirksey offered no restitution. 'There are just some folks who don't know how to be neighborly."

Todd LaJames. This surprises both of us, but he also makes a double appearance. Besides his listing as a survivor in his grandfather's obituary, he was written about and cited by police for disrupting a meeting/procession. In the Gay Pride Parade four years ago he came down from his Triple-Rainbows float and attacked a heckler, Lee Roy Adkins. They exchanged a series of blows. Mr. Adkins was taken by ambulance to the St. Jude's Hospital Emergency Room and later released. LaJames "defended the honor of my lesbian sister. Any brother with blood in his veins would do the same." Because the incident was precipitated by Mr. Adkins, the charge against Mr. LaJames was dropped, and Adkins was required to perform twenty hours of community service, waived for Mr. LaJames due to his professional employment in community service.

Jared Phillips. Various newspaper announcements list his positions at nonprofit agencies. The mini-surprise here is that police records contain one count of Abuse of Official Capacity, eventually dropped, according to the *Times*, because he successfully defended at a county commissioner's hearing his handling of a federal government grant while working at Partners, an agency that pairs at-risk children with adult mentors.

Ofelia Taylor has a long rap sheet, all to do with her drug addiction: possession of illegal drugs, possession of drug paraphernalia, manufacture of methamphetamine and intent to distribute. Her mug shot appears in numerous *Times* articles over a period of twelve years, but nothing for the past three, since she's been incarcerated at the Texas State Women's Prison in Gatesville. According to the Police Department's Track-the-Inmate review, "Ms. Taylor has successfully completed a voluntary six-month drug rehabilitation program, works in the prison print shop, where she is learning an employable skill, and has no visitors to the prison other than family members."

Casey Guthrie also has been arrested twice. His offenses include graffiti on the Grove Boulevard Middle School, resulting in a charge of Damaging a Public Building. A little over a year later he was convicted and sentenced to six months in the County Juvenile Detention Facility for criminal mischief and theft at a Thunderclouds Sub fast food restaurant. In the eighteen months since his release Mr. Guthrie's record is spotless, and his parole officer, Crystal Dutch, stated that "Mr. Guthrie has to date complied with all requirements in a timely and satisfactory manner. He is currently employed by the Plankton Oxygen Service."

It comes as no news whatsoever that James "Jimmy" Jolipson has a rap sheet several counts longer than Taylor's and Zapata's combined. Criminal Mischief. Driving with License Revoked. Theft, Residence, and multiple counts of Assault with Injury—Family. He has served time in both the county and city jails but is not currently incarcerated as far as we can determine, and nothing has appeared in either the *Austin Times* or the police records for the past six months.

Jamail Davis has multiple arrests and convictions for DWI and Public Intoxication, usually at Oilcan Leo's Drinking Establishment, but nothing for the previous eighteen months, except his volunteer service as a basketball coach for the eight-and-under youth boy's league. His team went 12-5.

Aunt Arrow says it's good timing that we've reached the end of the list just as she's run out of ink. While she refills Sally's pen, I search the list for our mole.

Delia's destroying her neighbor's planter and not paying him is offensive, but I don't see that action on her part as a forerunner of criminal behavior, just the ongoing narcissism. Even though it may have been justified, Todd LaJames clearly has a capacity for violence that's worth pursuing. Jared. Well, Jared's aura of suspiciousness lingers, though I wouldn't put him at the top of the list. As far as I'm concerned the data clear Casey, Jamail and Ofelia. James "Jimmy" Joplinson, however, is another matter.

When Aunt Arrow returns, reinked, she lists my new marching orders:

1. Get back into the library and check the downstairs stacks for any questionable activity by LaJames. "What do you mean by questionable activity?" I inquire.

"Conversations with persons on the premises who are not conducting library business, slinking around, that sort of thing," Aunt Arrow explains.

2. Discuss past and prospective potential for devious behavior by Jared Phillips with Detective Frederick.

3. Resolve the issue of the oxygen delivery and maintenance for Ruth Ann—who's coming and when, and what are they doing.

4. Confirm with Dahlia to the extent possible that Ofelia Taylor does not have ongoing communication with previous drug connections.

"You mean like their taking a birthday cake into the prison with a saw-tooth knife hidden inside?"

Aunt Arrow ignores me.

5. Talk to Detective Frederick in detail about James "Jimmy" Jolipson, thereby risking violating the confidentially agreement of the creative writing class.

6. With my having such a long list, she will talk to Nathan about getting to the bottom of the Zoloft bottle.

7. I add a seven to search for a bereavement support group.

"You know," I say to Aunt Arrow as I'm refolding the printout, "you could find yourself on this list of police records and in the *Times* Daily Crime Blotter. It's not exactly a stretch to imagine our discussing a dual appearance by one Aurora Cecelia Edge relating to her housewifely gardening and baking."

"1:18 a.m. Patrol officer dispatched to the one hundred block of Travis Main, the downtown branch of the public library," Aunt Arrow replies, flipping up the cover of her steno tablet. "Placed in police custody on the charge of Illegal Entry, Public Building, one Grace Edna Edge, C.P.A. and aspiring romance writer."

Touché.

~ Twenty-Two ~
Strawberry Crumpets

For tea. What could I have been thinking? That's just the problem. I wasn't. But Bertel caught me off guard, calling on Sunday afternoon to let me know he was back in town, wanted to meet as soon as possible, and he's catching up this afternoon from being away. If I have some time.

That's when I blurted, "Why don't you just stop by for a cup of tea? Babe's demanding a ball throwing marathon since I've had to ignore her most of the weekend."

Blame it on Babe, sweet, innocent Babe. All she wanted was some attention and exercise this afternoon since I've been so busy writing. I have Gersalina on the brink, having re-encountered the Good Captain, who is sadly in danger of losing his commission at the whim of her royal highness. He's turning to the voluptuous but vulnerable Gersalina for solace and comfort. She, in turn, is torn between a passionate intensity of feelings never before experienced, certainly not acted upon, and honoring the responsibility to return to her family in order to provide the material and emotional support she alone can provide.

But no more writing this afternoon, and now I'll have to go out and get something to serve with the tea.

I'm still dressed in what I wore to church, the ankle-length skirt in the McPherson plaid I ordered online from a shop in Edinburgh that fortunately had enough fabric to allow me to move the button over one and a half inches, green mock turtleneck that doesn't overwhelm the tartan, and blue blazer, also ordered from Scotland. The blazer has a crest on the front pocket with the clan motto, "Per Ardura," which means "through difficulties."

No one at church seemed to notice one way or another what motto I was wearing, and it hugged up quite nicely during the Passing of the Peace. At social hour after the service I managed to find Rita Eustis, Eddie's daughter and a bereavement coordinator for the Austin Metro Hospice.

Rita remembered me or pretended to when I brought up the subject of having some bereavement coordinated for my aunt, and I added that we had missed her father at class last week. Her fault. With her work schedule, it was the only time he could do the tune-up on her car.

From our conversation I came away with her business card and a brochure for the grief support group offered by hospice as well as Rita's understanding that grief was nonlinear and didn't fit into any definitive steps or models, although there were "common experiences such as profound disorganization, with accompanying physical, emotional, and spiritual responses." She emphasized the profound.

Before initiating the search for my teapot, which I rarely use because I ordinarily make only individual cups of tea, I go into the utility area to transfer the load of wash into the dryer and see that I've run the entire load with nothing in the washing machine. The separated darks and lights sit anxiously on the floor in respective piles, awaiting the decision of which gets to go first. Babe, who trotted in with me to sniff a few items, chooses a sock to take back into her corner of the kitchen. I load whites, add detergent and turn on the washer once again, lifting the lid to double check the tub.

The teapot can wait. I told Bertel two hours.

I shore up with lipstick and a touch of blush, and Babe agrees to help me pick out something to eat to go with the tea. After putting us both in the car I remember the gas bill I was supposed to mail yesterday and go back into the house to look for it. Not on my desk or on the kitchen table or the bookshelf by the front door. I finally find the envelope on top of the egg carton in the refrigerator.

"Don't ask," I tell Babe when I get back into the car, and she tactfully offers nothing about profound disorganization.

We briefly consider the strawberry pie at Threadbelle's, but the nearest one to me is way out on Langford, and I've taken so much time looking for the gas bill that there's not enough time to get there and back.

We opt instead for Krispy Krust, where providentially there's an available parking space on the side of the building. I run in quickly, wait in line, find I'm too late for the cinnamon rolls, but the fresh peach muffins are still available.

I calculate that I'll eat one, Bertel may want two, and I'll take a couple of extras for tomorrow's breakfast, but the counter clerk convinces me to make it an even half-dozen. Babe looks at me so mournfully, head tilted to the side, when I return to the car, I go back into Krispy Krust, wait through the line again and buy one shortbread cookie.

Whew. Bertel is parking in front of the house as Babe and I drive into the garage. I quickly pull her into the house on the lead and through to the front door as Bertel rings the bell, setting off a raucous round of barking and snarling. I make Babe sit. When I open the door, however, she leaps up vigorously and paws against Bertel's chest.

He rubs her ears and pulls her gently down, speaking in a calm voice, "This must be the lovely Babe. Such a lady in her starched white blouse." He glances around the room. "Thanks for the invite. What a nice place you have and great, old trees in this neighborhood. Mine just has the newborns."

"Acorns and pecans."

"My first smoke was in an acorn pipe," he says.

"Mine was cedar bark, wrapped in torn strips from a paper bag," which finishes that portion of the conversation.

Babe lifts her head, and Bertel obliges by rubbing under her neck.

"You seem to know what dogs like."

"From necessity. I have a feisty female golden retriever who could probably hold her own with this young lady. They're good company, aren't they?" He hesitates, then adds, "And more to the present point, protective."

"Babe's enabled me to sleep almost through the night. I'm only waking up seven or eight times."

"Officer Dunbar's substantially increased your neighborhood patrols. He and I will meet tomorrow, and then I'd like to set up a session with you and Aurora. I want to look through everything thoroughly. For now, let's ..."

"... have some tea," I finish for him, recovering my respiration and rubbing my hands together briskly. He follows me into the kitchen.

I glance at the list I've just happened to place on the kitchen table: Discuss devious behavior by Jared Phillips...Talk to Detective Frederick in detail about James "Jimmy" Jolipson... And patrols aren't enough to stop someone who really wants to harass me or worse.

Before I can launch into my list, he says, "I don't want to burden you with anything about the case this afternoon until I review matters with Dunbar," then adds, "unless there are particular things you want to discuss. Mainly, I wanted to touch base."

What base? I wonder. "I do have some questions," I say, noticing for the first time that he looks tired from the travels, I suppose. "But they can wait until the meeting with Aunt Arrow."

Opening the cabinet, I attempt to reach the top shelf where I spot the teapot behind the food processor. It becomes apparent to all parties present that I can touch the shelf but not the teapot.

"Allow me," Bertel says, putting one hand on my back and reaching up for the teapot with the other.

Bored with the damsel-in-distress proceedings, Babe pads over to her corner to chew on the sock.

"Let's see," I say, taking charge with a full survey of my cabinet. "English Breakfast all right with you?" It's all I have, except for some decaffeinated Typhoo, and I'm thinking we need the full tilt as I add water and plug in the electric kettle. With milk. Or should I offer sugar with lemon, which would mean bottled lemon, since I don't have any fresh, and that's artificially acidic. I prefer my tea with just the milk and a couple teaspoons of sugar. I'll warm the muffins in the microwave, one plus two plus the one extra so I don't seem stingy.

"We can have our tea and crumpets in here," I wave broadly across the kitchen, "or take them through to the living room."

"I think it's easier to eat tea at a table," Bertel chooses, which is something of a relief because I don't like crumbs down my front either, even though it means giving up the privacy of the preparations.

"How do you like your tea?"

"Not too strong," Bertel says.

Trying again, "Milk, sugar, lemon?"

"Milk and a bit of sugar will be fine. What are crumpets, anyway?"

I'm about to explain the British short pastry when Bertel laughs, and I realize he's made a joke. He settles at the round table while I efficiently make the tea, warm the muffins and bring everything to the table on a tray. Babe wanders over, accepts her cookie, sniffs under the table and settles by Bertel's shoes.

He eats three muffins and drinks two cups of tea while we talk about his trip to California, highlighted by the time spent with his son, who took time off from his alleged studies to show Bertel the campus, attend a basketball game at Pauley Pavilion, spend an afternoon at the planetarium and walk along the beach at Malibu. Bertel shows me some spectacular photos of sunset from the pier.

We walk out on the patio to take turns throwing the ball for Babe, and I talk vaguely about my work, concentrating on assets and liabilities but mentioning my fiction as an aspiration. When he notices the cement mixer, I'm able to shift to a detailed explanation of my plans to patch the cracks in the driveway, eliciting a few nods of admiration.

We even manage several periods of companionable silence, neither of us compelled to say anything at all to the other or to ask or explain. Whew.

"Grace, thank you for the afternoon," Bertel says when we come back into the house and he puts on his jacket. "Sundays are especially hard for me since Helen died. The time with Ben, well, it just made me feel the loss all the more. I keep busy during the week with work, and I do errands and chores around the house on Saturdays; but Sundays slow down, and I have so much time to think and remember."

Truth be told, I have trouble with Sundays, too, and I haven't had a spouse die. I've hardly had a spouse. And I've enjoyed the afternoon an unexpected amount, but where is Bertel leading?

Confused by the unexpected personal turn in the conversation, I say, "Kira's been a help to you, I know."

"Who?"

"Kira Mattingly. Officer Mattingly."

"She has? Oh, right. She's a first rate technician, best we have in the department for I.T. Was there something you wanted to bring up about Ms. Weathers?"

I shake my head. "Doesn't Kira come, I mean, aren't you and Kira seeing … uh, she said that the two of you were, oh shit, this is none of my business." What an idiot.

"Oh, I see what you mean."

You do?

"Kira's brought food over, and she's not the only one, me being the lonely widower, and OK, if we're being honest here, I'm no monk."

I don't recall anything about the desire for honesty.

"But Grace, here's more truth for you. I like to cook myself. It's something that brings me peace, caramelizing vegetables, chopping and dicing, inventing a marinade."

We've left Babe outside, so I'm on my own, walking with Bertel precipitously toward the front door.

I settle on, "Caramelizing, I can't quite get it. My onions always turn out either soggy or burnt."

Bertel holds my shoulders, bends forward and kisses my cheek. This time, there's no question about the moisture's source, and it's spread to other parts of my body.

"We'll have a caramelizing practice session for the crested Scot," he says. "My kitchen next time."

Bertel's cheeks are the same color as mine, and he hasn't used any blusher. He turns quickly and walks out the door.

Reluctantly leaving her post of supervising the robins' nest-building, Babe comes inside to help me clean up the tea things. Instead, I pour a large glass of red wine, sit down to drink it, and burst into tears.

~ **Twenty-Three** ~
U-Haul

Nothing from Bertel all day Monday, and by late Tuesday morning my anxiety level is soaring. The ever-energetic Babe refuses to go on yet another walk around the park, and even with her presence I jump every time I hear an unidentifiable noise outside my house.

My analysis of QuadRay is nearly complete, but my damsels and warriors refuse to engage. So I review my notes once again to take a fresh run at the mole.

If Tony is steering me right, the person we're seeking has a cover, appearing to operate in a seemingly safe and ordinary setting. But all the while, deep in the underground, he or she is performing criminal activity that is effectively masked and possibly fueled by the surface appearances.

Jared Phillips runs the seemingly safe and ordinary Senior Center, and we now know that he's had suspicious dealings involving finances. Both library employees qualify as to surface cover. But LaJames seems more likely as a suspect, still a slim one, unless I turn up something newly damaging in the library stacks, which I'm avoiding until I'm sure I'll have Bertel's backup. I'm not sure why, but I don't think the homeless man rises to the level of mole-ness. Or sinks.

Sally could have observed something in the neighborhood when she brought the ribs to Suella's. Casey would have seen her there, like he sees me now, and those two boys could have been the ones to pull off the note-drop at my house.

Dahlia's daughter Ophelia has both cover and connections but no means of which we're aware.

We don't know anything about Jimmy Joplinson's current involvements, but we have plenty of information about his criminal past, rendering him a candidate as well.

Reviewing Aunt Arrow's list of assignments, I find that I'm stuck. Much too much depends on communication with Bertel. Danm him anyway.

At loose ends, I call Aunt Arrow, who tells me she hasn't heard back from Nathan yet on the Zoloft dosage, but I'm welcome to come over any time. She's baking up a frenzy to assuage her own anxiety and imagines a snack would help with mine as well.

I thank her for the offer but pass.

Next in line for human connection is Jana. Remembering that she doesn't teach classes on Tuesdays and Thursdays, I call her campus number and am relieved when she picks up on the second ring and invites me to come visit the Bone Lab, which I've never seen.

Babe settles willingly in the back yard with a chew-bone, indestructible and good for your pup's dental hygiene, and I'm on campus in fifteen minutes.

Having navigated this campus quite easily as a student, I'm frustrated by the effect of its ongoing growth on accessibility. In desperation I park illegally in a well-marked University Vehicles Only space and roam a labyrinth of academic corridors to find Jana, smartly dressed in a white lab coat and examining a tooth. I lack the energy for a smart-ass comment and instead wait for Jana's explanation.

"Research on how Indians adapted to stress," she obliges, "by studying their bones, specifically the teeth. That's where you find the indications of stress."

I reach in my mouth and feel a couple of front ones, pleased that nothing wiggles. "Where do you get the teeth?" Jana's never told me much about her academic research, even though—or perhaps because—she's internationally renowned in academic circles.

"We keep them in storage here in the lab. What I do is select a tooth from the appropriate period, set it in epoxy and take out a slice," Jana explains in a menacing tone, "with the giant saw."

"Giant saw," I nod as if that makes perfect sense.

"A giant circular saw. I make two thin cuts through the tooth, yielding a slice to mount for observations under a microscope. In my work I'm looking for indications of stress in Arizona Indians at different periods, from the hunting and gathering phase on through the beginnings of agriculture."

"And were they stressed?"

"Oh, yes, it's not a question of whether, but what circumstances produce the most, and in their case it was in the transition, the time between hunting and gathering and the beginning of food production."

Tony Hillerman or I could have told her the transitions produce the most stress. Still, it's intriguing that Indians had the same experience so long ago. "I'm reading about Arizona Indians, too," I tell Jana, "especially some of their religious practices. We may be looking at much the same thing from different angles."

"Uh huh," Jana nods and checks the time. "I have a meeting at two, but let's grab a coffee.

We walk across the street to a campus coffee bar, and I have trouble with my order, changing from decaf latte to small Americano to large cappuccino and back to the Americano, medium.

"What in the hell is going on with you, Grace?" Jana's never been known for her subtlety.

"I have this new friend," I say, drizzling milk from a tiny cardboard container into my coffee. "Well, we knew each other slightly from working on a case together a while back. He's a police detective that Aunt Arrow and I are seeing because her best friend died in the library, you know, Sally Weathers, and we believe she was murdered by drug dealers, and I've received a threatening note, which affirms the connection to Sally, we think, it's scary stuff, and this detective is a descendent of Bertel Thorvaldsen, have you ever heard of him, that's where he gets the unusual name, Bertel, the famous Danish sculptor who did the Lion of Lucerne carved in rock in front of ..."

Jana makes a T-sign with her hands. "Back up to new friend. Let's start there. You told us about Sally Weathers when you came over to the house, and your suspicions about her death. I'm concerned, of course, but what I want to know about is this guy. What do you mean by friend?"

I sip, then gulp, burning my tongue.

"Friend. I mean friend. He has a golden retriever and is going to teach me how to caramelize onions."

Jana waits.

"We talk about things other than the case. In his office. At dinner. Mama Rosa's. He eats pigweed. Have you heard of it?"

Jana shakes her head, still waiting.

"He came by the house Sunday afternoon for tea. It all went well except for when he was leaving. I think he's lonely for his wife, who died. Couple of years ago. He has one son living in California, and he's just been out there, going around and looking at the sights. They saw a night sky display at the Planetarium and ..."

"So he's looking for female companionship," Jana ignores the travelogue. "Intimate companionship?"

"The first time was in the parking lot of Mama Rosa's, and we sort of bumped into each other when we were leaving. It was a mix-up, and he wound up hugging me ... but Sunday afternoon, it wasn't."

"Wasn't what?"

"'He's a professional police detective who came to discuss the case with me as well as the mail threat. I mean, he wasn't outside the bounds of his professional position or anything. It's not what it wasn't, it's what it was."

"Which was?"

"Dammit, Jana, I haven't felt like this for years, maybe ever. I'm acting like a teenager, will he call, won't he call," I say, pausing. "Not the professional woman I am, which in today's culture means you can just jump in bed or not. That's all you see in films, they're pulling each other's clothes off as they're walking through the front door. There's no ambivalence allowed, not like will he, won't he, what does he mean by that?"

She raises her plastic cup in toast.

"It's awkward, because we're supposed to be working together in a professional manner."

"I get that you're both professionals," Jana says. "You don't need to use that word again either as an adjective or noun."

I nod, smiling slightly. "He and I haven't talked since we were together on Sunday. I don't know why, no news of the case or he doesn't want to talk to me, and I don't know what I want."

Jana looks up at the clock and says, "Grace, I have to leave for my meeting. He'll call. Maybe not this afternoon, but he will. Or you will. There's no rule that says you have to know what you want. It took Daisy and me three back-and-forths with the U-Haul."

Jana's such a comfort.

On the way out of the coffee bar I get a piece of carrot cake to go and eat it on my way to the car, where I find a parking ticket under the windshield wiper. Shit.

~ Twenty-Four ~
News from the Front

My cell phone blinks with a voice mail message, and I wait to retrieve it until I'm successfully sitting in my car. It's from Jake inviting Babe and me to join him and crew for a dogs-swim in Lady Bird Lake, the body of water near downtown. It has alongside its shores the hike and bike trail Sally so loved to walk every morning. "No need to call back," Jake says in the message. "I'll be there with Sophie and Shorty at five-ish, somewhere between Kayak Rentals and mile marker four-point-twenty-five."

I swing by the house and check the mail box for bomb threats. Finding none, I load Babe, enthusiastic about an outing and evidencing her pride in having successfully destroyed the indestructible bone. "Good dog."

We spot Jake and his dogs with surprising ease, thanks to the stone markers at quarter-mile intervals along the trail and my finding a space in the roomy, free lot near mile marker three-point-seventy-five. Babe jumps in at about four miles, seeing Sophie and Shorty already in the water, and swims out to join her colleagues. Jake's right-on about her loving the water.

Patiently observing from the shore, Jake shares butterscotch brownies and cheese sticks from an *Austin Times* copy paper box. He often has something at the end of the day from office snacks. We munch, eliminating the need for conversation as we enjoy the dogs' half-hour swim and stick-fetching. One of the things I like best about Jake is that he's mostly nonverbal, choosing to express himself through his writing and selected activities, such as throwing sticks for the dogs. I've already talked enough today to last for a full economic cycle.

I do express out loud my gratitude for Babe's companionship, just as she bounds out of the lake and shakes water all over me. The point is, she comes to me and not to him, and he's all right with that, in fact "mightily pleased" by our "obvious bonding, damp though it is."

I dry us off with one of the oversized bath towels Jake has thoughtfully brought along, and we're readying to part ways when he says, "What are you and Aurora up to with this investigating? Every one of those people she had me background check is up to something, and not all of it is legal."

"We're proceeding cautiously, finding out what we can about some of the dicey people Sally may have had contact with. Thanks for doing that work—it's insightful. I mean, that P.R. lady at the library tussling with her neighbor and failing to appear. Who would have thought it?" Besides Aunt Arrow and me.

"She's not the one I'm worried about."

"We'll turn anything we find over to the police right away."

"Right away has already come and gone. I'm apprehensive about both of you taking unnecessary risks."

"Aunt Arrow won't do anything dangerous. I'll see to that. Cross my heart, needle in the eye."

"I'm concerned about you too, G.E."

He calls me by my initials because he says I light up Aunt Arrow's life. If anyone else said that it would come across like sentimental slop, but Jake somehow sounds genuine. Genuinely schmaltzy.

"Not to worry. I'm working closely with a police detective, and I wouldn't think of taking so much as a baby step without his approval." I lie with abandon, my inhibitions mellowed by some unknown force. "Thanks for the swim and the office treats."

"Oh, that batch isn't from the office. They're courtesy of your Aunt Arrow."

Correction. Mellowed by a known force.

Once home, the first item on the agenda is feeding Babe, ravenous after her swim. Having no need for dinner myself after consuming two lunches and the lakeside desserts, we settle down in my office, Babe to chew computer paper as it emerges from the printer and me to generate the pages, my rocking chair counseling session with Laverne-the-quilter having reopened the creative floodgates, with supplemental fuel supplied by Aunt Arrow's bakery.

The Good Captain presses softly against Gersalina with his body, moving her backward and himself forward, accidentally causing her to fall upon the bed in a prone rather than a sitting position. Quite accidentally, he finds himself fallen atop her, panting against her neck, then licking it and nibbling on her earlobe. "His mouth is so busy," thinks Gersalina. Reaching for balance, the Good Captain's hand mistakenly lands under her dress, which would ordinarily be filled with petticoats, but she had not yet completed that portion of her toilette prior to his arrival. Instead of petticoat he encounters a band of something silky. Clumsily, his finger catches on the top edge, and the only way he can seek release is to pull downward on her pantaloons...

Babe whines by the door. She doesn't make that noise unless she needs to go outside. I'm surprised to find that it's almost ten o'clock. I turn on the outside lights as a precaution, and as I'm letting Babe out I hear my phone, which I answer, expecting to hear Aunt Arrow's ten o'clock bed check.

Instead it's a cheery, "Sorry not to be in touch sooner. Been a madhouse of catching up around here since I got back. Can't believe how far behind I could get in two days, and I wanted to have all the reports in order before we moved on. Hope I'm not interrupting your beauty sleep."

Not exactly.

"Could you and Aurora come to the Department tomorrow?"

"I'll have to check my calendar."

I've practiced being coolly aloof, and it comes off pretty well considering the extenuating circumstances.

"There'll be some good news coming at you," he says.

"And Aunt Arrow's schedule," I say. "I'll have to check with her as well. I have no idea what she'll have on tomorrow."

"She always looks good," he says, and I'm thinking maybe he's been drinking.

"We'll have some news for you, as well, though not sure you'll find it altogether pleasant," he says.

Since we didn't talk business on Sunday, Bertel doesn't know yet about the suspects on our list and why they're there.

"And good evening, I think I forgot to say."

"Where are you anyway?" I ask, now almost sure about the drinking.

"Still at the office catching up," he says soberly. "Would four o'clock tomorrow afternoon work for the both of you?"

"Didn't you go to a seminar in L.A. where you had training in listening to the general public?"

"In California? I attended a conference on developing community relations. Yeah, I guess that would involve listening to the general public. I mean, when we're out on the streets or in meetings, we want the communication going both ways. Both parties talk, both parties listen, that sort of thing. Am I missing something here?"

Missing something here? Hello.

"It's good to hear your voice, Grace."

"Thank you, Detective."

"You're welcome, Author-Accountant."

He put the author first. "Babe says hello." She's slobbering on the fresh pages.

"And hello back to the young lady."

"But you've missed a few critical points."

"I'm here to listen," he says. "One of the seminars I attended was on tact and subtlety. The facilitator said I was so advanced that she's recommended me to head up a national task force."

He's making this up. "Point one," I continue, "I have to check my schedule and also confer with Aunt Arrow about her agenda for tomorrow. We're not just sitting around at your beck and call."

"Right. I'm taking notes. Not sitting around at beck and call. What in the heck is the beck of beck and call?"

"It's short for beckoning, as in summoning."

"Got it. Not responding to summons."

"Aunt Arrow and I haven't exactly been idle during your absence, since we have a murder to solve and a possible suspect hovering on my doorstep. When I say we have news, I would expect you to have at least a passing interest."

"Not a one-way street, point two. Sorry, Grace, you're right."

"Thank you."

"I didn't mean to be flippant. I'm very anxious to get with you and Aurora just as soon as possible, but only at your convenience. I may be able to relieve some of your concerns. I know you both have busy schedules. Please let me know what time is convenient for you and Aurora, and I'll do my best to accommodate it."

"How about four o'clock tomorrow afternoon?"

"Four o'clock tomorrow afternoon," he dutifully repeats.

If we meet in the afternoon, I'll be able to go to the library in the morning, something I've been avoiding until I felt confident we'd have some back-up in the event I find anything. I'm interpreting this meeting as back-up.

"And I was thinking," he adds, "depending, of course, on how your work week evolves and on what commitments you and Babe might already have on your separate and joint agendas, but I have to drop off some iPads that came to us by mistake at a precinct office in the Hill Country. We might grab a sandwich or something, find a quiet and peaceful place to evaluate my listening skills."

If he thought this was murder, he wouldn't ask me out on a picnic. But if I know it is, should I go?

~ Twenty-Five ~
Ashes for Lent

The basement stacks again, early Wednesday morning. Initially I see no one but am drawn to the clicking sounds in the microfiche area. It's Henry Schmidt, my old volunteer friend, the one who gave me the rundown on the library's security system. The emitting noises are the result of his restocking a large stack of fiche.

Just to get things started in a casual but professional manner, I fill out a request for Sally's U.S. Senate hearings fiche, "The High Cost of Prescription Drugs, Hearings before the Special Committee on Aging." Henry responds with an expression of minor irritation at the interruption but stops his restocking to consider my request.

"Pretty quiet down here this morning," I say customer chit-chattily.

"Usually is of an early morning."

"Just peopled by the one staff?"

"Oh, I'm not staff." He lifts the ribbon of his volunteer ribbon to show me. "Todd LaJames is staff. I'm Henry Schmidt, volunteer for tee to thuh."

He apparently doesn't remembering me from the tutorial he provided. "What section is tee to thuh?"

"Tuesdays, Wednesdays and Thursdays. That's what they call it here, the tee to thuh rotation."

"You take care of all this territory by yourself then?" I point in the general direction of the 000-200 stacks.

"LaJames supervises, but he's mostly upstairs. I call him down if I have a question I can't handle, but that's rare." Henry's volunteer ribbon ripples on his chest.

"I read about the death down here," I say. "Were you working when it happened?"

"No, but that's why I've added the thuh. I used to work just tee and wed, Tuesday and Wednesday, but thuh was Ms. Weathers' day, the deceased, and I'm filling in until we can shore up the thuh volunteers."

"That staff member LaJames you mentioned must have had his hands full that morning when she died."

"I wouldn't know, since I wasn't present. It'll take me a few minutes to retrieve your fiche."

Temporarily dismissed, I wander over to the stacks and am leafing through a copy of 251.007 *How the Sermon Made America: Exhorting the Republic from the Pilgrims to the Present*, when I see two legs extending on the floor at the end of the shelves. Faded jeans encase the legs, well-worn hiking boots the feet. I creep toward the legs and find an attached torso leaning against a shelf. Male. Caucasian. Flannel shirt. Astros baseball cap. Chin against chest, eyes closed, no body parts moving. Now his chest heaves. He's breathing.

I recognize my colleague from the overnight.

I hear the elevator open and footsteps crossing the room behind me. Not wanting to be seen staring at a sleeping man on the floor, I slide over three shelves as the footsteps move toward the stacks.

I see Todd LaJames bearing down on the aisle I've just vacated. He walks toward the Caucasian male and takes some bills out of his front shirt pocket. How many and of what denomination, I can't determine.

Crouching down to get a better view through the shelf layers, I watch as LaJames gently shakes the torso shoulder. Flannel Shirt awakens. Sees LaJames. Sees LaJames holds up some money. Awakened Flannel Shirt arises. LaJames hands bills to

Flannel Shirt, who promptly slips bills into his front right jeans pocket. LaJames shakes hands with Flannel Shirt. When he removes hand from handshake, LaJames is holding a plastic bag containing white powder.

Three bars across. I have just witnessed Todd LaJames, reference librarian, making a drug purchase from a seeming transient in the Main Branch of the Austin Public Library basement stacks. It was a clever transfer, at that, concealed by a handshake. All the while, Henry clatters innocently away.

Sally knew about these drug sales, here and possibly in other library locations. That's what she stumbled across, and they knew she knew. LaJames and probably someone else that morning, possibly this very same Caucasian male, did something that scared Sally into a fatal heart attack.

I have to stay alive long enough to prevent Flannel Shirt from leaving the library and LaJames from stashing his purchase. But how? They're here, and I'm here. Or they were here. Now they're walking toward the elevator.

From my night's sojourn I remember there's a telephone number for the "Technical Help Line" prominently displayed above the computer terminal, which I can see from my ferret's post. I memorize it, crawl into the farthermost corner and dial on my cell.

"Get me security immediately," I whisper to the answering voice. "We have an emergency."

"If you are using a touchtone phone, for circulation, press two. For technical assistance, press three." I listen through the entire menu to "Press zero or stay on the line for ..." I break a fingernail mashing the zero.

"Austin Public Library System, Main Branch, how may I direct your call?" as the two men enter the elevator.

"Security guard. Urgent."

Seconds later, "Stan Sinclair, please state your location."

Rapidly I explain that I have witnessed a drug purchase in the basement stacks between Todd LaJames and an unknown

Caucasian male. Both men have left the stacks, entered the elevator, and presumably are arriving at the first floor about now.

"Please don't let them out of your sight. Impede, using any means necessary."

"And you are?"

"Grace Edna Edge, General Public."

I rush to the stairwell as Henry calls to me, "I have your fiche now, Madame."

Stan Sinclair, neatly attired in a gray security guard uniform with nightstick and blue piping, has done his job. He stands, blocking the library entrance while talking to LaJames and Caucasian Male.

Gasping for breath, I rush over to New Acquisitions— Fiction, pull a book off the shelf and pretend to read it while monitoring the confrontation.

"… report, Mr. LaJames, from one of the library's customers that there was a suspicious exchange in the basement."

"Nothing suspicious, Stan. I gave Melvin some cash for his food today. He told me when he came in this morning he was bust. Like to help our regulars from time to time. Melvin rarely needs or asks. When he does, I respond if I can."

Don't listen to that rubbish. He took the powder. Search both men.

"Did Melvin give you something in return, Mr. La James?"

"Tic Tacs. Wants it to be an exchange, not charity. I give him a few dollars, and he gives me Tic Tacs."

Todd LaJames holds up a plastic baggie containing a few mints and shakes it. He opens the baggie, offers one to Stan and to Melvin.

"Don't mind if I do, keeps the breath fresh," Stan says.

"The lady can have one, too," Melvin says, pointing to New Acquisitions.

Todd LaJames turns to me. "Would you like a Tic Tac?"

I shake my head. Search them, dammit.

Flannel Shirt, a.k.a. Melvin, walks out of the library without a backward glance. Todd LaJames stares at me, memorizing appearance details, I'm sure, and goes behind the Reference Desk.

Stan asks me to complete some forms, which I do, mostly providing information about myself, which I imagine will appear on some sort of Public Library Most Wanted list. I can't tell him how I know Melvin, or don't, but I do attempt to persuade him, based on my observation, that something other than Tic Tacs may be concealed in his garments and possibly in LaJames', as well.

My attempt is unsuccessful.

I retreat downstairs, wash my face in the women's room, then vomit.

As a courtesy to Henry, as well as to settle myself, I take the fiche, which I'd already read that night in the library, and load it into a reader. Again I cover the material Sally had consulted the morning she died. The Senate hearings concentrate on the increasing cost of prescription drugs for those on fixed incomes, especially the elderly. Some forgo the medications they need, some sell their drugs to generate income, some take alternative products that may be dangerous, some reduce their assets and go on Medicaid. Nothing newly insightful, but it's no surprise Sally would be interested in these issues and want to help seniors who faced them.

I'm grateful for the library's side exit that allows me an unencumbered departure, not to mention an opportunity for repentance. Today is Ash Wednesday, and I have just enough time to make the noon service at St. Barnabas.

"Almighty and everlasting God, you hate nothing you have made and forgive the sins of all who are penitent. Create and make in us new and contrite hearts." I do not regret acting boldly on my observation or the preliminaries that brought me to them, only that I lacked the courage to risk admitting to Stanley why I suspect Melvin and that I called him Flannel Shirt. And that I set off the alarms when I exited the library and kept running.

Bertha's homily speaks of temptations, "not worldly temptations but inner temptations. Self-interest. Putting ourselves ahead of God. We have not loved you with our whole heart and mind and strength. We have not loved our neighbors as ourselves."

Have mercy on us, O God.

The service leaflet reminds us to feed those less fortunate than ourselves. I make a vow to donate to the downtown Trinity homeless shelter and to continue taking ribs to Ruth Ann, as my forehead receives its imposition of ashes.

~ Twenty-Six ~
Updo

Aunt Arrow finds me in the Police Department pew waiting area, where I'm reading a book, and she comments that my face is dirty. Do I want her to spit on a tissue and wipe it? Attired in a vibrant green and canary yellow caftan, she has her hair pulled up and tied at the crown of her head, with strands cascading out of the knot like a water fountain.

My hair falls unregulated in a plop over my ears, and the knees of my navy blue stretchy slacks show the effects of crawling across the library floor. And walking on my knees for a hundred miles through the desert, repenting.

"I had an incident in the library this morning, and the smudge on my face represents atonement, not dirt," I tell her, putting my book away.

She wants a blow-by-blow, and I oblige in what would be a canon were it set to music, from Henry's fiche, to finding the sleeping body, to crouching in a position that sprained my right knee, to observing the exchange of cash for white-product-laden sandwich bag, to responding so urgently that I didn't have time to feel panic and bone-numbing fear, to almost passing out from running up the stairs four at a time, to creative disclosure by the accused, to distribution of breath mints, to withholding in my reportage, to release of accused, to compilation of my vital statistics, to Henry's fiche.

I don't tell her that I set off the library's alarms, which I ignored and kept moving until I reached my car, where I found *Raven Black*, a novel by Ann Cleeves, unchecked out in my carryall.

Aunt Arrow listens carefully, asking me to repeat several parts. As I wind down she says with assurance, "You're not a wimp. Admitting you stayed in the library overnight would immediately shift the focus to you and your crime. You're maintaining the integrity of the real crime scene, which honors Sally."

"But gets us nowhere except that Melvin and Todd LaJames know I saw them." I don't especially like her emphasis on "and your crime."

Aunt Arrow nods her head supportively but asks again for my description of the Tic Tac exchange among Stanley the Guard, Melvin and Todd LaJames. Before I can finish, out rolls her laugh, moving up from the inside and gradually building momentum until our police waiting hall pew is vibrating. The shaking pew sets me off, in spite of my best efforts to honor the incident with the seriousness it warrants, and when one of us manages to stop momentarily, the other one is still laughing and shaking the pew, which gets the other one going again.

We are laughing in the vibrating pew like sixth graders when a uniformed woman sticks her head out an office door and says, "Are you here for the Weathers?"

Stopping cold turkey, Aunt Arrow manages, "Yes, Ma'am."

"Detective Frederick wants you to join him in the conference room. I'll show you," the uniformed woman says.

We follow repentantly along the hallway until she knocks on a door and opens it. There sit Bertel, Officer Dunbar and a foot-high stack of multi-colored file folders. Bertel stands and thanks Officer Mayhew as Officer Dunbar walks over to Aunt Arrow with a pumping handshake and an enthusiastic, "Aurora," to which she responds, "Boyd," after which Bertel says, "Aurora, Grace," Aunt Arrow says, "Bertel," and I say nothing at all.

Bertel invites us to sit and asks if we'd like anything to drink.

Vodka tonic, double, with a twist. I shake my head, and Aunt Arrow says, "No, nothing for me until five."

Bertel looks at his watch. "Let's start with the good news, and for that I'll ask Officer Dunbar to report on his portion of the investigation." He nods in the direction of Officer Dunbar/Bruce.

"Thank you for your patience, ladies, and especially yours, Ms. Edge." He looks at me and opens an orange file folder. "Ms. Grace Edge, I should say. You're both Ms. Edges." He waits to see if anyone smiles, but no one does.

"We followed up on your report of finding what I shall refer to as the threatening note, classified according to its tone rather than by any veiled or overt …"

"I remember the content," I say.

"After conducting a series of interviews related to said threatening note," he consults several pages in the folder, "based on information received from both you, Ms. Grace Edge, and you, Ms. Aurora Edge, we determined that the threatening note was not related in any way to the death of Ms. Sarah Weathers."

Aunt Arrow covers her mouth with her hand, and I exhale.

"It seems that Ms. Grace Edge serves on a committee in her Rosewood Neighborhood Association that has been working to enforce the 10:00 p.m. weekday and midnight weekend curfew in Rosewood Park." He looks at his notes. "Specifically, she serves on the Curfew Committee. Anyone can learn of the Association, its activities and its personnel by consulting the Yahoo Rosewood Group Listserv."

He's right. I do serve on that committee. All the association's minutes and internal communications are posted on the Listserv.

"Numerous violations of curfew have occurred in Rosewood Park, involving loud music and the consumption of beverages not legal to some. We learned through our investigations that every member of the Curfew Committee received a note identical to that received by Ms. Grace Edge, with the exception of gender. The two male members of the committee included the word asshole instead of bitch."

The park. The threatening note was about the park. This is a relief, I think. Or maybe not. I don't know what to think.

"Asshole," repeats Aunt Arrow in wonderment.

"Further," Bertel says, entering the conversation, "I knew we'd be able to relieve your anxiety today about any connection to Ms. Weathers' death, but now we can do even better. Late last night patrol officers arrested four males in the park who were violating curfew. After extensive questioning and some consultation among them and their attorneys, the four confessed earlier today to the note deliveries. I'm pleased to report that one aspect of this case is now fully resolved, and I hope to everyone's satisfaction."

He nods and folds his hands atop the stack of file folders, less one.

Officer Dunbar/Bruce reaches across the table to hand Aunt Arrow a business card in case we have further questions, and while that's going on, Bertel nods at me.

So when we talked last night, he already knew the note wasn't about Sally. He doesn't think it's a murder, and that's why he's all kissy face and picnic-y. It says right here in this book I've stolen from the library and read in the pew while waiting for Aunt Arrow that the detective in the story wouldn't kiss the woman he's smitten with because she was helping in the investigation of a murder case. He wouldn't even kiss her on the cheek as he walked out of her house. There's no kissing in murder.

Officer Dunbar leaves, and Bertel takes a light blue folder from the stack. "Let's get to it," he says, taking out a computer printout that looks similar to the one Kira gave me. Identical, in fact. "Officer Mattingly, I believe, ran some background checks for you, Grace. And Aurora."

I take the computer printout from under sermons and blackbirds, the printout about which Kira said there wouldn't be any follow-up.

"We have reviewed the findings of people you questioned with regard to some aspect of their relationship to Ms. Weathers and capacity for criminal behavior," he begins.

"Aunt Arrow and I have considered some possibilities, yes, but we aren't …"

"I understand. You're not accusing anyone, just doing some legwork and raising relevant questions, given the seriousness of all that's occurred and sadness."

"We're sad, but we're not stupid," says Aunt Arrow. "For your edification it's emerged that Sally's dosage of Zoloft was increased without knowledge of her physician. I haven't had a chance to tell you yet, Grace, but I've heard back from Nathan, who talked to her doctor. Sally's pills were fifty milligrams when the prescription was for twenty-five. The doc is checking into the problem with the pharmacy."

I add my observations at Suella's about the teenagers, one of whom is Casey Guthrie, the Hummer, the unused oxygen.

Aunt Arrow nudges me with her elbow. I tell Bertel about the morning's events in the stacks and Stanley's handling of the incident, my ongoing questions about his thoroughness. I'm especially concerned that the transaction I saw this morning could be identical to what Sally may have observed.

Bertel takes out a tan folder and writes on a page, reading what he's jotting: "50, not 25 milligrams. Teenagers in the vicinity of invalid on pain medications and oxygen but not connected to concentrator. Probable vagrant known as Melvin and library employee Todd LaJames dealing in claimed innocent substance but possible illegal drug. LaJames with known history of violence."

"You left out that the doctor prescribed twenty-five milligrams, not fifty," Aunt Arrow almost shouts. "The doctor prescribed one amount, she had another in her bottle."

"We in the Department appreciate your efforts, and we are considering this list very seriously. Where we are, follow-up wise, besides these new items is that we'll be bringing James

Jollipson in for questioning, and I am personally going to interview the Center Director, Jared Phillips."

So they do think it's murder.

"We are still persuaded that Ms. Weather died from an accidental drug overdose, but you've raised some shadows of suspicion, and we don't want to ..."

So they don't. I wonder if I'll have to give Babe back to Jake.

~ Twenty-Seven ~
Two by Two

It rains, starting around midnight on Wednesday, continuing through the day on Thursday. Neither Babe nor I likes being fenced in.

Ensuring that my gutters are down and functioning absorbs any time I would possibly have had to call Jake to report the all clear on the note, and who knows what Aunt Arrow might have told him by now. We had a minor tiff after the meeting in the Police Department. Aunt Arrow doesn't think Bertel is casting a wide enough net. I'm willing to give it a couple of days. Well, four, to be exact. Casey and counterpart are squirrelly, we agree, but that isn't a chargeable offense, and they're innocent of the note-leaving.

In the afternoon I slosh to the MLK Center with Babe temporarily mollified by a semi-smushed soccer ball. Only Aldeen, Tilly, Annie and Mark have come to class. Dahlia's babysitting, and Eddie's filling in at Murphy's Garage. No one knows anything about Jamail, but Mark thinks the new girl friend is quite a bit younger and likes "stuff."

Aldeen says, 'Uh oh," and adds that Jared is "tied up. The cops." The door to his office is closed.

For today's writing session I ask the class members to put "I Remember" at the top of the page and, without any further embellishment from me, let the writing flow from some strong memory—a person, a place, an event, a sensory experience. They set to work, but I'm distracted, watching Jared's office. About one medium-sized tulip into the exercise, the door opens, Bertel leaves and Jared's hair patch stands at sixty degrees.

In the time for sharing Tilly reads her piece about a hike in the Colorado Rockies with her disabled son Charles, who was determined to make it to the top of a steep maintain trail, converted to universal access, in his wheel chair. He wouldn't accept help, even in the most strenuous portions of the ascent. A couple of times he got out and pushed from behind the chair, crawling on his knees. Just pressed on and on until he made it to the top, never uttering a word of anything but gratitude about the spectacular views.

Mark remembers Matthias Williams, the basketball coach from his own teenage years at the YMCA, who taught him the value of discipline, "which is what I'm trying to pass along to Casey. My coach followed in the footsteps of his namesake, the apostle Matthias, who was elected to fill the role vacated by Judas. We never read any more in scripture about him after the election because Matthias wasn't into self-promotion."

Mark and Matthias probably wouldn't make it on the book tour circuit, I think, but would be welcomed as guest Lenten speakers at St. Barnabas.

Aldeen shares a story from the elementary school where she volunteers and reads to the children. "We gathered around in a circle before starting the day's story, and I told them they could ask me any questions about anything that interested them. Lucinda, the smallest girl in the class, raised her hand and asked, 'Why do you have lipstick on your teeth?'"

Everyone's chuckling as Annie begins her story about an incident involving an uncle, her mother's brother, when she was eleven. The laughter fades rapidly as she continues. Her mother had run out of milk, needed a quart for something she was cooking. The family had no car, and Annie's mother asked her to walk to the store about a half-mile from their house, but Annie resisted. "I didn't want to go to the store by myself, because coloreds had to go in from the back, and it was scary. Some of the workers in the store were mean to us. My uncle very reluctantly agreed to go for the milk, but he told Mama I was lazy, that's why I wouldn't do it. When he crossed the street down the corner from our house, two men drove by and shot at someone else in the street. They missed and hit my uncle, and he died. Mama and I ran out when we heard the gunshots, but he was already gone. There's a piece of me that's always felt like I killed my uncle. If I'd gone to the store like Mama asked, my uncle wouldn't have died."

Mark attempts to offer support by telling Annie, "We all know rationally it isn't your fault, but I have empathy because I feel responsible for what Casey got himself into."

I'm concerned about Annie and wish we had more time, but someone is waiting for me to help complete a tax return. As we're breaking up Tilly and Aldeen are talking to Annie, and I ask Mark how Casey is doing with his work at the oxygen company.

"Real well. That job's the making of him."

"What exactly does he do?"

"Goes around with his boss, delivers concentrators and portable tanks, services the concentrators, fills the tanks, gives instructions on use, monitors equipment. It's just the two of them. Ramon Plankton, he's the owner, and Casey. Ramon says he's good with the equipment and the people. Mostly old folks, like me," he beams. "Guess I've taught him something."

"Does he ever service the oxygen customers on his own?"

"No, always with Ramon, the two of them together. Casey doesn't drive; had his license revoked when he went into juvey detention and isn't eligible until he completes parole. The boy still needs supervising."

I don't report my sightings. Mark has enough data without mine. So does Jared, whom I see crossing the center in a direct line to our area. He's interrupted by Greg Hockings, who oversees the Center's ping pong and pool tables. I'm thankful Greg engages Jared with pool cues long enough for me to make a soggy get away.

En garde.

Tempted as I am not to make the ribs run, I honor Ash Wednesday's promise and proceed to the drive-through at Bud's and on to delivery, not bothering to attempt a call. Getting out of the car at Suella's, I step into water above my ankles and wade to the front door.

Several hard knocks renders the presence of Suella. "Aren't you the duck?"

Dripping and tracking, I step inside.

"Hi-dee-doo, Miz Grace," comes from the recliner.

"Hi, Ruth Ann, how are you?"

"We didn't think you'd make it, but I sure hoped so. This is what I look forward to all week. I'm watchin' the weather channel, and we're under a flood watch."

"No longer a watch," I say.

"We got an old raft in the garage we'll pump up for you to get home," she says, laughing and slapping the table next to her chair, rattling the pill bottles that cover its surface this week in lieu of beer empties.

"Thanks for the offer," I say, "but I'll just leave the food and be on my way in the Suburu Ark."

Ruth Ann slaps the table again, knocking bottles to the floor, which roll in myriad directions.

Suella hustles to pick them up. "Ruth Ann's hurting, hurting. She'll be needing these and more. It's gonna be a rough night in Jericho."

"No, San Marcos," Ruth Ann says. "That's where the front's passing. And on to Luling."

I hand Suella the food, which the Bud's crew has thoughtfully encased in plastic.

"I've called that oxygen boy to come help us," Suella says. "She can hardly breathe in this humidity, may not make it in the storm."

"Is there anything I can do?" I ask, not sure what she's implying about Casey's help. It's not oxygen, according to Mark.

"No, you bringing the food is plenty. I keep telling Ruth Ann it's too much trouble for you." She looks out the window.

"Schulenberg," shouts the weather center. "Under water. Won't be able to get a hamburger at Frank's tonight."

Suella moves all the pills to a larger coffee table with the food bag. "Thanks, and you'd better get going."

"Lucky for us we have ribs. We'll be in red within the hour."

"You're welcome."

"Steady as she goes."

Carrying my shoes, I make it back to my car, relieved that it starts. Four blocks down river, I see the Hummer, two boys full.

~ Twenty-Eight ~
Shutting Down

The rain continues through Friday, no golf, and on into Saturday. Aunt Arrow and I resume telephone contact. We're collectively perplexed by the events at Suella's, and Aunt Arrow speculates that the boys could be buying pills from Ruth Ann, which I don't want to believe because of Mark's hopes and Casey's encouraging parole reports. Aunt Arrow's awaiting more news about the Zoloft dosage via Nathan, and I agree to discuss the ribs scene with Bertel.

Jake sends an e-mail to Babe, asking her to remain on sentry even though the problem of the tainted note has been resolved. Babe promptly responds with an affirmative yip.

During the flood I work on the bank teller case, which involves two employees at Brazos Springs State Bank who've apparently stolen $1.4 million from customer accounts over the last several years. Pamela Louise Moody and Rosie Fawn Danken, both forty-three, were arrested last week on suspicion of forgery and felony theft and are facing fifteen to twenty years, if convicted, which is where I come in. Bank representatives are declining comment, according to this morning's *Austin Times*. I bet they are.

Babe shows no interest when Rosie's and Pamela's pages come off the printer but perks up with Gersalina, who's building a moat, metaphorically speaking.

Saved by the dinner bell in the almost-encounter at her Hen and Egg chamber, Gersalina's developed a cunning savvy in her contacts with the good but lusty Captain. Simultaneously dawning on said Captain, startled by the imposition of a gauntlet, is the rueful recognition that this one might be more than a one-afternooner, much more. He plans to take the sweet Gersalina into the mists for a repast upon the bonnie fields, aside a babbling brook, with roasted joint of lamb and disposable chalices of malt beverages.

What I don't know is how wide to build the moat, and we'll not be finding out anytime soon because the anticipated trip to the Hill Country, which I've agreed to attend in order to continue building our case with Bertel, will probably be rained out.

But Sunday dawns bright and clear, sun and blue skies replacing the gunmetal gray. Bertel and I find ourselves similarly attired in long-sleeve Lady Longhorn t-shirts, supporting today's university women's NCAA tournament basketball game. A few minutes of negotiation as Bertel is loading the dogs into the shell-enclosed back of his truck produces a treaty to postpone discussing developments in the case until the drive home so we can listen to the second half of the game on the radio.

Bertel assertively places the picnic cooler in the passenger seat. "Too hot in the shell." I'm cozily seat-belted into the middle. I'm so thrilled with the overtime victory that I lose my head and invite Bertel to accompany me to Jana's and Daisy's commitment ceremony, which he accepts.

We make the stop at the police station to deliver the iPads and then head out to the state park, where a dispute erupts over the location of the picnic site. I favor the shade of a willow and Bertel the rising damp of the river bank. We ultimately settle on the slope of a hill overlooking the river, where we can see miles and miles of flowered and clovered fields in all directions. Bertel opens with an off-key round of "I'm Looking Over a Four Leaf Clover," while attaching the dogs to a long double lead. That song is so last century. The dogs immediately pull in opposite directions, knocking Bertel down and blessedly stopping the singing in its tracks.

While he lifts the plastic thermal cooler lid, I spread a blanket on a bed of Bermuda grass between two live oak trees.

Bertel announces he's graduated from the pigweed study, coming in first-place among the participants' ratio of good to bad cholesterol. The study director has encouraged the pyramid for continuity.

"Watch," he says, pulling each item out of the cooler. "From the milk group, we have wedges of baby Brie and sharp cheddar cheese. For meat and beans, slices of rare roast beef and jalapeño bean dip. Our vegetables include marinated carrot coins and artichoke hearts, as well as these lovely leaves of arugula," which he flutters. "On the fruit panel I offer the season's finest fresh strawberries and a bottle of chilled Fumé Blanc."

It's a stretch, I think, to categorize the latter as fruit, but oh, well. Bertel opens and pours the wine. "Not to ignore our grains, we have gourmet dog biscuits, onion-flecked whole wheat rolls , handcrafted corn chips and freshly baked oatmeal raisin cookies, all packaged for your convenience by the nice folks at Terry's Deli-and-Take-Away."

Even with his unbalanced proportions, Bertel somehow manages to array the food in a sort of pyramid on the blanket, with a cookie at the point. "And I brewed the coffee." He pulls a thermos and Styrofoam cups out of a paper bag.

Successful in chewing open a mustard packet, I prepare an onion roll, roast beef and baby brie sandwich, avoiding the arugula. The pyramid and I have been wary of one another from the get-go. "I don't remember ever seeing the fields as thick with wild flowers so early," I observe. "Must be the rain."

"Something in the atmosphere's definitely different this year," Bertel says.

We let that one sit while we eat and sip.

"Did you ever see that movie, *Out of Africa*?" Bertel asks. "It was on the classic movie channel last night."

I nod, sleepy from the wine.

"You look a little like Meryl Streep in that film except for the hair color," he says.

And her height, build, face and temperament.

Bertel smiles in anticipation, I'm guessing, of my saying he looks like Robert Redford, which he does except for the hair color, hair style, eyes, height, face and shape.

"Umm," I say. "Nice animals in that film." Babe and Maggie have reconciled their differences and are running coordinated laps through the bluebonnets and paintbrush. "Elands. Isak Dinesen wrote about the elands. What exactly are elands?"

"A variety of antelope." Bertel shifts position, spilling his coffee on a corner of the blanket, which he begins sopping with paper napkins.

"Don't worry," I tell him, "this blanket goes in the washing machine. Since the coffee doesn't have cream, I'll just pour hot water over the stain before I wash it, or I can soak it in a solution of warm water and hydrogen peroxide. Miracle liquid, peroxide."

"We might share a bottle."

Share a bottle of peroxide? Is this supposed to be a romantic lead-in?

Apparently so, because Bertel says, "The time with you is the best thing that's happened to me in many months. I realize that although we're, uh, somewhat constrained at the moment by our professional considerations, that is to say, limited in our respective capacities to ... oh, what the hell." He slides forward on the blanket, reaching out an arm to gather me in. As he does, he puts an elbow into the remnants of carrot coins and artichoke hearts, sloshing marinade onto the blanket to join the coffee.

Robert and Meryl, we're not. We leap up to avoid the spreading dampness as the dogs, sensing promise, run over and lick eagerly. They quickly move on toward the river in relative tandem.

"Glycerin will work on that," I say, thinking I'll be all the way through the periodic table by the time we finish this picnic.

"Let's walk to the river," Bertel suggests, as if it's a spur of the moment idea instead of a necessity to prevent Babe and Maggie from escaping.

This is my chance. "There's something I need, just a minute." I reach into my carryall, pull out a tape measure and follow along.

We walk down the hill and along the river for a quarter mile, keeping the dogs in view, and stop at a scenic overlook. "Would you be willing to try an experiment?" I ask.

"What kind of experiment?" Bertel says warily.

"I'd like us to separate by walking away from each other, you to the east, me west, and when I say now, we turn around and walk toward each other. Then, as you approach I'd like you to stop when you reach a comfortable chatting distance from me."

"A comfortable chatting distance?"

"Yeah, like when you sense you're the right distance away for a friendly conversation, that's where you stop." As if there's a moat between us. "It's research for my writing. I'm looking into cultural differences in contact. For instance, I read a study about pairs of people from around the world, talking to one another. In Puerto Rico couples maintained a distance of seven inches, fifteen in Paris, forty-seven in Gainesville, Florida. You get the idea? Spatial needs vary culturally." No available data from Edinburgh.

"You can start," I instruct, turning my back to Bertel and walking along the edge of the river for fifty paces. "Now," I call, readying the tape measure. "You can stop now, Bertel." I turn around, and Bertel is directly behind me, having crept along noiselessly in my footsteps.

He gently puts his hands on my face pulls me toward him. "No inches."

"That's not what you're supposed to do."

Bertel takes the tape measure and kisses me, pressing with the full length of his body. And breadth, no moat.

The savor of the vinaigrette is interrupted by a clap of thunder, followed by opening drops of what promises to be a deluge, judging from the darkening clouds that have assembled overhead, unnoticed in our reverie and spillage. Which takes care of distance control, as the four of us run back uphill as fast as we can. Bertel and I scoop up the picnic gear en route and hurriedly load ourselves into the truck, dogs and cooler in the back, people in the cab.

All creatures settled, windows up, wipers flapping, Bertel wants music that fits the occasion. I suggest Handel's "Water Music," which he ignores, sliding the Beach Boys into his CD player, a gift from his son Ben on the L.A. trip, "at low volume, so we can have our conversation." He guns the engine and manages to spin us out of the mud. *"Let's go surfin' now, everybody's learning how, come on and safari with me."* I'm not sure AAA would ever find us here.

Finally managing to achieve paved highway, Bertel opens his mental police file, reporting first on his conversation with Jared Phillips, whom he finds "a bit slippery in personality but no current suggestion of any criminal behavior or connection to Ms. Weathers other than her volunteer work at the Center. Our comptroller verified the Center's finances. They're clean.

"James 'Jimmy' Joplinson, however, is another category altogether, a real scumbag, to use the vernacular, but for the last three months he's been living in Elgin and working at a sausage factory. One report from the Elgin P.D on a domestic violence, but the woman wouldn't press charges." Bertel dissuades me from the notion that sausage could hide a multitude of drug particles.

I counter with my observations about Casey, his teenage male friend, Ruth Ann and her non-oxygen, the pain pills, Suella's odd behavior and Mark's hope for his grandson. "Ruth Ann could be selling her prescriptions to those boys."

"Or they might be coming by to offer help to Ruth Ann like Suella says, a friend driving Casey, since he doesn't have his license. We ran a check on the Hummer. Registered to a former high school buddy of Casey's."

"How could you run a check?"

"Believe it or not, Grace, we have procedures that we follow at the Austin Police Department. There aren't that many Hummers in Travis County matching the description. You reported the sighting of the boys, the vehicle, your suspicions, and we found it. Our procedures help us solve cases, and they sometimes save us from making big mistakes and causing harm to innocent people."

"And the oxygen ruse?"

He has no answer for that but seems unconcerned.

"Do you believe what Mark is telling you about the progress his grandson is making during his parole?" he asks.

"I know he believes it."

"Officer Dutch, his parole officer, insists the boy is doing well, unusually well, and some of it on his own steam," Bertel says. "She reports that Casey has developed a form of community service on his own, helping the elderly he serves with oxygen by going back to do small household and yard chores for them. Officer Dutch has on record some of their thank you notes. Exemplary."

That leaves us exactly where?

Bertel's cell phone vibrates, and he pulls into a convenience store parking lot to check it and make a return call.

How is this afternoon going to end with such enormous disparity between us?

"Grace, I'm sorry," he says, getting back in the cab. "That was Officer Mattingly, who has station duty today and needs help with a spate of abandoned vehicles. She's asked me to come in, because the on-call officer is having twins. "

"Have you followed up on the reference librarian? The possible drug deal?"

"Ms. Weathers wasn't murdered, Grace. We have followed every lead, and there is no conspiracy, drug or otherwise. We value and appreciate everything you and your aunt have done, but I have to tell you, officially, the case is closed."

Tach it up, tach it up, Buddy gonna shut you down.

~ Twenty-Nine ~
Building Blocks

Eddie calls from the Center on Wednesday afternoon. Jamail had promised to meet him to work on the library shelves and contribute some of the supplies, but he hasn't shown up. Eddie would keep working if I brought the reinforcements. He's sorry to bother me, but it's his only free day this week. "GI bug's hit the garage where I substitute."

I take his list to Hemming's Hardware and acquire the requested items without interference, unusual at Hemming's, because the store's we're-here-to-help staff lie in wait for customers like me, who they believe have limited knowledge of construction implements. What I can do, besides operate a cement mixer, is change out the innards of a toilet tank. I know my balls and sockets.

When I park in the lot that serves the MLK Center and several offices in the area, I see Jared pacing behind the Center building and can't imagine what he's doing out there unless he's putting something in the dumpster. Nothing else related to the Center resides in that vicinity. But he just keeps walking, back and forth, between a photinia shrub, blooming bright copper, and a mulberry tree, like the one on my bike ride to elementary school that armed me with juicy weapons for the playground.

An elderly, orange Pontiac puffs into the parking lot, emitting fumes and hydrocarbons. It halts at the slot closest to the pacing arena. An elderly, silver-haired African American man in a three-piece gray suit exits the vehicle. Carrying a battered, honey-colored briefcase, he moves to join Jared, and they meet at a southwest branch of the mulberry tree.

Not a particularly warm greeting, I appraise, as they don't shake hands, hug or smile at one another. At least Jared doesn't smile. I can't see the other man's face, but the back of his neck doesn't suggest smile. They do confer intently, Jared gesturing and electrifying his hair. The African American man appears calmer, though he, too, at one point waves his closed hand like a politician on the stump.

Jared looks around nervously, as if to see if anyone is watching, but he doesn't notice me, possibly because I duck down every time he turns. I'm thinking this is the library basement déjà vu, as I await the exchange, only this time for real.

What's going to emerge from that briefcase, drugs? Weapon? A cache of small, unmarked bills? How is it that I manage to come upon these furtive meetings? They must happen at times other than when I show up, mustn't they? Jared turns. I duck, I peek, I rise. Jared turns. I duck.

I peek above the glove box in time to see papers emerging from the briefcase. A handful. Jared takes them, looks and nods. No handshake. Jared folds the papers in half and half again, puts them in his back pocket and goes into the Center. The elegant male, who receives nothing in return, gets in his car and drives away. Tony would have blown something up at this point.

Not to tip Jared off, I wait a few minutes before entering through the Center's front door. I notice new signage: "Check in with the Office."

Walking across to Jared's office, I wave to Eddie and pass several tables of bridge and canasta. A new sign on Jared's office reads, "Ask for help only from authorized personnel." The only authorized personnel currently in the Center is not in his office. I spot Jared by the coffee bar.

Seizing this as probably my only chance, I slip into the office and scan the desktop for papers, of which there are a variety but none that have been twice folded. Ditto for the credenza top behind Jared's desk. Dare I risk opening drawers?

"Why are you here of a Wednesday?" Jared's voice startles me.

"Bringing supplies to Eddie so he can finish the library shelves. The memorial for Sally Weathers. I was looking for you, uh, to check in." Which doesn't exactly explain why I'm between his desk and the credenza unless I thought he was on the floor.

"You've found me, and so did that cop. Are you the one who put him on my tail?"

"Detective Frederick?"

"Whatever."

Whomever. "No, he came all of his own accord. I have no influence with the police force at all. Were you able to help him with the investigation?"

"He did plenty of prying about how I run things here, which is none of his damn business, and he had information that had to come from someone like you."

There is no one like me.

"S'water under the bridge." Jared leans back against the door frame, mashing the bulge of papers in his back pocket, to let me pass. "And I saw your bait and switch in the parking lot."

Uh oh.

"I spilled a jar of nails on the floor."

He shuts the door. How is anyone else going to check in?

Sighing, I weave back through the card tables of bridge to where Eddie is hammering. Four hearts are going down, vulnerable.

Eddie greets me cheerfully and looks through the bags from Hemming's, pleased that I've brought everything on the list as well as a small box of Russell Stover's, on sale from Valentine's, which we share.

But he's a tad worried about Jamail. "This is the old pattern when he gets into trouble with women and addiction, quits showing up at the places that nurture him." He's tried phoning

Jamail's apartment, but like Aldeen, reached a full answer machine.

I offer to stop by the diner. Eddie thinks that's a good idea and gives me directions. As long as I'm playing mother hen, I phone Dahlia to tell her we missed her last week and ask after her family.

"Ophelia's been accepted into a program to train dogs," she tells me. "It's a joint venture with the local animal shelter. Inmates work with the dogs, and that helps them get placed in homes. The dogs. One of the few programs that consistently reduces recidivism. Plus the printing she's already learning."

"Sounds like a great idea."

"I'm relieved she's in it. Better salvation rates even than finding Jesus."

At the diner no one seems to know anything about Jamail. I talk to the manager and one of the waitresses. He's missed his shift the last two days. A counter waitress has gone missing, too. "You interested in a job?"

Aunt Arrow buzzes about her trip to San Antonio, where she's lectured at an elderhostel, and the new bereavement support group she attended last night. Without me.

"Sea change," she says. "There's a topic every week, and last night's was secondary losses, about what's missing our lives besides the deceased person. One widow in the group comes home from work every night, counting on television for companionship, and when the television went on the brink, she fell apart. I've lost Sally, but I've also lost my longest friendship and my Thursday breakfast partner. You see what I mean?'

I nod supportively

"After the topic, participants can bring up whatever they want, any problems, like how hard it is to go into the grocery store where you see someone on the bread aisle, but by the time you get there they've disappeared because they don't want to talk to you, or they don't know what to say. Or wearing one black shoe and one brown. Can you believe I did that, standing up in front of an entire group on the River Walk in San Antonio? It's helpful to hear the other stories and know I'm not crazy."

"Oh, Aunt Arrow, I'll meet you for breakfast."

"I know you will, honey."

"Does anyone put their bill payments in the refrigerator?"

She laughs. "You're not crazy either."

I appreciate the affirmation. "But not tomorrow morning. I have a client meeting, the QuadRay destiny. We need some face-to-face much sooner than that anyway. Threadbelle's now?"

She'll pick me up.

A lively rock group sings to us as we open with the fried pickle spears, and I move on to catfish bronzed with butter and Cajun spices, okra gumbo, broccoli and rice casserole, honey butter biscuits. When the waitress sets everything out on the table, I assess a grain shortage in my pyramid and take on some of Aunt Arrow's hush puppies.

She's heard again from Nathan about the doctor who prescribed Zoloft, who confirms a definite discrepancy. Sally's doc prescribed twenty-five milligrams. Aunt Arrow confirms that Bluebonnet Pharmacy has a 'scrip on file for fifty milligrams, doc's pad and signature. Apparently Bluebonnet uses a system for filling prescriptions that would not allow for a mistake. The tech records the prescription on a computer, the pharmacist checks both the computer and the hard copy of the prescription. Impossible to make a mistake. Aunt Arrow says, "The doc sent the wrong dose, according to the pharmacist, and it's Bluebonnet's mistake, according to the physician, who's documented what he prescribed."

I suggest we talk to a pharmacist ourselves when we meet for breakfast.

"Which brings us to new business." Aunt Arrow offers to serve as recording secretary. We spread our notes and papers on the table, and she writes Delia Ingram-Kirksey, Todd LaJames,

Jared Phillips, Ophelia Taylor, Casey Guthrie, Jamail Davis, Jimmy Joplinson

"Delia Ingram-Kirksey," I begin. We agree with some regret that Aunt Arrow should draw a line through her name. After a minimum of discussion and rehash, Todd LaJames meets with the same fate.

"Jared Phillips," leads into my description of the bizarre dumpster-photinia-mulberry incident and our speculations about why he met the man outside rather than inside the Center or even somewhere else in Austin.

"It's obvious that Jared didn't want to be seen with this man, who might be a criminal and, in fact, the connector between Jared and the drug underworld. I believe we're looking for a mole."

Aunt Arrow nods, glancing furtively around the restaurant, where all the customers appear intent on their food or the music.

"I mean, am I way off base here? He was so rude afterward in the Center, as if I were a mosquito to swat."

Aunt Arrow circles Jared Phillips.

I tell her about Ophelia Taylor's participation in the animal training program at the women's prison and Dahlia's assessment that it offers a lower recidivism rate than taking Jesus Christ as personal savior. Aunt Arrow draws a line through Ophelia Taylor and places a small cross beside her name.

"Casey Guthrie," I read. We decide to make a list of pros and cons. Aunt Arrow records:

Pro: Job. Positive ratings by parole officer. Initiating help for seniors. Strong family support. Did not leave note in Grace Edna's mailbox.

Con: Past history with drugs. Unexplained appearances at Suella's. Her exaggerations regarding Ruth Ann's oxygen usage. Involvement of unidentified woman. Plethora of available pain pills.

"The cons have it," Aunt Arrow says, and I ruefully allow her circling of Casey's name.

Jamail Davis is a sad one for me, as well, but I acknowledge that his history of addiction and interactions with Sally over many months move him at least to an underlining.

Aunt Arrow's instinct is boldly circling. "He needs money, we think. The new girl friend. Not working. A long-term pattern of behavior, according to those who care about him."

"And his own recognition of addiction's lure," I reluctantly add, remembering the rap that we had so relished in the group.

"If he's been doing and dealing, Sally could have found out, and Jamail's attending the class as a way to see if anyone else suspected, which no one did. Right?" Aunt Arrow asks.

"Until now."

She circles Jamail Davis. And blots Jimmy Joplinson with fish-fry grease after hearing Bertel's report on the Elgin residence and sausage factory.

"Are we leaving anyone out?" she asks.

We sit quietly for a few moments, and I slowly shake my head.

"And then there were three," Aunt Arrow says. "Any point in going back to Bertel?"

"He's into abandoned cars with Kira Mattingly."

"I take that as a no. That leaves me more apprehensive than ever about your activities at the Center and environs."

"They're in broad daylight."

"Which didn't save Sally."

~ Thirty ~
Destinies

Armed with financial reports, several pages of analyses and a can of cola, I ready the Thursday morning attack on QuadRay. My client, Collie Sue Reynolds, has driven over from Houston to discuss my recommendations and to visit her daughter, a student at the university. We're meeting at the bed and breakfast where Collie Sue is staying, a lovely three-story 1907 plantation-style house located in a pecan grove of Harris Park about a mile south of the campus.

On a first name basis from e-mails, Collie Sue offers a choice of spaces, either of two elegant wraparound porches or the antique furnished sitting room with twelve-foot ceilings, original woodwork and leaded glass windows. Regretfully, I pass on the porches, the upper of which was voted by *USA Today* readers as one of the ten best porches in the U.S. on which to sit and rock, because it's a bit brisk this morning, and I don't want to lose my numbers in the wind. I decline coffee and open the soda that I hope will settle my stomach, rocky, I'm speculating, from last night's dinner.

Collie Sue exudes about her job environment at QuadRay Energy, where she works in health services as a nurse, and how much she benefits from interacting professionally with such smart people and for a company that's on the front pages every day, not just the business section. High marks for greenness. Diversity. Employee satisfaction. Contributions to the community. Volunteerism. And soaring financially. The C.F.O showed all the staff a recent video of Wall Street analysts discussing QuadRay's future, "and wow, I mean wow. But I heard the same guy in one of my health cubicles on his cell phone expressing concerns over credit ratings and limited partnerships and financial restructuring. My daughter's taking these classes in finance. She's all into investing, learning about cautions and diversifying, you know how it is when they all of a sudden know more than their parents," she laughs.

Actually, I don't.

"It's a big deal for my daughter, and that's why I contacted you after conferring with Bernie Schwartz, who says you can find your way through any financial morass, not that there's one to find. I mean, I'm certainly not worried about losing everything I've invested in QuadRay stock."

Certainly not. Sipping calmly from my can, I explain the analytical procedures I've used to address her questions about the security of her job, her 401K and the outlook for investing family funds in QuadRay.

"That's exactly what I want," she says, showing me the most recent QuadRay Energy annual report she's brought from her office. Collie Sue flips through the glossy pages with their slick, colored pictures of the board of directors, the employees at work, the people around the world benefitting from QuadRay business and the sidebar graphs documenting the company's many successes.

I take her report and point out to her the plain paper section at the back with the financial statements and notes. "Here's where I look for the answers. Do you ever read mystery novels?"

"My favorite Houston bookstore is Murder By The Book," Collie says, referring to the Bissonnet Street emporium that sells only mysteries.

"What I do in my work is like solving a mystery. You have your red herrings, like the displays in the front of your report," I explain, "but to get to the solutions, in this case determining the real financial condition of QuadRay, you have to dig underneath all that fluff to find the clues."

I've made a chart with several key ideas I want to discuss: revenue relative to profit, provision for bad debts, cash flow from operations, and a football stadium. She leans over the antique table to see my list.

"As you know," I say, holding up a table I've prepared, "revenue is what QuadRay takes in, and profit is what's left over after all the expenses have been paid."

"That's right, and QuadRay has plenty left over."

"They do," I agree, "but the profit is not growing as fast as the revenue, and their operating income—that's before all the extra stuff, like interest—is declining. The mystery here is why, what's happening in between the revenue and the bottom line? What I think is that your company may be growing too fast, or costs could be out of control. Those aren't the only explanations, but they're some important possibilities."

"Uh huh." Collie says in a this-is-boring tone.

I rev it up with, "QuadRay makes sales on credit, just like you and I buy things on credit. We pay our bills, but some folks don't. So companies that sell their products on credit have to allow for some expected bad debts."

"That makes sense."

"QuadRay is selling more and more energy on credit but allowing for less and less bad debt. You solve the mystery here."

"They're showing more profit than they deserve."

Well done. "Exactly. This next one is a little trickier, but you're with me so far. Your company sells on credit and counts the revenue from the sale even before the cash is collected," I say. "In other words, the credit sale is recorded as a plus in the books before the cash is received."

"So if the money from the sale doesn't ever come in, we're in trouble."

"In a way, yes. QuadRay shows income in its financial statements that doesn't bring in any hard cash. And there are other transactions affecting revenues and expenses where there's a difference between accounting income and cash income. What they're using is an acceptable system of accounting, but in some periods your company's cash from operations has actually been negative."

"They need cash to pay us," Collie Sue says. "Covering it up with bandages and antibacterial ointment won't help."

"You're a quick study. I hadn't thought of the medical angle."

"Just another version of the mystery," she says with a smile. "But where does that leave us?"

"Companies have gone bankrupt, all the while showing rosy net income figures," I say. "It may not be a problem for QuadRay, because your company's swung back to positive cash flow. For now. But what you've overheard in the cubicles about the debt and restructuring and unusual partnership arrangements certainly suggests potential problems underneath the gloss, as does my analysis. Your firm makes the explanatory parts so complicated," I flip through the report to the financial statement notes, "that Agatha Christie, P.D. James and the Surgeon General in collusion couldn't figure them out."

"But all those hot shots in New York are touting our stock," Collie Sue says.

"The analysts may very well be right," I say, " but they also may be buying into the hype."

"Like these?" She goes back to the slick photos and sidebars.

"And Wall Street may be buying into what your company's leadership tells you. Your guys make a compelling case, I concede. I've heard your chairman speak myself, and he could sell me about anything."

Collie Sue mulls and nods. "I'm interested in this other item on your chart," she says, "the one about the football field."

"Your firm paid to put its name on a football field, QuadRay Stadium. There's a bizarre history of companies' failing after they put the company's name on a sports arena. Fruit of the Loom, Trans World Airlines, WorldCom, Adelphia

Communications," I offer a list. "All collapsed after paying for rights."

"You're kidding."

"Not really," I say, but we share a laugh. "Venues aside, my recommendation is to invest elsewhere."

Collie Sue sits quietly, reviewing my tables as I finish the soda, which is not soothing my rumbles.

"I think I'll update my resume," Collie Sue says.

When I arrive at the Center later that afternoon, I find Aldeen, Tilly, Mark, Annie and Dahlia stocking Eddie's newly completed shelves and making admiring noises. No sign of Jared. We unload two remaining boxes of books before gathering around the table.

Annie observes that the books aren't in alphabetical order, "or in any kind of order. A real library has little numbers on its books."

I make a note to donate a copy of the *Dewey Decimal Classification and Relative Index* by Melvil Dewey.

Annie offers to organize the collection, as well as to make a list of what we have and develop a system to check out books "instead of the hit-and-miss we've been doing, take what you want, bring it back when you remember."

"You're hereby appointed our official librarian," Aldeen says, and Annie beams.

Dahlia reports a spotting of Jamail by one of her cousins at Oil Can Leo's, with several unsavory companions. "He's sinking." We brainstorm interventions but don't make a definitive plan.

"Are you ready for your assignment?" I ask.

They respond with a rustling of papers and writing implements.

"Today I would like you to write a memoir."

"A memoir? That's a whole long book, Jasmine, we don't have time to do all that much in twenty minutes," Aldeen protests.

"Unless you're gonna keep us after school," Dahlia adds.

"You're right in saying that the memoir can be a long book, but it can also be quite short. Here's the deal. What I want each of you to write today is your own life story in six words."

"Our entire life in six words. Right," Tilly says skeptically.

"Here's an example. You all know Ernest Hemingway. Well, when he was asked to write a novel in six words, he did it. Said it was probably his best."

"A novel in six words. I gotta hear this," Mark says. "He's one of my favorite authors, but I haven't read that one."

"For sale: baby shoes, never worn." I read Hemingway's novel.

"Say again."

I write it out for them and pass the sheet around.

"Ah," Annie says. "I get it. There's a whole story here. Someone's selling baby shoes, but there wasn't any baby to wear them. Could be abortion. Could be baby died in childbirth or the mother miscarried. Baby died before it needed shoes. Someone's broken hearted. Couple breaks up. Affects their whole lives. Or a single mother gave it up for adoption. You could go on and on, all triggered by the six words."

"That's the idea, and it's what I want you to write. Your own life story or a piece of it. Six words worth."

We all set to work, and twenty minutes later I call time. I can see that their sheets, like mine, have multiple drafts and crossings out. "Any volunteers?"

Mark raises his hand. "I'll go." He reads, "Two roads. Chose path. Ever forward."

"Uh huh."

"That's good, Mark."

"You da man."

Tilly reads, "All that I am, I sing."

Nods around the table.

Annie goes next: "Bad marriage. Broken. Good Friends. Healing."

"Yes."

"Yes."

Dahlia raises her hand. "Daughter down. Dogs to the rescue."

Communal humming of music from the *William Tell Overture.*

"Your turn, Jasmine."

I read, "Smart teacher learns from smarter students."

Laughter. "That's a cop-out."

"Alecky. Smarter-Alecky."

One I don't share reads, "Girl meets boy. Yes or no?" Because I don't want any advice.

Aldeen goes with, "Still talking after all these years."

More laughter.

They agree on a group response. It's a hot exercise. And cool.

Jared surfaces through the back entrance of the Center. He walks briskly over as I'm getting my things together to leave.

"You have a phone message from Suella Reams," he says. "She said to tell you not to bring the food."

I guess I'm relieved, given the deteriorating state of my intestinal tract.

"Thanks, Jared. How are you, today? I didn't see you when I came in. We've set the library up, and Annie's volunteered to do some organizing."

"I told you the class would diminish in numbers."

Jared has a real talent for *non sequiturs.* Someone calls to him from the back of the Center, and he leaves our area without further comment.

The group disbands with ongoing expressions of concern for Jamail, and I hesitate only briefly, because I'm alone, before heading to Oil Can Leo's to see if I can find him.

Because it's a popular watering hole for a wide spectrum of Austin's populace, I've shared more than a few pitchers there over the years, beginning the night I turned twenty-one and drank one with Nathan. Tonight it's going to be a Sprite.

Leo's attracts serious pool players with regular tournaments, a diverse element of ages and ethnicities and who knows what sorts of transactions. Animal heads from locales near and far adorn the wall above the bar, and I slide in next to two women under an antelope, whose eyes make me wonder how anyone could choose to hunt.

The women at the bar glance at me only briefly before returning to their conversation, and the bartender pours my soft drink from a spigot attached to a container that offers a multitude of beverages choices.

My eyes roam the premises, and I spot Jamail with a group of African American males seated at a round table with several empty pitchers and bottles, already well into their evening even though it's early. The surprise attraction is one of Jamail's table companions is the silver-haired man who brought the papers to Jared behind the Center.

Jamail hasn't seen me, or if he has, he's ignored my presence. Should I go over to the table? Probably not, it could be embarrassing for him. I wave to him from the bar, but he's conversing earnestly, and I succeed only in attracting a waitress who tells me, "You can order right from the bartender, hon."

My stomach, which had improved during the class, begins to churn uncertainly, and I know the ladies' room at Oil Can Leo's well enough to decide I have to make it home. My exit route intentionally takes me between Jamail's table and the booth behind, and he looks up, meets my eyes as I walk by, but doesn't speak. I nod a greeting.

Because it's so close, I detour by Suella's en route home. Parked in front are the taxicab yellow Hummer and a black Silverado. As I'm pausing to write down the license plate number of the Silverado, I see the two boys and the woman emerging from the house, and I have to speed off without it.

~ Thirty-One ~
Outward and Visible Signs

If one of my characters becomes ill, I surely won't give them projectile vomiting and recurring spasms of diarrhea. Just doesn't make good copy.

The only bright spot is having an in-house nurse. Collie Sue would be impressed. Babe keeps watch all Thursday night, never leaving my side as I crawl back and forth between the bedroom and the bathroom. On the bed she snuggles close, conforming her body to my contortions, and trots along diligently on necessary journeys, but much preferring the walks we take to the kitchen for our fluid replacement.

The siege continues through Friday, ebbing but ever-lurking. I'm alternating between ice chips and diluted Gatorade while the ladies are driving, chipping and putting their way around Penick Park without me.

Around mid-day I gather the energy to call Aunt Arrow and report the various sightings from my soiree at Suella's and Oil Can Leo's.

Aunt Arrow diagnoses a stress-enhanced intestinal virus, for which she recommends solace and the BRAT diet, which she'll bring. Bananas. Rice. Applesauce. Toast. I recoil, postponing acceptance until maybe tomorrow, when I hope I'll no longer be contagious and might have some appetite for solid food.

"Definitely something suspicious with that crew and Ruth Ann at Suella's," Aunt Arrow speculates. "Both boys there and a woman. Strange. No wonder they told you not to come with the food. What the hell is going on over there? And now we have the link between Jamail and Jared, whoever he is."

Aunt Arrow brings the provisions by on Saturday morning but doesn't linger. She'll text message the solace.

Bertel leaves a phone message suggesting a movie, but I don't return the call. One, I don't feel like going to a film. Two, I don't feel like having a conversation with Bertel. Three, I don't feel like seeing Bertel. Four, I don't feel like Bertel's seeing me. Five, he can just wonder what the hell I'm thinking about since our post-picnic discussion.

Popcorn. Sightings. Yuck. Ants ruin picnic.

On Sunday I'm improved but still too dehydrated to go anywhere except the back yard, which suits Babe just fine. I eat a banana and some toast. She eats the rice and applesauce to shore up her strength for chasing the tennis ball, mourning doves and a family of mice. I had signed up to help with refreshments at St. Barnabas today but leave a message on the church machine that I'm sick and can't make it.

Around one o'clock Aldeen calls from St. Barnabas. Bertha included me on the morning prayer list, so I've been prayed for. She and Helena Roberts want to bring me communion. They're the lay Eucharistic ministers for the week and will be visiting all the shut-ins this afternoon. "And you're shut-in."

"You'll bring communion to my home?" No one's ever offered that in the entire history of my Episcopalian-ism. I accept, even though bread and wine don't fit the BRAT diet.

"The peace of the Lord be always with you." They begin around two-fifteen after reverently setting up the elements on a small table in my living room with a minimum of bustle and conversation. Chalice and paten in miniature ceramic. Their home service starts with a gentle passing of the peace.

"And also with you."

Aldeen prays the Collect of the Day, which seems to speak directly to my condition, "Almighty God, keep us both outwardly in our bodies and inwardly in our souls, that we may be defended from all adversities which happen to the body, and any thoughts that assault and hurt the soul …"

From Luke Helena reads the appointed Gospel for this Sunday, Jesus' parable of the fig tree. Fig trees and fruit. Wasting soil. It's about living our lives prolifically, not sterilely, I think as she reads. Producing fruit may take time, may require some digging and fertilizing. No cutting the tree down because we're not finding our satisfaction in the moment.

"No support for instant gratification here," Helena says as if reading my mind.

We confess things we have done and left undone and pray the Lord's Prayer.

The body of Christ, the bread of heaven. The blood of Christ, the cup of salvation. The gifts of God for the people of God. And the creatures. Babe accepts a large chunk of the communion bread.

Together we offer our thanks for the God who embraces all people and for the bread and the wine, the outward and visible signs of inward and spiritual grace.

~ **Thirty-Two** ~
Borders Up

I wake up Monday not exactly filled with vim but incrementally better. Babe and I opt to spend our morning productively in ways we hope will yield eventual fruit.

We have a two-pronged attack with an objective to demonstrate nobly the loving of our neighbors as ourselves: engage in bantering with Gladys and Joe Ray Marks from next door, and patch the cracks in the driveway. Babe is thrilled with the prospective involvement with the cement mixer, which she thinks is alive, circling and barking, approaching and retreating, as I bring it around, set up on the sidewalk and plug in.

Gladys bites right away, arriving with a Jesus is the One coffee mug. When she lifts it to drink, Jesus Saves is on the bottom. "Whatcha doin there, Grace? Would you like a nice hot cup of coffee? I've just made a fresh pot. Joe Ray won't drink it past thirty minutes of setting. Says it gives him acid stomach."

"Thanks, Gladys, but I'll have to pass. Had a mean G.I. bug over the weekend, and I'm still on tea."

"I keep a jar of sun tea, always on the ready. Let me get you a glass. Do you prefer it sweetened?"

"Hot tea," I clarify and hold up my Life is Good mug with the golfer completing her swing on one side, and Do what you like, Like what you do, on the other. Jana gave it to me for Christmas.

Babe indicates by ducking her head and rubbing up against my leg that she would accept a biscuit, but Gladys doesn't offer one.

Joe Ray arrives and booms observantly, "Notice you have a dog there, Grace."

Babe bounds over to Joe Ray to be petted, and he willingly complies. "We can't have a dog. The wife. Allergies. Miss 'em. Always had a dog as a kid." Babe stands alertly beside Joe Ray, who scratches her ears.

As if on cue, Gladys takes a tissue out of her apron pocket and vigorously blows her nose.

"She's semi on loan from a friend. You know, that business about the note in the mailboxes around here, came for protection, and we've bonded. It'd be hard to give her back. If you want to take her for a walk in the neighborhood sometime, Joe Ray, she's available at no charge."

This chit-chat is going well, I think, even if I don't drink coffee from salvation mugs or iced tea.

"Whatcha doing there, Grace?" Gladys repeats her opening salvo.

"You can see the cracks and hollowed out spaces, how they're enlarging. Want to keep up my end here," I explain, "appearance of the neighborhood and all. So I'll be sealing them up with my trusty mixer. By tomorrow, after they harden, you'll never know it was anything but smooth out here."

"Your own mixer, yeah, I remember." Joe Ray walks over to the machine, looks in, goes back to the driveway and checks my spread of implements.

"I never heard of anyone having their own individual cement mixer," Gladys says. "It's usually done with a big truck, goes round and round in the back. I see 'em, driving around town, twirling their buns."

"Oh, this one goes round and round when I turn on the motor." I demonstrate. Babe barks and feints. "I'd be willing to do a loan on this, as well."

Joe Ray ponders that offer, walking over to evaluate his own driveway, pronounced by Gladys to be smooth as silk. "But thanks anyway, Grace. We'll be getting back inside. Joe Ray's on wallpaper duty today. You'll have to come see it when we finish bordering the guest room with little Gabriels, all blowing their horns. Just darling."

"Sounds sweet."

"Well, yes and no. If you're ready, they're sweet. There's a message in that border, if you know what I mean. Are you ready?"

"Ready?"

"Ready. Have you taken Jesus Christ as you personal savior? That's the only way, you know, to salvation. When Gabriel blows."

"Oh, I see. Yes, I can say with complete assurance that Babe's ready. She sealed the deal by taking her first communion just yesterday."

"No, I don't mean the dog," she shakes her head as Joe Ray returns.

"I did notice a couple of small fissures that could use some …" he says as Gladys pulls him by the arm toward the house, like a bad comedian being hustled off the Comedy Central stage.

"I'll let you know when the border's up," Gladys says. "It's never too late."

"All dogs go to heaven," Joe Ray calls.

Having completed the first step of my project, which is to lay out all the tools—pick, shovel, wood, level, carpenter's square, trowel, vegetable oil—and the second step, which is to appraise the situation, I move on to step three, a trip to Hemmings.

No way you can do a job like this one without a trip to the hardware store. Right, Babe? Babe hops up from the grass, where she is rolling, and heads for the car.

We travel to Hemmings via Aunt Arrow's, who invites us in. "You two just come right on up and so glad, glad, glad you're better, Grace Edna," she says in hyper-chipper, which means she's baking again. "Your color was pasty green. Green, green, green."

She greets us at the door with a treat for Babe, containing who knows what, and a "Hi-dee, hi-dee, hi-dee." She seems to be talking in trios today. "Speaking of pasty green, I'll have some pistachio muffins on offer, emerging in about," she walks out on her balcony, looks skyward, "seventeen minutes and one cirrus passage."

Cirrus passage. This clearly isn't the best time to work our suspects. Babe stays out on the balcony, cheerily munching greenery.

"Try, try, try as hard as you can," Aunt says, "and explain to me what those cars were doing at your friends' house. If the boys are helping Ruth Ann, why would a woman be with them?"

"I don't have any explanation. Bertel would say she was helping, too. A job that needed six hands. Or she came by to give Casey a ride, not knowing the Hummer-owner, probably her son or nephew or younger brother, was with him. Or the alleged son, nephew or younger brother had to go to basketball practice."

"I think they're buying drugs, and the woman's involved. That's why they didn't want you to bring barbecue, a drug deal was going down."

I don't disagree.

She asks me about Jared and Jamail. "Could it be Operation Double-Jay?"

"Well, yes, they could be in collusion." It's possible that in her loopy condition Aunt Arrow's onto something. Jared would certainly know of Jamail's history with addiction, meaning Jamail has some sort of built-in network. For acquisition, certainly, and possibly for distribution and manufacture. And the silver-haired conduit is a link worth pursuing. But how and when? Not in Aunt Arrow's current state, for sure.

The timer goes off on her stove, and Aunt Arrow runs to the kitchen with Babe in pursuit, smelling fresh meat. When she returns to the living room, Aunt Arrow repeats the offer of muffins, which I decline, pleading BRAT. Further, I shake my head when she picks one up and blows on it for Babe.

All we're able to accomplish is scheduling a breakfast meeting on Thursday, which Aunt Arrow dutifully records in her day planner. "Tacos, tacos, tacos."

Hemmings requires forty-five minutes—five to browse, ten to confer with staff, five to check out with my sack of Ready-Mix and twenty-five for Babe to chase the Hemmings Hardware tabby Rufus around the store, me to apologize for not securing Babe more tightly to the metal flag pole at the entrance, and the woman at the cash register to daub my arm with alcohol where Rufus scratched me when I rescued him in the southwest corner aisle between ceiling fans and light switch covers.

All that works up an appetite, which heartens us both as it's my first surfacing. We pull into Sonic Drive-in to order a lime slush and supersonic cheeseburger for me and a crispy bacon toaster sandwich for Babe.

Back at the construction site I use a pick and shovel to clean out the areas where I'll patch. Next I prepare to pour in some ready mix and add water from the hose, which I discover is not attached, because it's coiled on the back patio. That distracts Babe, who requires ball-retrieving before she can return to her post of engaging with the cement mixer. We delight in the lubrication with vegetable oil in the screw top on the back. Finally, I'm ready to mix and pour, adding the water alternately with the mix, liquid and dry, the dry creating great plumes, like smoke pouring out, until I achieve a soupy consistency.

The machine hums merrily for a few minutes, and I pour a batch into one of the smaller cracks, just to get warmed up. The mixer's set so the hole allows me to spill its contents directly into the desired spaces.

Babe wanders over, watches intently as I smooth the mixture with the trowel, but gets bored and falls asleep at the base of the pecan tree. I feed several more cracks, mixing, pouring and smoothing, surprised that Joe Ray doesn't emerge to supervise. Gladys has him cowed.

I rinse out my mug and fill it with water, drinking a couple of cups, diligent about staying hydrated. Having finished the cracks, I have one more area to fill, a worn section by the curb that began as Rhode Island and has grown into Montana. This one's more complicated and requires the form, which I make from pieces of wood screwed and nailed together, then squared and plumbed over the space. I mix what I estimate to be the last batch, pour and begin leveling the output over the crater.

Out of the corner of my eye I see Babe leap up, and I hear her growl, a sound that competes with the whirr of an approaching motorcycle. Sensing something's amiss, I stand up to see what's wrong and move toward Babe as the growls turn to snarls.

What's wrong is that there's no Doppler effect, whoosh, from the passing cyclist, and that's because there's no passing. The cyclist veers off the street and bears down on me, but in the approach, instead of hitting me where I was before I moved toward Babe, hits wet cement, causing the bike to spin and slide down.

The helmeted rider rights the bike as hurriedly as is possible in wet cement and rides away, having ruined my afternoon's work.

Joe Ray, an ambulance and two fire trucks arrive simultaneously in response to his calling 911. "That dog saved your life."

She did, indeed.

~ **Thirty-Three** ~
Second Verse

"It could have been much worse," Aunt Arrow says, outraged and solicitous. "Gawd Almighty, Grace, you think they'll believe us now?"

Aunt Arrow and Jake came immediately, arriving less than ten minutes after Joe Ray phoned, the only call I had the energy to request. I've never figured out their rhythms, which is none of my business anyway, but they were together at her condo on Monday afternoon, an alleged work time for Jake. Their skin glows like the transfiguration.

We're all in the yard: Babe, me, Aunt Arrow, Jake, Joe Ray and Gladys, four firemen,two EMTs. From across the street are Sarah Jane and Phil Simkins, who received one of the asshole notes. The counter man from Trader's Coffee around the corner. The Pattersons' two Siamese cats from four houses east. Vehicles at the curb. Two police cars. Jake's car. Aunt Arrow's car. Two fire trucks. One ambulance.

And Officer Boyd Dunbar, who's accompanied by Officer Thalia Peabody, a police department family counselor who can't be more than twelve. "For emotional support. Standard procedure in a trauma case like this one," Boyd Dunbar explains.

"Although you can't make interpersonal comparisons of traumatic experiences, we're prepared for some of your common responses, such as your pallor," Officer Peabody adds. "We'll need to treat for that."

Aunt Arrow and Jake put their arms around me from either side. "Well, of course it's a shock, duh," she says not entirely under her breath.

Officer Dunbar appraises the section of the driveway by the curb. "What were you doing when this happened, Ms. Edge?"

"Montana." I point to the driveway.

With an authoritative sweep of his arm, Officer Dunbar dismisses the fire trucks, the ambulance and accompanying personnel. Neighbors and animals stick. Mail carrier arrives. Officer Peabody offers to wrap me in a blanket and without waiting for an answer retrieves and methodically unfolds a yellow blanket stamped Austin PD in large blue letters from the trunk of her police car.

"For the shock. We'll go inside and lie you down."

Negative to both offers. I'm sweating profusely. In shorts and a short-sleeve denim shirt, beads are running down the back of my legs, absorbed by the knee pads I'm wearing for the patching.

Joe Ray walks Officer Dunbar over to the cement mixer, retracing for him my steps in the concrete process. After Babe barks and lunges several times at Boyd, Jake puts her on the lead. Enticing her with biscuits, Jake spreads out Officer Peabody's blanket and attempts to settle Babe on it.

We all meet at the section by the curb, except Babe, who pees on Officer Peabody's blanket.

I describe what I remember. "But it all went so fast. Babe barked and growled, I stood up and moved toward her, heard the sound of the motorcycle, and there he was, spinning between Helena and Bozeman. Took out one of the Tetons."

"Is there any brandy in the house?" Officer Dunbar inquires politely.

I shake my head.

"We've got some," Joe Ray shouts.

"We do?" Gladys says.

Jake appears with a few lawn chairs he's brought around from the back, and some of us sit while we wait for Joe Ray, who comes out of his house with a tray, a bottle of brandy and several iced tea glasses.

"I meant just for Ms. Edge," Officer Dunbar says as Joe Ray pours an inch or so for me, Aunt Arrow, Jake, the Simkins, the Trader's Coffee counterman and himself. The mail carrier declines, pleading duty, and Gladys asks Joe Ray where he had the brandy hidden.

"Down the road to sin."

"To Babe," Jake offers a toast, and we drink.

Frustrated in his attempts to conduct an orderly investigation, Officer Dunbar goes back to his car and does something with his radio. Officer Peabody hovers, and Joe Ray refills our glasses, draining the bottle.

"Now, Boyd," Aunt Arrow says to Officer Dunbar when he rejoins our group, "we want to help you, but Grace Edna is our first priority."

"Understandable," he agrees, then asks everyone but Aunt Arrow, Joe Ray and me to leave. Jake takes Babe around to the back yard, and the Simkins cross the street to their house with promises of, "Anything we can do, you just holler, Grace." Gladys backs up to her rose bushes, the mail carrier and Coffee Trader counter man return to work, and Officer Peabody turns on the hose and sprays her blanket.

Jake whispers to me as he's gathering up Babe that water won't wash the scent out. "Probably permanent."

Good dog.

Another police car pulls up in front of the house. Out steps Detective Bertel Fredrickson.

"All that's missing is the theme music from *Bonanza*," Aunt Arrow says. Now we know what Officer Dunbar was doing with his radio.

Bertel ignores everyone except Officer Dunbar, with whom he confers extensively. Officer Dunbar motions to Joe Ray, who joins them at the intersection of the curb and the driveway.

They learn what Joe Ray has already told us, that he saw the whole thing from a ladder between the corner windows facing the street. He had just completed pasting an especially challenging fourteen-inch section of the Gabriels blowing their horns, difficult because they had to run right up to the corner precisely. He'd looked up from the work, taking a breath break before turning the corner.

"If the driver completes his mission, Grace is a goner," we can hear his report "Heading right smack for her. She jumped out of the way, thanks to Babe, and he hit the wet spot. I'm taking down all those little tooting bastards. They're a bad omen."

Bertel glances over to where Aunt Arrow and I are seated.

He bends down next to my chair, pats my arm until it stops shaking, then stands up again. Bertel asks for a description of the driver and the vehicle, readies a notebook and looks at me.

"No idea," I say. "Big and loud."

Joe Ray replies immediately, "Harley Sportster 1200, white gold pearl and vivid black."

"Anything on the driver?"

"Aral Viper helmet, blue and silver. Roadgear gloves. Fox Creek black leather jacket," Joe Ray describes.

"You could see all this detail from your window?" Bertel asks.

"I know the bikes and accessories intimately from catalogs. That's as close as the wife will let me get."

He might just make it as a witness.

"It's a big help. Thank you."

"Narrows it down to about two thousand motorcycles in the area," Joe Ray estimates.

"Any idea where he went from here? We can see from the concrete prints that he left the premises, heading east, but they fade out after a few houses," Officer Dunbar says.

"Couldn't see. Just sped off down the street away from Seaton Hospital," Joe Ray says. I climbed down the ladder, slid the last few rungs, called 911 and ran out here, but he was long gone."

"Uh huh," Betel says to Officers Dunbar and Peabody, who have now gathered on either flank. He and Officer Dunbar walk back out to the street, Boyd steps off some measurements, and we lose him in the ess-curve between my house and the hospital.

Bertel makes a call on his cell, then comes back and asks Joe Ray about traffic on the street, if vehicles take the curve too fast in any sort of pattern. Joe Ray affirms the curve as a common problem and that he's seen all kinds of vehicles careen, cyclists included, but not usually land in my driveway.

"So it could have been an accident—just taking the curve too fast? We're trying to run the table here on what we might be dealing with."

"If that were the case, he wouldn't have sped off," Aunt Arrow points out.

"Maybe, maybe not," Officer Peabody says. "There could be psych-social issues with the driver of which we are unaware, causing him or her to want to avoid conversation, confrontation or being connected with a motor vehicle accident."

"You know he attacked Sally?" Aunt Arrow interrupts. "Same thing. Barely missed her, too."

"We have the report," Bertel says, "along with everything else in the record, and we will be giving it a meticulous review."

"What I don't understand is why they'd go after Grace, since you'd dropped the case, and stir up the suspicions again," Jake says, arriving with Babe, who runs over to Bertel.

Bertel kneels down and rubs her head.

"This isn't an official response," he says, "but I'm guessing either it was truly an accident, and the driver rode off for reasons unknown, alcohol or a stolen bike. We'll check. Or it was intentional, and the driver thought he could get away with a hit and run, that we wouldn't make a connection to any case, just a street accident, driver going too fast and losing control, woman working in her yard. Wrong place, wrong time."

"In her driveway," I correct.

"But he had to have been watching for an opportunity," Aunt Arrow says. "Couldn't just be coincidence that he rides by at that precise moment when she was near the street."

"Have you seen this rider before?" Bertel asks Joe Ray.

"Motorcyclists up and down the street all the time. Probably have. They convene at the park."

"Do you have a regular schedule for working in your yard, Ms. Edge?" Boyd asks, returning from his measurements.

"Not really. Weekends. But I do take out garbage and clean up anything in the yard on Monday afternoons to prepare for the city truck's pick up Tuesday morning. "

"OK. If you were under observation the rider would be aware of your Monday afternoon schedule. The cement mixer was just a bonus, giving him more time."

Gladys peeks through the rose hedge and proceeds to our grouping to collect the iced tea glasses and tray, offering us a salmon and potato chip casserole that she could have ready in "just a jiffy" for our supper.

Aunt Arrow declines on our behalf, disappointing only the Siamese cats. Bertel uses this transitional moment as an opportunity to dismiss Officer Peabody, the wet blanket, Joe Ray and Gladys. The cats resist direction.

He moves Aunt Arrow, Jake, Babe, me, Officer Dunbar and himself into the house, welcome for me, as I'm now shivering in spite of the near-ninety-degree heat. The pooled sweat feels like ice droplets.

Aunt Arrow insists on covering me with my ships-at-sea quilt, and the others convene uncovered in a surrounding semicircle, reminiscent of the scene from a Dorothy Sayers manor house. Tony Hillerman, on the other hand, would never put so many disparate voices in such a small and contained space.

Bertel announces the commencement of the interrogation, not in words so much as in demeanor as he stands, hitches up his blue serge slacks, asks Officer Dunbar to hand him the notebook, opens the notebook, takes a pen out of the front pocket of his shirt—light blue, button down collar—loosens the knit yellow tie with the tiny blue scales of justice and sits stiffly in a chair Jake has brought in from the kitchen.

"You're with the press?" he asks Jake, not having met him until today.

Jake offers a plate of sandwiches he's assembled in the kitchen with a large pot of hot tea. "I'm managing editor of the *Austin Times*, but I'm here in my capacity of support crew for Aurora and Grace Edna. And Babe's assistant trainer," he adds. "Anything discussed here is off the record, I assure you. I'll arrange for a reporter to interview you and the other principals later."

Seemingly satisfied, Bertel turns to the assembled parties and says, "Where to begin."

"By admitting you were wrong," Aunt Arrow suggests.

Bertel hands the notebook back to Officer Dunbar and asks him to take the notes. Officer Dunbar obliges by dutifully recording something.

"If this incident today with the biker relates to the prior incident with Ms. Weathers on the hike-and-bike trail, it suggests that both women were targeted for attack. Further, the possibility exits that the reason for the attack was to eliminate someone with knowledge, accidental or otherwise, of illegal activity. The cause of Ms. Weathers' death is the interaction of two drugs for which she had prescriptions."

He looks up from his notes. "At this point anything else is conjecture, but today's event suggests the need to reopen the investigation into Ms. Weathers' death, as well as to pursue the notion that she had gained knowledge of criminal behavior related to drugs." Bertel says all this so rapidly he runs out of breath.

Aunt Arrow intervenes with a translation. "A motorcyclist tried to kill Grace Edna this afternoon. You have an eyewitness. Sally Weathers escaped a similar attempt in a different location and ultimately died under highly suspicious circumstances. Even the drug dosage was wrong. Sally was murdered, and my niece is in extreme danger until we find the killers. They think she knows whatever Sally discovered."

"The possibility also exists that the incident was purely accidental," Bertel says as Officer Boyd's stenography is interrupted by his cell phone. "Be right out," he says. "Motorcycle officer one minute from ess-curve. Excuse us just a moment."

He and Bertel go outside, and we hear the sound of a motorcycle, don't hear it, then hear it starting up and passing by.

The men return. "We confirmed that a motorcycle traveling at seventy miles an hour could spin out on the curve," Boyd tells us.

"Hello," from Aunt Arrow.

Officer Boyd sits and writes something on the pad.

"We aren't concluding anything except that we have considerable work to do," Bertel says. "If Grace feels like it, I would like to return to the list of people who were connected to Ms. Weathers and the MLK Center. We've completed background checks and some interviews, but given the developments of today, we'll be revisiting that list and possibly broadening it."

I rise up between schooners and whaleboats to relate what I've seen, smelled and tasted on Casey, Jamail, Jared and the potential silver-haired link, with Aunt Arrow adding detail and speculation. Boyd records, and Bertel knots his tie. He asks about other possible suspects as if what we're offering might actually constitute a murder investigation.

Or maybe not. "We'll follow up diligently, but also bear in mind that Grace may be the victim of an accidental miss and run."

"Grace will need protection, regardless," Aunt Arrow insists.

"We've already ordered increased patrols around the clock."

"But she's here by herself, and if they're watching ..."

"I've got that covered," Jake says. "Six neighbors sharing a twelve-hour watch, 8:00 p.m. to 8:00 a.m. Phil from across the street, Joe Ray next door. I've talked to them, and Leroy in the 4-B townhouse will organize his three roommates. I've just gotten off the phone with Leroy next door."

"Leroy is?" Bertel asks.

"Leroy Noah Joakim, all-American linebacker. He's out of spring drills because of a torn hamstring. His mother works at the paper, sports writer, Noella Joakim. First female reporter to enter the university men's baseball locker room. She's the one who was welcomed with the dropping of a towel by Jim Hansborough, first baseman, and her response was 'No wonder you lost the game.' Never had a problem since."

"I remember it well," Aunt Arrow says. "We had a luncheon in her honor at the Professional Women's Writer's League."

"Leroy's six-four, three hundred forty pounds, the baby in the house. He'll have the other three on board for two-hour stints for several days anyway, until we can get a system installed that connects directly to the station," Jake says.

Babe's ears droop.

"You're still our main gal," Jake reassures her with one of the pieces of liver he's zapped for her in the microwave while assembling the sandwiches. She signals the need for a pit stop, and he takes her outside.

Aunt Arrow walks out with Boyd. "You'll be keeping an eye on things here, right?"

"Vigilant patrols," he assures her.

Which leaves Bertel and me in the kitchen with tea remnants.

"I had hoped to make connection before now," he says. "Left some messages."

"Sorry I didn't return your calls, but I had an intestinal crisis. You don't want the details."

"Our basketball ladies won, and they're playing again Friday."

I turn my back and begin unloading the tray into the dishwasher. He stands behind me, massaging my neck and shoulders.

"I'd like to be in the cheering section with you," he says.

"They're playing in Palo Alto, California."

"I meant in front of the television."

I can feel Bertel's breath on my neck. Just for a second I'm wishing I could be like those characters who rip each other's clothes off before they even get inside the relevant premises or medical supply closet or elevator. What they miss, though, is the thrill of losing inhibitions, because they have none, not that it's relevant here, because I see the KPRX-TV truck pulling up outside my kitchen window. Someone's got to talk to them, and it sure as hell isn't going to be me.

~ Thirty-Four ~
Ravens and Moles

The guys managed to contain the press, Bertel and Boyd assuring the television reporter and camera crew that there was no story. A motorcyclist out of control, didn't stay to apologize, all too common in today's metroplex.

What about a human interest piece about a woman with her own concrete mixer? Nixed. Maybe later. The relevant powers at *Austin Times* opted to report only a sentence in the police blotter, no names, no addresses. "Driveway in Rosewood Park area reported damaged by unidentified motorcycle, under investigation." Maybe later.

"Premises Patrolled By Neighborhood Watch." Leroy and Jake have the signs posted by early Tuesday morning. If I'm under observation, I just hope the observers observe Leroy. What's nagging at me, though, is that they don't relent.

Single telephone conversation with Bertel late Tuesday afternoon. Masterful police-speak. "The task force investigating the death of Sarah Weathers has reconvened, and the Department is pursuing all leads thereto," those donated by Aunt Arrow and me as well as "certain other possibilities which I'm not at liberty to disclose at this juncture."

Juncture of what?

Bertel has met again with Crystal Dutch, Casey's parole officer, and personally read all the sweet notes submitted by Casey's clients about his volunteer services in and around their homes. The high school associate, Claude Murphee, has no offenses on file other than a citation for exceeding the speed limit shortly after obtaining his driver's license. "Common for teenage boys, fortunate it wasn't worse."

Jamail, Silver-Hair and Jared "remain active, pursuit-wise." A confidential one, as Bertel cannot at this stage reveal the investigative plans for that trio, other than their receipt of "due attention."

As an aside Bertel wants me to know two things from his solo perspective. First, and also in all confidence, there are those above him in rank within the Department, as well as a few below, "who aren't pushing this thing, still not grasping the murder and drug ring connection."

He's somewhere betwixt and between, pulling out all the stops to ensure my protection, recognizing the parallels between Sally and me, acknowledging the appearance of certain suspicious behavior, but "limited in resources by evidence to support your contentions, or as they see it, the lack thereof to this point."

Bertel's awarded five stars for ambiguity. The "few below" would be Kira Mattingly. Aunt Arrow has talked to Boyd Dunbar privately. He's with us, hinted at the departmental head-butting, and believes Bertel's doing all he can.

Second from Bertel, his son is arriving for a long weekend during his spring break, and would Babe and I like to watch the women's basketball tourney at his house? Fenced yard. Caramelizing demonstration. Meet the family.

Game on.

On Wednesday morning at seven-thirty, I park a block away from Plankton's Oxygen Company, the second stake-out of my career, if you count the Jared Mulberry Tree incident, and I've improved my preparations, this time packing a thermos of coffee and two chocolate cake doughnuts. Three-quarters of a doughnut in, I see the man I assume to be Ramon Plankton arrive, followed by the woman who must be Louise, to whom I talked on the phone yesterday about the company's business hours in the event

I wanted to stop in for an informational brochure on the fees and services. At a doughnut and a half, Casey arrives.

A large gray truck with an enclosed cargo area leaves the office storage shed as I'm cleaning my fingers with a Handi Wipe. I follow along, maintaining a distance of about three-quarters-of-a-block, and record the first stop at 8:27 a.m., where Casey and the assumed Ramon Plankton open a sliding door on the side of the truck.

They carry a large cylinder of liquid oxygen and smaller apparatus to service the customer's equipment. Casey returns to the truck for several portable cylinders. They repeat these operations at various locations that I record at approximate thirty-minute intervals plus driving time. At each stop I park several houses back from their servicing location.

As the traffic picks up I find it even easier to tail them unobtrusively with vehicles between us, the truck's size and color facilitating distance sightings. My only problem, having to pee, I solve by running into an H.E.B. while the truck is parked on a side street perpendicular to the grocery store.

When the guys break for lunch at Taco Bell, I retrace their route to visit the four houses located in the low-income neighborhood of Suella and Ruth Ann. At house number one I introduce myself to the elderly Caucasian woman who answers the door as Louise Perkins, telling her I'm new to the community and looking for an area in Austin to live with my eighty-seven-year old mother, who's feisty and independent and in relatively good health except for some C.O.P.D. that requires oxygen. My housing budget is limited, so we want to rent a place where she might find some compatibility with neighbors, as I work all day. The nice folks at the MLK Center sent me in this direction.

Louise tells me it's a mixed neighborhood racially. "Red and yellow black and white, we are precious in His sight. My husband's on oxygen, too. Thought we'd have to spend down the assets and go on Medicaid, but I got the house in my name now, and we eke along with the occasional financial windfalls here and there. Know what I mean? You're not from the government, are you?"

"No, I work for Belle Computers."

At house number two the nattily attired Latino male door-answerer, early twenties, encourages neither conversation nor my moving into the neighborhood, as he's busy caring for his grandmother, who's too sick to talk to any new neighbors. He doesn't invite me inside, but I see a set-up somewhat reminiscent of Ruth Ann's with a woman in a recliner, table of pills next to her chair, an oxygen tank in the corner, super-size flat screen television. Salsa music plays on an upscale Bose sound system.

At house three the African American woman who comes to the door tells me she thought I was the hospice nurse, who's due any time now to treat her husband. So she won't stop to talk but wishes me well in my search.

House four renders a situation similar to house one, genders reversed, with the caretaker an elderly Caucasian male, Buzz Creighton, the invalid a woman. An immaculately detailed late model Buick LeSabre sits in the driveway. He allows me in briefly, and I admire the modern furnishings. "It's a stretch just living on my social security, but we make it, the wife and I. Don't know what I'd do without her."

What's evident from my survey is that, with the exception of the hospice case, each situation hints of a financial disconnect. Windfalls, décors not meshing with expected economic circumstance. Or is that my judgment talking?

I decide to phone Nathan for an objective consult and begin by inquiring about his own grief. "It's like trying to swim through seaweed," he says. "Some days an opening, some days not." But he's always willing to discuss our efforts, which he appreciates mightily. We've exchanged some e-mails, but this isn't something I want floating in cyberspace.

Nathan affirms my endeavors and agrees that these oxygen customers could be the link to drug sales. It would be a simple means of supplementing income, selling pain pills each week to

Casey & Co. with the revenue potential continuing to rise, especially from Oxycontin. "After the manufacturer of Oxycontin, Purdue Pharma, won a patent infringement suit in Federal Court disallowing generic versions of that drug, its street value has soared," he says, "in direct proportion to the danger for you and Aurora."

He appreciates the neighborhood patrols and especially Leroy, whom he's seen play on television. He hopes he's still injured for the Texas A&M game but expresses dismay over the lackluster support of the Austin P.D.

"As you know, I can take care of myself."

"Actually, I don't."

One of us will be in touch after we talk to the pharmacist at Bluebonnet, which is on tap for the following morning, our Thursday breakfast.

I wait on the front porch for Aunt Arrow to pick me up. She's not fully trusting my capacity to meet her under my own steam. Thanks to inner stress and outer humidity, my hair looks like sliced roast beef piled high on a sesame seed bun.

Joe Ray walks over and tells me he's been down to the station to identify the bike and apparel from a color photo line-up, which he had to supply because the Police Department's catalogue selection was badly out of date.

He waves as Aunt Arrow pulls into the now hardened, but unsmoothed, driveway entrance. It'll be a complete pick, shovel, form, level, plumb-lining for Babe and me. Wyoming's now involved.

While en route to Bluebonnet, I confess to Aunt Arrow my reconnaissance of Casey's oxygen activities and customers. She's a bit hurt that I excluded her from an event we had loosely planned to perform together but hadn't scheduled for a definite time.

Aunt Arrow would certainly have accompanied me, had she known, but I argue that there was less chance of being spotted on my own. She could have blown my cover, sitting in the car, since she could never have passed for my eighty-seven-year old, oxygen-dependent mother. Plus, I had to leave my house at 7:00 a.m., which she concedes is not her finest hour.

Aunt Arrow concurs with Nathan's assessment that Casey has access to a population of relatively low-income elderly people in compromised health who are, like Ruth Ann, in possession of "a table full of potentially valuable prescription drugs. We know for sure he visits them at times other than when he's servicing their oxygen concentrators. How do they get the liquid oxygen from the big tanks into those concentrator things, anyway?"

"They don't. The concentrators use room air. That's what they're concentrating, the air around them."

"You're quite the expert, missy."

We let that one ride.

"Question is, do we take this to Bertel now?"

Aunt Arrow believes that my stake-out and follow-up give us useful knowledge of Casey's customer base and prospective financial connections but nothing that would interest the Austin P.D.

At Bluebonnet we go directly to the prescription drop-off window, where no one is attending. One of the pharmacists, Chad Wilbarger, according to the name tag clipped to his crisp lab coat, apologizes that the tech is out of pocket.

I'm about to step up and explain that we're following up on the death of a friend and yada, yada, yada, when Aunt Arrow elbows me aside.

She introduces herself to Chad, asks for some help but not to have a prescription filled. Does he have just a minute? He indicates he does.

"I'm a professional writer and will be leading a writing workshop at the Mystery Writers of the West next month in

Portland, Oregon," she says, lying creatively as she goes, "on the necessity of accurate documentation when writing about the investigation of a murder. You just wouldn't believe the ways a hack writer can botch a murder."

"What's your question?"

"Here's an example: The dosage on a med gets upped without the victim's knowledge or that of his doctor. The author has to be able to explain that scenario. You can't just kill off the victim from the overdose."

"I've tried my hand at writing those things," Chad says, picking up interest. "That's the part I do well. I know my poisons. What gives me fits is the front loading. I put too much at the start and don't know what to do with the rest of the story."

"Yes, pacing can be a challenge," Aunt Arrow says, "and what I want to do is give these novices some practical suggestions. What would be the answer on that one?"

"Spread it out. Like fertilizer."

"I mean on the increasing dose, although I appreciate your simile."

"Never happen. We double-check at every step, first the tech in the initial recording and then the pharmacist in the filling. If the dosage has been changed, the tech would call the doctor to verify and make a notation in the record."

"The tech would record the change?"

"But it would also have to be in the 'script, and most of those are faxed over from the doctors' offices."

"It could be handwritten, though, right? With the milligrams."

"Would have to be confirmed by the doc."

"And that's done how?"

"You may not remember, Aurora, is it? But I just explained that. The tech would call the doctor, verify the change and note that in the record, and I would double-check the dose when I fill it. All recorded in our system."

"With the incorrect dose."

"No, the correct dose. What are you killing this guy with anyway? Not many of our common meds will wipe somebody out with a prescription dose unless there's an underlying medical condition or an interaction."

"Ummm," Aunt Arrow says, nodding. "Yes, an interaction. That would be an interesting twist. Could you suggest a couple of drugs I could use for the group that would produce a lethal interaction?"

"No, ma'am, I cannot. Ethical considerations." The phone behind the counter rings. Cliff picks it up and asks the caller to hold just a moment, turning back to Aunt Arrow. "But good luck with your workshop. Seattle's a great walking city. We had our pharmacists' convention out there a couple of years ago. The library has books about drugs, if you're so inclined. Do you hold any of your workshops around here?"

"Nothing's scheduled, but I'll let you know if I do."

He hands her a business card.

We both go for a double order of today's special: migas, salsa, hot and fresh flour tortillas. I'm tempted to supplement with the peanut butter rolls but pass, thinking ahead to my appearance at the basketball-caramelizing fest.

Our inclination, based on Chad's contributions, is to hone in on the tech rather than one of the pharmacists. Whoever documented that dose change with the doctor's office could be involved in this thing, making a dose-change call for the pharmacy's records that never occurred. The tech would have access to Sally's prescription history, at least those filled here at Bluebonnet, which all of hers were, as well as to any information coming into the pharmacy about the potential interactions of the two she was taking. One of us has to get to that record and see who confirmed the change.

We're fortunate the pharmacy isn't as busy as usual. Aunt Arrow sashays back over to the drop-off window, her aqua caftan billowing, and I see her successfully engaging Chad once again in conversation. Putting one hand on her chest, she takes a tissue out of her pocket with the other and wipes her eyes. He tilts his head to one side and pats her shoulder. Telling him about Sally, no doubt.

She speaks some more, and his head bobs up and down as if he's sighing deeply. Sketching something on a pad, she points and talks, showing him a story arc, I'm guessing, because he duplicates it with his hand, rising action to crisis to falling action. Aunt Arrow puts her palms together in what appears to be a gesture of collegial pleading, asking to see the records. Real detail for her students plus closure for her on her friend's death, eerily similar to her example and his suggestion about the drug interaction.

He responds by cleaning his glasses, taking time to consider his response to whatever she's pled. He smiles goofily, obviously charmed and apparently persuaded as he opens the top drawer of a file cabinet, shuts it, opens the second drawer, takes out a folder, looks through documents in the file, takes one out and returns to the window where he holds the paper up for Aunt Arrow to see. She shakes her head as if in disbelief or despair, wiping her eyes again with the now wadded tissue.

Seeing the record causes her to tear up. What'll she do for the falling action?

As a customer approaches the window, Aunt Arrow mouths something to Chad. Before returning to our table she spins the display of paperbacks next to the magazine rack, selects one, pays for the book at the front register, writes something on the inside cover and takes it back to Chad, who smiles broadly and shakes her hand. Gift of a perfectly paced novel, I'm guessing.

"S.B.," she announces to me when we are out the door. "That's whose initials are on the dose change. He let me see it just briefly."

Simone, the first name of the tech with the dangling earrings, who waited on me, the one I know from somewhere. We'll need to find out her last name. I can do that.

"Now back up," I say to Aunt Arrow, "and tell me how you persuaded the pharmacist to cooperate."

~ Thirty-Five ~
Fire Ants

Annie sits at the table, consulting a list and barking orders while Aldeen, Tilly, Eddie and Mark scurry to comply, each carrying a pile of books to locations designated by Annie's matrix. Aretha Franklin sings to us from the jukebox about respect. *Find out what it means to me.*

"We're real busy, Jasmine," Aldeen says, setting her stack momentarily on the table.

"I can see that. Don't let me interrupt." Annie called me last night to ask permission to use this Thursday afternoon class time to organize the library. Not ruling out that Dewey guy, and thanks for the book, but she's developed her own system.

"Give me some instructions, Sergeant," I say to Annie, who giggles and offers me a tour of the shelves.

"We're keeping it simple. Here's our section for fiction divided into general, mysteries, westerns, romance and everything else. Like the downtown library, the genres have icons: mysteries, miniature magnifying glass stickers; westerns, a lariat; and romance, little hearts." She's drawn them herself and attached them to the binding of each book.

Annie brings me over to a shelf holding the hearts with a space at the end. "Now this is for yours, Jasmine. We're keeping it open for your first book."

My eyes water.

What's your title?"

"*Gersalina's Dilemma.*"

"Which is?"

"Gersalina's a commoner, come from the Scottish lowlands, caught the attention of a handsome captain in service to the Queen, and she's smitten. But that's just it. What kind of service does he provide to all the women who cross his path? Does Gersalina commit to the dashing captain or go back to her day job at home in the lowlands to support her family or follow another steamy direction altogether?"

"I'm saving your heart for the outcome," Annie says, holding up a small sticker, and slides to the next section. "Here's for poetry. We don't have many of those yet, but I'm hoping Jamail will show up one of these days and help me. And in nonfiction our only separate category is biography." Annie points to the relevant shelves "I'll be writing one about Sally— that's my new project," she adds proudly. "I've already contacted her son Nathan. He's offered me access to her letters, which she kept from all parts of her life. That's what you do in researching biographies. Read the letters and talk to people who knew her. I'll want to interview you and your aunt."

From the jukebox Aretha belts out, "You make me feel like a natural woman," and Eddie sweeps Aldeen up for a dance.

"Look here, we have cards in each book," Annie shows me. "When someone takes it out, they write their name and the date and put the card in this box. We're not computerized yet." The box has a photo of Sally, taken at the Center, holding up one of the round, wooden numbers from the Bingo carrousel, and a small sign that says Sally Weathers Memorial Library with the instructions for checking out material. I wipe damp cheeks.

Later, on a break, I ask Aldeen for a favor. Would she accompany me to Suella's when I take the food today? I want to have a private conversation with Ruth Ann about something, and it's impossible with Suella hovering. She understands perfectly.

"No way you can talk to Ruth Ann with Suella even in the house," she says, and she will.

Jared never emerges from his office, where he's conferring, not looking pleased from the looks of his hair, with an unidentified suit the entire time I'm in the Center. Just a guess, but if Bertel has interrogated him again, this man's his attorney. That suggests Jared's worried, and good news for the home team.

Suella's surprised to see us, reminding me she'd left a message last week for me not to come any more. I apologize for the misunderstanding, thinking the message applied only to the one week. Now that we're here, her sister will appreciate the food, but they don't want it any more. The doctor has put Ruth Ann on a low-fat diet.

Suella says, "He's doing everything he can for her pain, and the extra weight don't help. More and more pills. Hard on her system. Those things make you constipated, and I'm having to give her enemas at night. Phew-ee."

True to her word, Aldeen entices Suella outside to look at the fire ant mounds, for which Aldeen has a new plan of attack, having been devoured when she was working in her yard last week end. Aldeen scratches her right calf vigorously. Although Suella maintains it's a hopeless pursuit, she agrees to go along with Aldeen. I offer to fix a plate for Ruth Ann so she won't have to wait, but Ruth Ann's nowhere to be seen.

"In the john," Suella says. "Don't talk to her when she comes out. Tires her too much. Just fix the plate and leave it on her tray table."

Finding dishes and utensils on the kitchen counter, I make a serving of ribs, beans, potato salad and slaw. Then I pour sauce in a little pitcher I find in the cupboard and add a corn bread muffin to a separate plate with a pat of butter and plastic container of honey. Bringing it all out, I cross paths with Ruth Ann returning from the bathroom.

"Sorry I wasn't here to greet you. Doing my daily duty. Prunes in the oatmeal keep me regular. How about you?"

"Granola for breakfast."

"Umm, does this look good. Missed you last week."

"We've had a breakdown in communication."

"Won'tcha join me?"

"I have an order to take home. My dog Babe's waiting for her rib."

Ruth Ann waves hers.

I can see Aldeen fully engaging Suella at the largest mound in the far northeast corner of the front yard and ask, "How have you been feeling, Ruth Ann? Are the meds keeping your pain under control?"

"My pain's a figment of Suella's imagination like the oxygen. I do fine, mighty fine. Jes don't get out like I used to. Figment. It was on *Jeopardy* last night. The category was fruity phrases, like American as apple pie."

Having cleared the tray table of meds in order to serve Ruth Ann's food, I've inventoried the stock. Oxycontin and Percodan, each with two or three pills left from original quantities of thirty each, both from different doctors. Nexium, the ubiquitous Zoloft, and Woman's One-A-Day multivitamins, all half to three quarters full, and just a few remaining rattles in the bottle of Atavan.

"That reminds me, I've promised to look into that online *Jeopardy* contestants quiz for you. Sorry, I've forgotten to do that."

"My mama always told me to tie a string around my finger when I forgot to do stuff," Ruth Ann suggests.

"Good idea, and about these pain meds," I hold up a couple of bottles, "your supply is low."

"That oxygen boy, Casey, and his friend who comes, Claude, they buy 'em from Suella. Just the ones I don't need, which is about all of them. Then he helps less fortunate souls, sells 'em, I think, at a low price same as what he pays Suella or maybe even gives some of em away to old folks who don't have much money."

She pauses to eat some more of her dinner.

"Such nice boys. Suella helps by calling in refills so we have a plentiful supply. She's busy, busy, busy, working on those meds, calling different doctors, using those keypad instructions to reorder. If you want to refill a prescription, press two. Enter your five-digit zip code. Enter your mother's maiden name followed by the pound sign. If this is correct, press four. If it is not correct, hang up and dial 911." Ruth Ann hoots with laughter. "You won't find me wasting my time with that foolishness."

"No, I wouldn't think so."

"They come every Thursday, same as you. Fruits of the spirit. You just missed them, here early today."

"And to service your oxygen."

"No, that's separate. With Mr. Plankton. He doesn't know about the pills. Casey says to keep it a secret so the people he passes the pills on to won't get in trouble with Medicare."

"Right."

"They come back separate for the pills."

"How do you know Casey isn't selling the pills for a profit, making some bucks for himself and his buddy?"

"Tells me so, you know, like that song about the Bible. For the Bible tells me so," she sings. "That was on Monday's *Jeopardy*. Scriptural ditties."

" … from the researchers at Texas A&M," I hear Aldeen's voice of warning as she and Suella come into the living room.

"Fire ants love cables and electricity. Last spring they ate the wire to my radio," Ruth Ann says. "Come over here just a minute, Grace. I have something for you." She reaches down beside her chair, lifts up a sewing basket, takes out a spool of thread and cuts off a section.

"Now, give me a finger."

I hold out my left index, and she ties a bow with green thread.

When I call police headquarters from my car, a dispatcher informs me that Bertel's leading a training session in Bandera, returning tomorrow. Would I like his voice mail? Officer Boyd Dunbar's not on duty again until Monday. Would I like his voice mail?

I'm thankful that Aunt Arrow is in place to receive a phone call and hear what I've learned from Ruth Ann about Casey, the Good Samaritan, which Aunt Arrow doesn't buy for one second.

"Helping the less fortunate," she sputters. "Gag me. Those boys are running a business with big profits."

"Bertel's not due back until tomorrow, Boyd on Monday, and I don't trust anyone else at the department with this."

"Even your friend Kira Mattingly?"

"Especially not Kira."

"Well, now I know," Aunt Arrow says, "so there are two of us who do."

Just in case.

~ Thirty-Six ~
Endorphins

Rain pelts the roof. Again. Friday's golf is in peril. I turn on the Weather Channel for Babe and me to evaluate the forecast. Seventy percent chance of rain until noon, clearing early to mid-afternoon. Radar shows us in a thick green band, unmoving. Temperature in the mid-forties. A bit chilly for March, wind chill in upper thirties. Huh.

"It doesn't sound all that bad," I tell Babe, who agrees, trotting outside eagerly, changing her mind, dripping back in. I dry her with my largest bath sheet, which she resists by chewing a hole in the corner, then running away and hiding under the bed. One of the ladies I'm scheduled to play with, Ethel Trowbridge, phones to let me know she's canceling.

"Weather is terrible," Ethel says observantly.

"Oh?" I respond. "Do you think anyone will show up?"

"Fish got to swim."

No return call from Bertel. I go outside. Pouring rain. I go inside, put on a rain-repellent hooded jacket and add a down vest layer underneath. Out in the garage I check my golf bag in the car trunk, confirming winter golf gloves. Back inside and tempted to stay, I find a wool cap to wear under my golf hat. Acceding to my need for mental and emotional distraction, I drive to golf course in an unrelenting downpour. Maybe it's just raining on my side of town, I think, but soon discover it's raining on the golf course side of town, as well. Really raining.

Parking in the golf course lot, I watch the water on my windshield, coming down too hard even to make a break for the clubhouse. While I sit, another car parks next to me. It's my friend Emma, who's driven down from near Round Rock, over an hour to get to the course.

"It was dry when I left my house," she says, rolling down her window, "and by the time it started raining, I was stuck in traffic. Then I had to pee so badly I just came on to the course to use the ladies room."

"Good decision," I say.

Rain slows from pouring to a steady drizzle, and we break for the clubhouse, finding Kira and a second flighter, eighty-two-year-old Darlene, sitting at a table, drinking coffee and watching the Weather Channel.

"You four can go out at the regular ladies start time," Chub Lewes, assistant pro, tells us, laughing boisterously. "In fact, you can have all the tee times."

None of us joins in the laughter, but the rain slows from a steady drizzle to spitting. Darlene and Kira opt to ride in a cart for weather protection, but Emma says, "I'm from Wisconsin, what the hell."

We tee off. The plan is to stop after nine holes or the return of drizzle, whichever comes first. Everyone's fairway shots include a flight-altering combination of mud and clumps. Even though the ball doesn't seem to travel as far in the heavy, damp air, my shoulders are turning nicely.

After four holes the clouds persist but yield no more spitting. Emma cries out as the cart ladies glide by us on the way to the fifth tee-box, "What a great day for golf," and Darlene yells back, "Any day's a great day for golf when I'm getting to play." We applaud.

Our bodies warm up. At the clubhouse turn, there's no more rain falling or threatening, and the wind has died down. We decide to finish the round.

Kira's up by two in our flight, hers and mine; Emma and Darlene are battling it out at even for their flight. On the back nine Emma and I have several opportunities for discreet high fives. Each hole we complete is announced by Darlene, as in

"That makes twelve, ladies," and even Kira joins us in cheering as if we're the final group in the Women's U.S. Open.

On the Achilles heel fourteenth I tell myself there's already so much water, a little more won't matter. I clear the lake and land my ball four inches from the cup for a tap-in birdie.

In my university years I occasionally ran 10-Ks and experienced a runner's high, the feeling that comes of exhilaration and well-being, apparently related to the secretion of endorphins associated with extended exercise, but I've never had a comparable experience in all my years of golf until today. Emma tallies the scores. Darlene Lytle, 102. Emma Burkhart, 97. Kira Mattingly 91. Grace Edna Edge, 89.

I pocket the Titleist Distance DT So Lo after taking it out of its little stocking and tossing it in the air a few times.

Definitely deserving a treat, I remember the peanut butter rolls, which will also give me the opportunity to talk to the prescription tech if she's in. I park in the lot behind Bluebonnet Drug and enter from the back through a hallway that goes by the rest rooms and employee break room, from which Simone emerges as I approach. No last name on her tag.

I say brightly, "Hello, Simone," but she retreats into the break room without acknowledging my greeting. The ladies room offers a plethora of paper towels for drying off and a well-lit mirror for displaying my remarkable resemblance to Ratatouille. When I pass by the break room, Simone is whispering into her cell phone.

About ten minutes later I've ordered, paid for and consumed two peanut butter rolls and a large glass of lemonade. I'll have to discover Simone's last name for the initials. Not as clever as Aunt Arrow, I've decided to take the direct approach, walk up to Prescription Drop-Off when she gets back and ask her.

In profile, now pouring herself a drink from the snack counter spigots, she looks even more familiar. Recognition erupts. Not from church, not from the political caucus, not from a writers' workshop, not from a Rosewood Neighborhood Council meeting, not the public library.

She's the woman with the boys, Casey and Claude. Hummer. In the street. Chevy Silverado.

Holy shit.

~ **Thirty-Seven** ~
Missing in Action

Once again traversing the back hallway to my car, I sense a shadow, Simone at three o'clock. I know it's three o'clock, because that's where I'm supposed to take the back swing on my pitching wedge for the forty-yarders. Three o'clock to a nine o'clock finish. Or is it nine to three?

Hard metal in my right rib cage. That would be five o'clock sharp.

"Keep it moving, sister, and not a peep," Simone says, as if we're in playing parts in a western movie.

Me, peep? I glance at my rib area. It's surprising how a pistol that small and rounded at the, at the .... I can't think what that part's called, where the bullet comes out. But it feels sharp, like it's pointed, which I know it's not. I jump, wincing at the pain, which earns me a shove forward between my shoulder blades.

Barrel. It's the barrel where the bullet shoots out. Now I remember.

Out into the parking lot for a cozy reunion with Claude, to whom I've never been formally introduced, and Motorcyclist, whom I've also never met personally. I know it's the same one, because I identify a speck of concrete in his front tread. And Claude's standing next to the taxi-cab yellow Hummer.

Cement-specked motorcycle on one side of my Subaru, Hummer on the other. I spot the deep blue Silverado four spaces left. You see what I mean by cozy? The four of us and the four vehicles all together. We're only missing Casey. I wonder where he is. Working, probably. And whether I should introduce myself and shake hands with Claude.

He looks a lot less ominous than Motorcyclist and smaller. If Motorcyclist weren't hunching over, locking his cycle, he'd be about six-feet-two, two hundred seventy-five pounds. He has coal black hair over his ears, I can tell now that the helmet's off. Huge thighs. As it is, leaning down, he's about three-feet-four. Leroy could take him either way.

Hello, my name is Grace Edna Edge. Aren't you supposed to be practicing basketball at the Y or street lot? I could say to Claude, just to get the ball rolling.

They all seem to know what to do, but no one tells me.

Wrong. Now they do.

"In your vehicle," instructs Simone.

I just wasn't patient enough. Lifelong problem.

Simone opens the front passenger door but apparently wants me to drive, which means I have to slide over the console, not such an easy task with my hips and the gear box en route, ouch, and all with a gun poking in my ribs. The damned thing could go off accidentally.

Accidentally, what am I thinking?

Of all things, I remember from the writers' conference that scene with the eyes staring from the back seat, I think he said. Now, I have it, too, Motorcyclist's eyes. He's in the back. Not just the eyes, though, the big body, too, and a weapon of his own. You'd think we were in a war zone. Motorcyclist changes his mind and gets out of my car, leaves an odor behind. Garlic, I think.

Hummer follows me, motorcycle hugs my left. By follow, I'm referring to exiting the parking lot, which is what I'm doing now, taking a left out of the Bluebonnet Drug Store parking lot, to be specific, leaving civilization as I know it behind.

"Where are we going?" I ask politely.

"Shut up," says Simone.

OK, I can do that.

"You'll stay on this street for a few blocks," she says more nicely. Good cop, bad cop, all rolled into one body with stringy blond hair. I wonder if Chad's noticed his tech is missing. What if he needs a dosage change checked?

That's not all I'm wondering about. I'm wondering who in the bloody hell knows where I am. Mentally I go through my list of everyone in the universe who might know where I am at the moment and come up blank. No one knows where I am except Simone, Claude and Hugh. That's his name, Hugh, which is something of a letdown. I heard Simone call it when he exited my car. I expected his name to have three or four syllables.

"Right turn at the light, stay in the curb lane."

Yeah, the curb lane so Hugh and his weapon can stay close. The only weapons I have are my golf clubs, and they're in the trunk.

There's so much traffic, I don't make the light. Simone drums her fingers, the ones that aren't holding the gun, which she eases out of my side. With Hugh on my left, there's no escape, I'm guessing she's figuring.

Another thing I'm guessing is that we're on our way to another murder. Where will they leave my body. The light changes, and we move on in the traffic flow.

I'm so grateful that Aunt Arrow likes that new grief group. She'll need to continue. Odd, the things you think about when you're about to die. I've always read that your life passes before your eyes, but on this journey what's passing are my old haunts, like the Austin Public Library on my right. I can see it clearly, my windshield spotless thanks to Eddie's system.

Bertel. I won't ever get to meet his son, see what he looks like and whether he has the cute butt. We never even got as far as the STD talk. He was going to Jana's wedding with me, and now I can't go. But I promised Jana. No lace or chiffon.

My writing. The world will never know Gersalina's decision. Nor will I.

My clients' work won't be completed, maybe ever. I'll never know what happens to QuadRay. My church, St. Barnabas. Yes, it is my church now. Will Aunt Arrow know where to hold my memorial service?

And Babe. I can't stand it. Who'll give her the pan from the fajitas? She'll go back to Jake. Will she miss me? Will she remember me? I'm sobbing. Simone is unmoved unless you count that she's allowing the gun to sit in her lap. That must be her concession to my blubbering.

I reach down to my own lap, and my hand finds the golf ball I won, which I massage in my right pocket, wishing for a sling shot so I could launch it. At least I'll go out a champion.

"Casey identified the clients," I say, "from his oxygen service rounds with Plankton's. That's right, isn't it? People who had the pills you could market."

Simone looks straight ahead in silence.

"He and Claude did the buys from seniors who needed the extra income. Screened carefully, with you overseeing who to target and continuing to check back with them. Keeping it secret. That's why you were often in the neighborhood with those boys."

Simone doesn't answer

"Who did you tell them you were? Ruth Ann, for instance. What did you tell her was going on, something like a goody-goody agency helping the poor by redistributing the pills?"

No response.

"You and Hugh resell the drugs to dealers."

Nothing.

"You might as well tell me."

She glances at me.

"Casey makes the first contact," I press on. "He knows his customers, talks with them, does a few favors. Whose idea was that, you or his parole officer? He learns about their financial status and what drugs they have. Suggests there might be a way for them to earn a little extra income and help someone else at the same time, a fellow sufferer. But they need to keep it secret. You confirm. The boys buy the pills, weekly or however often they're made available. You and Hugh take them to market. Ingenious plan."

Barely perceptible nod. That confirms my death certificate. Otherwise, she wouldn't admit it.

"How much to do you make a year, six figures?"

She holds up seven fingers.

"So you have other sources, other areas besides Casey's route. Claude's a busy boy. Anyone else involved?"

"Don't need any more," Simone finally says something. "I have the pharmacy's computer network at my fingertips."

"Why Sally?"

"Snooping, just like you."

"How did you effect the drug interaction?"

Simone sits forward—proudly, I suppose. "In her orange juice that morning at breakfast. She was clockwork with her schedule. Always ate breakfast at the same time. You're not. That's about the only way you two differ. And she always drank orange juice. "

"Put what in her orange juice?"

"Thorazine. Comes in liquid. I poured it in while they were gabbing with the counter help and waiting for their tacos. A wallop. Plus the build-up of Zoloft. Worked to perfection, just like the drug alert warned.

Thump. Thump again. No thump.

We pass the parking garage, several blocks beyond the library, where my Subaru lived briefly. Next, the Whole Foods Market. "Would you like to stop for a chicken salad on whole wheat?" Hugh revs on my left. Claude behind. Gun in Simone's lap. Not hungry.

Live Oak Park is coming up soon on my right. Live Oak Park, where Aunt Arrow and I had our picnic after my library stay. We watched Walter doing all that watering while we ate.

Live Oak Park on my right, populated by aged live oaks with the enormous trunks, some deep within the Park and some close to the street.

Some close to the street. It's my only chance.

Relying on a maneuver I learned from motorcyclist Hugh, I veer and jump the curb. The last thing I see is the trunk of a massive oak.

~ Thirty-Eight ~
The Things They Brought

Through the fog Aunt Arrow walks toward me, carrying a Styrofoam cup, its contents emitting steam through the low-lying clouds. Now she's leaning over me, her hand on my forehead, saying words I can't hear clearly about patience stirring.

I don't know why she's in this rising mist with me or where we are, but we need the heavier cloaks. It's so cold, and I'm shivering. Now I'm not, as she or someone else has covered me with a blanket the full length of my reclining body, and when I try to move my arm to reach out for her, it won't move because of something cumbersome. I look up beside Aunt Arrow's head, where a plastic bag hangs on a metal stand, and I hear more voices.

Regaining consciousness. Coming to.

Aunt Arrow stands next to another woman, who wears white pants and a shirt covered with characters from a Winnie-the-Pooh story. Tigger and Eeyore and Piglet frolic across the fabric landscape, and I'm lying in a bed with foreign objects attached to my body, plastic tubing and tape on my arm and a line leading up to the bag next to Aunt Arrow's head, and it hurts in my chest when I try to rise up.

Aunt Arrow presses me back gently and kisses my cheek. "You're in the hospital, sweetie, but you'll be fine. You're going to be just fine." She says it in a way to convince me and herself.

The hospital, that's why the apparatus and the pain.

"You had an accident with your car in the park, do you remember? Your car hit a tree, and thank God for your seat belt and air bag. Thank God, period."

Aunt Arrow doesn't pray often, so it must be serious. Me, the patient stirring, not patience.

The ride with Simone and crashing into the tree, my only hope to wreck the car. I must have succeeded.

"You have badly bruised ribs and a dislocated shoulder and a sprained wrist, gashes and abrasions everywhere. Now that you're awake, though, we have hope for your head. Nothing life threatening, you'll heal," she assures me.

The lady with Winnie-the-Pooh *et al* wraps her arm around Aunt Arrow. "Your aunt hasn't left your side," she tells me. "Two days and nights."

"Resurrection on day three," Aunt Arrow says, smiling now, "just like it's supposed to happen."

"It's Saturday?"

"No, sweetie, Sunday. You had the accident on Friday afternoon. You've been in the hospital since then, two nights, Friday and Saturday. This is the morning of third day, Sunday morning."

"The others?" I ask.

"All in custody except Simone, who's still in a hospital bed, under guard. Casey Guthrie, Claude Phillips and Hugh Detweiler. Bertel's locked them up. You're safe now. Not sound yet, but safe."

A few minutes later I'm feeling less groggy and sipping the bouillon Aunt Arrow's brought through the mist. She tells me more about the accident and its aftermath. "Our old friend Walter, the oak-watering groundskeeper, called 911. Police and ambulance responded immediately, followed by four fire trucks. EMTs stabilized you. The air bag broke your ribs. Simone's gun was never a factor, thank goodness, or the men's weapons either. They had to keep moving with the traffic past the crash scene."

"How did they get Claude and Hugh, if they rode away?" My brain is waking up.

"Police had Claude under surveillance. That's about the only thing they got right in all of this," Aunt Arrow says. "Quite a caravan witnessed the tree crash. We still don't know the intended destination."

"And Casey?"

"Boyd Dunbar arrested Casey. Sad about his involvement. He'd hooked up with Claude after release from the Department of Youth Corrections and started using again. An easy recruit with the promise of income and drugs, but the good news, if there is any, is that he's addicted to Oxy and not meth or heroin. He's in deep trouble but on the periphery relative to the others, or so they think. And hope."

I also learn that my Subaru's already in the shop, Walter thinks the live oak will survive, and Leroy's caretaking Babe, who's remaining at my house. Jake offered, but he's acknowledged that Babe has a permanent home with me, and the guys have invited Babe to join the neighborhood patrol watch.

Bertel will fill me in on the other suspects when he comes, after I rest. Aunt Arrow has already called him, per instructions, "at the first hint of an open eye."

He walks in carrying a chocolate milkshake. Aunt Arrow asks the CNA to step out into the hallway with her to discuss a confidential matter, which I'm alert enough to recognize as consideration. Bertel busies himself tearing the paper end, taking the straw out of its paper enclosure and placing it through the plastic cover and into the milkshake, which he puts on the tray table. Sitting beside the bed, he reaches for my hand, which he holds, neither of us able to speak for a few moments as we listen to the sounds of the hospital's paging system, carts moving in the hallways and the hum of machines monitoring my vitals. All we're missing is the violins.

"For sustenance," he finally says, offering me the milkshake, which tastes fabulous, especially since the CNA has several times referred to a clear liquid diet.

Bertel claims never to have doubted, after the motorcycle incident, that one or more of the persons on our list was involved in the ways we suspected. The emphasis on Casey's charitable work was his attempt to reassure me, to steer me away so I wouldn't endanger myself further.

That tactic worked well.

He gives me credit for leading them to the drug ring. Boyd Dunbar had put a surveillance team on Claude and Casey. Members of the team tracked Casey and Claude on their evening rounds, observing one exchange between them and the middleman who turned out to be Hugh, and Hugh's subsequent transaction with a suspected dealer. Patrol tailed Hugh to Simone's house after the accident. He had both a record and a Harley Sport with cement in its tires, parked behind Simone's house in a gazebo between the porch and her swimming pool. The property's value and location in an upscale suburb were not exactly what one would expect of a pharmaceutical technician, all other things being equal.

About Jared, Jamail and Silver-Hair, I'm relieved to learn that Jamail wasn't immersed in anything other than too much alcohol. He's already back in A.A. The man with the silver hair turned out to be a process server, doing his duty after Jared's wife filed for divorce, and the suit in Jared's office, his divorce attorney. I had the lawyer part right, anyway.

Bertel's working with Casey's grandfather Mark, and they are hopeful of Casey's entering rehab while he awaits trial. Casey's helping his case, as well as the police investigation, by cooperating fully, a veritable lava flow of information.

Aunt Arrow returns to the room with the doc in tow. Assuming continued improvement, the doctor plans to release me Wednesday or Thursday. He confers with a nurse about administering my pain medication, and I refrain from offering a consult.

From my outpost I watch and listen to the stream of humankind through the hospital room over the next hours and days, bemused but grateful for what they bear.

Along with her near-constant presence, Aunt Arrow brings a lifetime's spirit of compassionate rebellion, baked into a poached pear upside down cake and oatmeal-walnut cookies. For once I'm able to suspend my disaffections and savor the attitude.

Nathan brings his expressions of admiration and appreciation, tempered by the knowledge that his mother was murdered for doing those things to which she had devoted her entire life.

The writing group arrives en masse on Tuesday afternoon, all except Eddie, who's in another hospital with a recurrence of pneumonia. Annie proudly displays a photo showing the splendidly completed Sally Weathers Memorial Library on her new laptop computer, which she has acquired to monitor the library's holdings. They rap to me, in a composition by Jamail, with themes of apology, regret and promise.

Emma Burkhart and a collected assortment from the Penick Park Ladies Golf League come armed with multicolored tulips and news of my upgraded first-flighter reputation as intrepid.

From St. Barnabas the Eucharistic ministry team of Rev. Bertha and Aldeen arrive not only with bread and wine but the list of St. Barnabas core values that they are encouraging each member of the congregation to read, digest and meditate on during the run up to Easter. "We're a church founded by black Christians who were not welcome at white churches," Bertha summarizes, "and the community strives to be a church where God's children can worship in a spirit of loving acceptance, practicing hospitality and rejoicing in diversity."

These, I tell her, are values I can digest as I offer them a slice of poached pear upside down cake.

Collie Sue's daughter brings news that QuadRay has declared bankruptcy.

Jake smuggles Babe in on a gurney, fully covered by a sheet, and claims that not a single person asked him on the way though the hallways who he had or where he was taking the body, even when it wiggled slightly. He hands me the soon-to-be-hot-off-the-press article in the *Austin Times*.

I read, fascinated:

Sinking Seniors Sell Pain Pills
by Gates Stafford

Ruth Ann Estes, 89, wrapped in six feet of oxygen tubing, was arrested last night, fingerprinted and placed in the Austin Corrections Facility along with her sister ,Suella Preston, 84. The women are two of several area seniors charged in a crackdown on drug trafficking. Detective Bertel Frederick of the Austin Police Department claims this kind of abuse is a growing problem in the area.

"I hope Ruth Ann and Suella have a television in jail." I put the paper in my lap.

"It's not just them," Jake says, recognizing my fatigue and taking the article back. "They've arrested a number of elderly people, all allegedly caught selling prescription pain pills and other medications. And here you are." He reads:

Simone Beckley, 44, and Hugh Detweiler, 41, along with Claude Phillips, 19, have been charged with the abduction of Grace Edna Edge, 47, a local forensic accountant who was aiding the police in their investigations. Ms. Edge is listed in good condition at a local hospital for injuries sustained in the alleged kidnapping and assault.

So her last name is Beckley. "How did they get my age?"

"Reporters have their ways," Jake says, smiling. "Readers want detail on the heroine."

"What else?"

"Charges are pending in connection with Sally's death against Simone and Hugh. There's quite a bit about seniors and others on fixed incomes selling pain killers at inflated prices, especially OxyContin, because the street value has soared following the elimination of any generic alternative. Its manufacturer won a series of patent infringement suits."

"We all knew that early on, Nathan, Aunt Arrow and I," I say, pausing, "and Sally before all of us."

Jake nods, not verbalizing what he must be thinking about possible outcomes.

I'm grateful for the silence and am almost dozing off with Babe licking my hand when Jake gets back to Ruth Ann. "Your friend claims to have been duped into selling her pills 'as a way of helping those less fortunate than herself,'" he tells me, reading a direct quote. "'Those turkeys told me they were giving my pills away to poor people'"

"What did Suella say to all that?" I ask.

"Her sister, Ms. Preston, declined comment," Jake reads

"What's the legal process for them?"

"Apparently, the Austin Corrections facility is in turmoil. The head jailer's reporting a strain on the staff, needing to call in doctors to care for seniors' medical needs and special dietary requirements and certain emotional issues that aren't explained."

"Uh huh," I comment.

"The County Prosecutor is apparently working on a probation plan for the entire group," Jake says, "if they enter a guilty plea since it's unlikely they would replicate the crime."

"Uh huh," I repeat quietly.

Having been forewarned by Aunt Arrow of my hospital release, all seven members of the neighborhood watch team await my arrival at home on Thursday, standing in a line at the curb, wearing matching blue bandannas.

~ **Thirty-Nine** ~
Passover

The group assembled for the Saturday afternoon celebration of Jana's and Daisy's commitment includes both sets of parents, Jana's two sisters, Daisy's brother, a rainbow spectrum of friends and colleagues, several students who have wandered in for the music, and the university chaplain who conducts the service in the interfaith chapel on campus. Although plainly furnished so as not to offend any denominations, the chapel's setting is lovely. Large windows on each side of the interior space open onto crepe myrtle, climbing wisteria vines, blooming honeysuckle bushes and a spacious parking lot.

After the service I show Bertel how to bite off the end of a honeysuckle bloom and suck out the juice. "Brilliant," Bertel exudes, having missed the interaction with honeysuckle in his Minnesota childhood.

Ned Lutherford, head of the anthropology department, says, "Lovely service," as he and his wife walk by the bushes.

"Care for a bite?" Bertel asks, biting, spitting and sucking.

"No, I'm afraid my wife and I can't make it to the reception," Ned replies. "We have another commitment."

As does Bertel. Per usual when Kira is the officer on duty, an emergency has erupted, requiring Bertel's presence at the P.D. This time it's his department's criminal task force, now in conflict with the county drug task force over a big fish hauled in this morning. Kira's managed to get herself appointed subaltern to Bertel on the department's entry. The relationship between the two task forces, which cooperated so well in the senior sting, has quickly evolved into inter-agency bickering over mackerels and bass.

Answering the vibrating page, Bertel missed the mid-ceremony music, Austin's Black Angels psychedelic rock sextet playing and singing from their album *Passover*.

Bertel drops me off at my house to pick up my car and Babe, who's been invited to the reception to help entertain Jana's cat, Small Change. "Sure you're all right to drive?"

I spit out a yes.

He'll be tied up the rest of the day and evening, sorry about that, but would I like to drink some tea or an adult beverage with him tomorrow?

"I'm not sure if I'll be thirsty by then."

Jana's mother has taken over Jana's and Daisy's' condo for the reception and decorated it lavishly with fresh flowers and hanging baskets. The champagne punch is served in a silver punch bowl she's brought from Sublime in spite of Jana's protests that they just wanted a few tubs of beer iced down with veggies and dips. There's more Sublime silver in the form of slotted spoons to serve nuts from her mother's crystal bowls.

Jana whispers to me that her mother thinks she can make anything, even this relationship with Daisy, all right if only there's enough silver and crystal. In addition to a three-tiered, white wedding cake, there are tiny finger sandwiches layered with different colors of cream cheese, contributed by Daisy's mom, who's brought no containers or utensils.

I wander outside, where Small Change is offering a demonstration to Babe on how to bathe herself. A quick study, Babe laps at a front paw, rubs it over her face and looks up at me. Spotting Daisy's father at the redwood refreshment table, I walk over and introduce myself as he attempts to spoon some nuts onto a white napkin that has "Jana and Daisy" printed in silver letters beneath two silver bells, hinged at the top. "Damn thing's worthless," he says, putting the silver slotted spoon down and grabbing a handful of nuts.

Jana and Daisy appear on the porch, radiant in their going-away outfits: plaid shirts, jeans and their only concession to white, Reebok walking shoes.

They both aim their bridal bouquets of yellow and pink tea roses directly at me and fire. I blink and lean left.

"Reload," someone behind me shouts.

It still hurts to bend.

Meet Author Lyn Fraser

Currently residing in western Colorado, Lyn Fraser spent much of her childhood immersed in the musty aroma of favorite library books in her hometown of Uvalde, Texas.

Her first publication, a short story on hula hoops, appeared in the local newspaper. Lyn's love of reading, writing and libraries has never wavered. She is the author of short stories, two books on the Psalms and a popular business book.

Lyn has taught at Texas A&M University and Colorado Mesa University and has served as a hospice and hospital chaplain. Learn more about Lyn and her work at www.LynFraser.net.

— avid mystery reader

CPSIA information can be obtained at www.ICGtesting.com
Printed in the USA
LVOW12s0419150414

381723LV00001B/1/P